PRELUDE TO DEATH

Other Blaine Stewart mysteries by Sharon Zukowski:

THE HOUR OF THE KNIFE
DANCING IN THE DARK
LEAP OF FAITH

PRELUDE TO DEATH

A BLAINE STEWART MYSTERY

Sharon Zukowski

A DUTTON BOOK

DUTTON
Published by the Penguin Group
Penguin Books USA Inc., 375 Hudson Street,
New York, New York 10014, U.S.A.
Penguin Books Ltd, 27 Wrights Lane,
London W8 5TZ, England
Penguin Books Australia Ltd, Ringwood,
Victoria, Australia
Penguin Books Canada Ltd, 10 Alcorn Avenue,
Toronto, Ontario, Canada M4V 3B2
Penguin Books (N.Z.) Ltd, 182–190 Wairau Road,
Auckland 10, New Zealand

Penguin Books Ltd, Registered Offices:
Harmondsworth, Middlesex, England

First published by Dutton, an imprint of Dutton Signet,
a division of Penguin Books USA Inc.
Distributed in Canada by McClelland & Stewart Inc.

First Printing, January, 1996
10 9 8 7 6 5 4 3 2 1

 REGISTERED TRADEMARK—MARCA REGISTRADA

LIBRARY OF CONGRESS CATALOGING-IN-PUBLICATION DATA
Zukowski, Sharon.
    Prelude to death : a Blaine Stewart mystery / Sharon Zukowski.
       p.   cm.
    ISBN 0–525–94079–0
    1. Stewart, Blaine (Fictitious character)—Fiction.   2. Private
investigators—New York (N.Y.)—Fiction.   3. Women detectives—New
York (N.Y.)—Fiction.   4. New York (N.Y.)—Fiction.   I. Title.
PS3576.U44P74   1996
813'.54—dc20   95–30206
                                                        CIP

"The Ties That Bind" copyright © 1980 Bruce Springsteen. All rights reserved. Used by permission.

"Highway Patrolman" copyright © 1982 Bruce Springsteen. All rights reserved. Used by permission.

Printed in the United States of America
Set in Plantin Light
Designed by Leonard Telesca

PUBLISHER'S NOTE
This is a work of fiction. Names, characters, places, and incidents either are the products of the author's imagination or are used fictitiously, and any resemblance to actual persons, living or dead, events, or locales is entirely coincidental.

This book is printed on acid-free paper. ∞

For Zeke

Thanks to Elizabeth Cavanaugh and Nicholas Vorolieff for dinner—and the title. Special thanks to Carol Eisenman for being my cheerful Key West tour guide and innkeeper.

PRELUDE TO DEATH

Chapter 1

Sunday was winding down to a lazy end. Dennis and I were spending the last hours of our weekend in bed. Dennis slowly made his way through the *New York Times*, a chore he'd started early that morning but never finished. I rested on my side, watching him, admiring the way his chest rose and fell with each steady breath.

Dennis broke the spell. He folded the newspaper and draped it over his chest, spoiling my view. Then he really ruined the mood—he started an old argument. Even though we'd been married for less than three months, the discussion was already old.

"Blaine, let's look at apartments this week. I think we should move." He looked at me and said, "I really mean it."

The feeling of contentment I'd been trying to hang on to slipped away. "Not again. I thought we settled this before we got married."

Rolling over onto my stomach, I covered my head with a pillow, closed my eyes, and thought about our wedding. Not very romantic, sneaking off in the middle of the day to get in line at City Hall, but it was what we wanted: quick, no fuss. No families exclaiming over us—or comparing the ceremony to my first wedding.

Dennis continued talking about moving. The pillow muffled

his voice but didn't distort the message. I tried to listen without losing my temper. ". . . we didn't settle a thing. We only postponed the debate. Every time I try to talk about it, you stop me. Blaine, listen to me. I want to move. I don't feel comfortable living here."

"This was my house before I met Jeff. It's *our* house now. I don't understand. You didn't mind staying here before we got married."

As soon as the words escaped from my mouth I knew I'd gone too far. I lifted a corner of the pillow and peeked at Dennis. A flush of anger spread across his face. I waited for the anger to reach his mouth. The ringing telephone saved me.

Dennis is an FBI agent. I'm a private investigator. When the phone rings at eleven forty-five on a Sunday night, it's usually business. Dennis reached for the phone. I dropped the pillow back on my head and waited. Was it business for Dennis? Or for me? Dennis asked the caller to wait. He nudged my back with the receiver and said, "It's for you—collect."

"Collect? Who is it?"

Dennis didn't answer. He lifted the pillow from my head and held the phone out in front of my face.

Propping my head up with one hand, I grabbed the receiver with the other and said hello. An impersonal operator's voice answered. "Collect call for Blaine Stewart from Dick Aldridge. Will you accept the charges?"

I stammered a surprised yes. The operator said, "Go ahead, sir." Then I heard my brother's voice. It hadn't changed in the two years since my last call from Dick.

"Hi, Blaine. Your new husband didn't sound too happy to hear from me. Hope I'm not interrupting the honeymoon. Sorry I didn't send a card; I haven't had time. Hope you understand."

The lack of a card didn't bother me; there were other things that bothered me. Things like why he had cut himself off from the rest of the family. Why he had self-destructed and spent the years floating from one dead-end job to another. Why he was always one small step ahead of trouble.

Dick has a habit of hanging up on people who challenge him, so I didn't ask any of those questions. I said, "Sure, I understand. Hey, Dick, last I heard, you were in Key West. You still there?"

"Yeah, I'm still in Key West." Dick's voice turned somber. "Blaine, I need your help."

That didn't surprise me. I knew my brother hadn't called with belated congratulations on my wedding. Deliberately keeping a light tone to my voice, I said, "Sounds serious. What's up?"

"This isn't funny. You have to help me. I can't trust anyone else."

Dennis was getting bored. He ran his index finger along my backbone, attempting to hurry me off the phone. I shivered and tried to ignore the goose bumps his finger raised.

Anticipating a request for money, I asked, "What kind of help do you need?"

"You have to come down here. As soon as you can."

"I'd love to see you, but I can't just drop everything and fly down for a visit. What's so urgent?"

"I'm in jail. Is that urgent enough for you?"

Over the years, as Dick moved from job to job and city to city, I had expected a call for help. I had never dreamed that Dick's call would come from inside a jail. My throat tightened. I had trouble keeping my voice calm. "What's the charge?"

Dennis's finger stopped moving and gently rested against my skin. He didn't make any attempt to hide his interest in my conversation.

"Murder."

Dick had a history of skating around serious trouble—but murder? I didn't believe him. I laughed and felt some of the tension leave my body. "Dick, you have the wrong sister. You need an attorney, not a private investigator. Call Eileen. She's the one who can help you."

"If I were guilty, I'd need a lawyer. But I'm innocent. I need you. You're the only one I can trust."

I stopped laughing. My throat tightened; the tension came rushing back. "You're serious. You're really in jail? For murder?"

"Yes. I'm not fooling around, Blaine. I need help."

The tremor in Dick's voice convinced me. Despite the warning pressure of Dennis's finger, I agreed. "Okay. I'll be there tomorrow. I'll take the first flight I can get."

Dennis gurgled as he strangled on a protest. I continued to ignore him.

"I knew you'd—"

"Save it. Do you have an attorney? What about bail?"

"Yeah, the cops let me call somebody. I don't know about bail. The arraignment's in the morning."

"Who was murdered? And why were you arrested?"

"Well . . ." The hair on the back of my neck rose. "Well" has always been Dick's favorite lead-in to really bad news.

"We were living together. I guess that makes me the number one suspect."

Disbelief that we were having such an outlandish conversation mixed with annoyance at the way information crept out of Dick's mouth. I impatiently asked, "Who was killed?"

"Corrye Edwards."

"Corrye Edwards. Am I supposed to recognize that name?"

"You've never heard of her? Corrye is—was—a famous poet down here. Not just here, all over the country. She even won a Pulitzer prize."

"Sorry, I haven't kept up on Pulitzer prize–winning poets. When was she killed?"

"The cops say it happened early Friday morning. They arrested me yesterday."

I was about to ask why he hadn't called sooner when Dick asked, "Aren't you going to ask if I'm innocent or guilty?"

"Should I? You said you were innocent."

"I'm surprised, that's all. Everyone else thinks I'm guilty."

I squeezed the receiver and counted. By the time my silent count reached four, Dick got the message. He laughed. Maybe it was the long distance, maybe it was the echoes of childhood battles that made the laughter sound brittle and harsh. The muscles in the back of my neck tightened.

"Ready to fight. Just like old times, isn't it?"

"Yeah, just like old times. I'll see you tomorrow."

Dick thanked me. I grunted, said goodbye, and passed the telephone to Dennis. Then I buried my head under the pillow again. I was beginning to enjoy hiding under its soft darkness.

"I have to go to Florida."

"So I heard. Corrye Edwards . . ." Papers rustled as Dennis snatched the *Times* from the floor and flipped through it. "The obituary doesn't mention murder." When I didn't respond, Dennis asked, "Do you want to hear this?"

"Not really."

"She was fifty-three. How old's your brother?"

"Thirty. Does the article mention Dick? Give me the phone—I should call the family."

Dennis tossed the paper on the floor and leaned over me. He pulled the pillow away from my head and kissed my neck. "Listen to me. You don't have to call your family. Even if your brother's name was on the front page in three-inch type, you do not have to call your family. Let someone else handle those chores for once."

"Give me the phone. I should call Eileen."

"Call her in the morning. Someone should get a good night's sleep. I know we won't."

I couldn't let go of the idea that I had to call someone. After thinking for a few seconds, I said, "I have to call the airlines. Who flies to Key West?"

Dennis, who always knew the fastest way to get anywhere, mentioned a few airlines. When I didn't move to pick up the phone, Dennis did. He dialed; I drifted away thinking about my brother.

I'm the middle child in what most people consider an all-American family. Eileen's the oldest; Dick's the youngest. Like most all-American families, we have our problems. Up until tonight, my drinking had been our biggest problem—and I hadn't had a drink for three years.

A finger jabbed me, bringing me back to the bedroom. I looked at Dennis. He was smiling. "Your flight leaves JFK at eight o'clock tomorrow morning. First class. You change planes in Miami and get into Key West at one. There will be a car at Avis. Take your fishing pole—the reservation agent said June is when Key West holds its Hemingway Fishing Tournament. What about a hotel?"

I felt too drained, too tired, to do more than say thanks and

I'd find a hotel when I got there. I closed my eyes and started dreading the morning.

Dennis pushed my hair aside. He kissed the back of my neck and started down my spine. "I wish I could go with you."

By the time his lips reached the base of my spine, I was in complete agreement.

Flying first class has two advantages: quick check-ins and extra room between the seats. Since I'm a very tall, very impatient person, I'm willing to pay extra for both.

The clerk at the check-in counter took my credit card and my bag. In exchange, he gave me a ticket, a boarding pass, and my used credit card. Done. Checked in. Twenty minutes until they'd let me on the plane. Just enough time to get a cup of coffee and call the office. That's the order I followed: coffee first, office second.

Eileen answered, as I knew she would. She's always the first one in. I tried to sound cheerful. "Hey, Eileen—"

"Hi, where are you? I thought we were meeting this morning for breakfast and to plan—"

I cut her off. "Sorry. You know that cliché about the best-laid plans? Well, it happened. Mine have gone astray. I'm on my way to Florida. I don't know how long I'll be gone." I heard a sharp intake of breath and quickly said, "Dick called late last night. He's in trouble."

"So you're going to bail him out."

Eileen's courtroom voice didn't betray any emotion. The cool tone didn't bother me; it's her way of maintaining control.

"Exactly. If the judge allows bail."

Even after a dozen years of delivering bad news, I still get sweaty palms when I face that unpleasant chore. My wet palms slipped on the receiver. I tightened my grip, took a deep breath, and repeated my conversation with Dick.

Eileen listened, then crisply said, "I'll handle the rest of the family. I'll also see if I know anyone in Florida who can help you. Call me when you land."

I knew what Eileen would do. As soon as we hung up, she'd pull a battered address book from her briefcase and start making calls. By the time I phoned from Florida, she'd have a list of law school buddies who were waiting to hear from me. I hoped they'd be able to help.

On my way to the gate, I stopped to buy the New York papers. Tucking them under my arm, I went to the gate and joined the line of impatient travelers inching down the passageway to the plane. While we shuffled along, I scanned the front pages.

The *News* and the *Post* featured pictures of the corpse du jour—a headless cadaver found floating in the pond in Central Park. The head was still missing. Neither paper mentioned Corrye Edwards. New York City provides enough bodies; they didn't waste space on one found in Key West.

A small box on the front page of the *Times* noted Corrye's death and promised a full obituary inside. After settling in my seat and buckling the seat belt, I opened the paper and found the article.

Pulitzer prize winner. Unofficial poet of the Keys. Famous for reading poems at the last presidential inauguration. Widow of a famous painter and Cuban expatriate who had committed suicide on their tenth anniversary. Police sources say death occurred during a late-night mugging. A private memorial service would be held in Key West later in the week. No children. Ten volumes of poetry left behind.

I read the short obituary over and over again, searching for hidden nuances that would explain Dick's role. By the time the plane touched down in Miami, I had a pounding headache. It started at the base of my neck, ended at my eyebrows, and was accompanied by strong feelings of doom. As I hurried through the terminal to my Key West flight, the headache intensified.

Chapter 2

I shared the plane with one family: Mommy, Daddy, one crying baby, two fighting children. The plane had only a dozen seats—I couldn't get away from the noise. I sat as far away as possible, closed my eyes, and made believe I was asleep. I woke up when the wheels touched ground in Key West.

I climbed down the short ladder from the plane to the tarmac and wiped sweat from my forehead. By the time I had walked to the air-conditioned terminal, a journey of less than one hundred steps, the backs of my head and blouse were uncomfortably wet.

In my drinking days the Conch Traveler, a bar set off to one side of the terminal, would have been my first stop. A cold beer . . . I pushed away the memories of icy beer sliding down my throat and hurried to the row of telephones lining the front wall.

"Hi—where are you?"

Eileen's voice was still too even, too unemotional. I didn't ask if she was okay because I didn't want to worry. Long-distance worrying is pointless.

"I'm in Key West. What do you have for me?"

"I've been waiting for your call. You have a meeting with Dick's attorney in half an hour. Reginald Brown is his name. He's going to meet you in front of the Key West police station.

He'll get you in to see Dick." Eileen hesitated, then quickly said, "Blaine, I want to be there. I'm going to fly down in the morning."

"What are you going to do when you get here? Are you going to follow me around and get in my way? Or are you going to sit in the jail and lecture Dick? Let's handle this like we would any case—"

"This isn't just any case."

"I know," I said soothingly. "But remember all those lectures you've given me about not letting emotions cloud my judgment. I'll do the investigation. You stay home—until we need you down here."

Eileen flatly said, "You mean wait until it's time for the trial."

We were silent for a moment. I pictured myself sitting in a courtroom watching my sister defend my brother. My voice shook a little as I answered, "If I do my job right it won't get to a trial. What do you know about this Reginald Brown? Is he any good?"

"He's from a large firm in Miami that specializes in criminal law. Where are you staying? I'll fax a complete bio as soon as we put it together."

I rested my head against the top of the telephone. "I don't know yet. I'll call you when I find a place." I glanced at my watch. "Eileen, I'd better get going if I'm going to make this meeting. I promise to call you as soon as I can."

I'd never been to Key West before; I probably would have liked the town if I had been there on vacation. As I followed the Avis lady's directions to the center of town, I found myself vaguely disappointed by the narrow strips of sand—I had expected wide beaches. After turning off the road that ran along the ocean, I drove through a stretch of grocery stores, bars, and houses. As I sat waiting for a light to change, I nervously drummed my fingers on the steering wheel.

I parked in the shade of a palm tree and trotted across Whitehead Street to the jail. I should have taken my time—no one was waiting for me. I paced up and down the sidewalk, feeling my nerves stretching tighter with each minute.

A few months ago, I would have smoked a few cigarettes and

tried to enjoy the sights. Now that I was a nonsmoker, waiting was intolerable.

Giving up smoking was proving to be as difficult as giving up drinking had been. I wake up every morning craving a cigarette, then a drink. Some mornings the order of my urges reverse themselves: I want a drink, then a cigarette. I found three socially acceptable ways to overcome the cravings: work, exercise, and sex.

Whenever I complain about missing smoking, Dennis smiles. Eileen's happy about my increased working hours—our billings have climbed to record levels. I was the only unhappy person. I wanted a carton of cigarettes and a liter of scotch. Instead of giving in, I walked around the block, counted tourists wearing Hawaiian shirts, and finally stopped in a store to buy the local papers. I spent the rest of my waiting time reading about Corrye Edwards and her death.

Sometimes you take an instant and irrational dislike to a person just because of the way she says hello or because the smell of his cologne gives you a headache. This was one of those times. From the moment the man in the wheelchair approached me, dislike raced through me. Reminding myself to be fair, I fought it down and tried to smile.

"Laska Brown. You must be Blaine. You and Dick look alike." He ignored my outstretched hand and pointed to a bench near the curb. "Why don't you sit over there? It's easier to talk when I'm eye-to-eye with people."

Reginald Brown—Laska, as he called himself—might have been an attractive man; I couldn't tell. His blond hair hung in greasy strands that flopped around his ears and in his eyes. Two or three days of stubble grew out of the pockmarks on his face.

I followed Brown's directions and sat. He parked his wheelchair next to the bench and squinted at me. "What, no questions about the chair? Don't you want to know how a cripple got through law school?"

The antagonism I felt rushed to the surface. I took my sunglasses off and stared into his eyes. "Nope. I'm assuming you managed to get through law school. My questions concern your experience with murder cases and your track record. How good are you?"

Either Laska didn't understand me or he was too intent on telling his story to hold it back. "It happened two days after I graduated college. I got drunk and drove my Camaro into a concrete pillar. The overpass is still standing—I'm not."

"That's too bad. I used to drink too. Dumb drunken luck kept me in one piece." The bright sunlight aggravated my headache. I put my sunglasses on again and said, "Now that we have our sordid stories told, let's get on to business. How much experience do you have with murder cases? What's your track record? How much do you charge and who's paying you?"

Brown's quick grin masked a flash of annoyance. "Is that it? A brief AA meeting, then let's discuss my résumé?"

"Listen, Mr. Brown, Key West might be paradise for a lot of people, but not for me. I've been here for an hour and I'm not impressed. It's too hot and too crowded. I have a headache and I don't know where I'm sleeping tonight. All in all, I'd rather be in Manhattan."

"That's good. We don't need any more tourists retiring down here, clogging our streets and sewers. So you dropped everything and rushed down here to rescue your brother." He made it sound like an insult. I clenched my teeth and waited. "You ever been inside a jail?"

"As a visitor or inmate?"

"And I was hoping your brother was the only asshole in your family. But I see they sent in reinforcements."

"I've been called worse. Is this your typical get-acquainted consultation?"

"Ms. Aldridge—"

"Stewart." The blank look on his face set me off. "Listen carefully—I'm only going to explain it once. I got married and changed my name. Are you this dense about the law too? If so, when Dick's convicted we'll be able to appeal because of incompetent representation."

Brown shook his head. "Nonhandicapped bias. It happens all the time. People can't see beyond the chair."

"You're wrong. I don't mind your wheelchair. I have a better reason to dislike you: your personality sucks. Now can we go see my brother? Maybe he'll be able to answer my questions."

"In a minute. I'm not finished. Do you work, Ms. Stewart?" I nodded, he nodded. "What kind of work do you do?"

"Why?"

"I'm not a public defender wasting time on some poor slob because I can't get a job at a real firm. I'm expensive. I did some work for your brother once, so when he called, I came down. I'd like to know if I have any chance of getting paid."

"What kind of work did you do for Dick? Who paid you then?"

"I can't tell you that. Attorney-client privilege. But I do have some experience with murder trials. Did the Webster case get much airplay up north?"

"Is that the one where the husband killed his wife and her lover and tried to feed them to the sharks? The details appealed to the New York City tabloids, and the trial made headlines for weeks. It was impossible to avoid it."

A grin of satisfaction flew across his face. He nodded happily. "My case. I got him off, you know. I specialize in jealous lovers who are accused of murder."

"So, my brother's a murderous, jealous lover. Is that what you think?"

"It's all the police have been able to come up with. I haven't found anything to shake their theory."

"Where do you practice?"

"Mostly Miami. My firm has a small office here that I use sometimes. I flew down when Dick called. Enough about me—back to you."

"I'm not very interesting. I'd rather talk about my brother."

For the first time, Brown's cool demeanor wavered. He snapped, "We'll get to your brother when I'm ready. I'm running the show. Not you."

The God Complex. *Don't question my authority, just follow my instructions.* Attorneys are famous for it. So are doctors and accountants (at tax time). I've had enough experience with Eileen's displays of omnipotence to not be impressed.

I shrugged my shoulders. "That could be a problem—if we were working together. Since the chance of that happening is remote, I'm not worried."

"Your brother tells me you do a little investigating for a living. How good are you?"

"Good enough to pay the bills."

I sat back against the warm wooden backrest, crossed my legs, and smiled the smug grin that always sets Eileen off. The attorney's face and neck turned crimson. My grin deepened. I love getting attorneys mad. Brown teetered on the edge of losing his temper but managed to hang on—with great effort.

"Let's be blunt here." He tapped the armrest of his wheelchair and said, "One, as you can see, I'm not exactly inconspicuous. I need someone to be my legs. Two, your brother doesn't have a hell of a lot of money. Three, you have more experience than anybody we can afford to hire."

I laughed until tears slid from the corners of my eyes. "I'm sorry . . ." I took my sunglasses off and rubbed my eyes. "Your enthusiasm is underwhelming. I'm flattered by your belief in my abilities. Let's see if I can sum up my qualifications: I can walk. I'm cheap. And you hope I learned something from the little investigating I've done."

"That's it. Deal?"

"I don't know what my brother's been telling you, but let me set this warped record straight. I run a business that booked several million dollars in fees last year. There are half a dozen investigators and another half a dozen lawyers on my staff. I'll work with you, not for you. Equal partners or we don't have a deal."

"Headstrong."

"People who know me prefer to call me pigheaded. Fill me in on what's going on down here, then let's go inside. It's too hot to sit out here and wrangle with you."

"No, let's visit your brother first. Then we'll talk. I want you to listen to his story and make up your mind without any prompting from me. I want to hear what you think."

My stomach dipped. Laska's tone did nothing to inspire confidence in Dick's claims of innocence. Could he do better when Dick was facing a judge and jury?

I waited in a barren room that wasn't much bigger than a small closet and watched the ceiling fan struggle to move the humid air. The fan lost the battle. Sweat dripped down my back and soaked my cotton shirt.

The door opened. Dick stood in the doorway and stared at me. I sat, incapable of doing anything but stare back. In the two years since we'd last seen each other, Dick's hair had thinned. Constant exposure to the sun had turned his hair golden and his skin bronze. The fluorescent coverall that's become haute couture in jails all over the country gave his face a sallow tint that reminded me of a rotting pumpkin.

Dick stepped into the room. Mindful of his duties, the guard followed my brother—or tried to follow him. Laska Brown sharply maneuvered his wheelchair to block the entrance. The attorney looked at me over his shoulder and nodded. With a faint smile on his face, Brown pushed himself, and the cop, out to the corridor. He pulled the door closed. I was alone with my brother.

I pushed myself to my feet and rushed across the tiny space. Dick and I awkwardly hugged, then broke away.

Dick backed up until he was against the wall. "Calling you was a mistake. Go home."

It's difficult to argue with a carbon copy of yourself, but I tried. My jaw snapped into the same intractable pose as my brother's. "I didn't volunteer for this assignment. Remember? You called me. Here I am. I can't leave; I just signed on as your lawyer's errand girl."

"I'll tell him to fire you."

Before the words "Grow up" could escape my mouth, I sat at the narrow fake wood table. Instead of looking at Dick, I carefully traced a cigarette burn with my index finger.

When we were kids, I'd get so mad at Dick that I'd pound on his chest or head with my fists until an adult tore us apart. I knew Dick half expected me to rush across the room to hit him. I didn't get up; I delivered my knockout punch from my seat.

"Do you know that Florida has the death penalty? The district attorney says he's going to plunk you down in the electric chair."

Chapter 3

Dick recovered and repeated, "Go home," but his voice had lost its vigor.

"I read the newspaper stories. Now I want to hear your story."

"A story—that's all this is to you, isn't it? A story that you don't really want to hear."

Dick folded his arms across his chest and glared at me. The scowl on his face was lonely and scared—not angry.

"Corrye Edwards was murdered early Friday morning. Her blood-covered body was found on Smathers Beach. She'd been shot. Smathers Beach is near the airport—I drove past it on my way into town this afternoon. I imagine it's deserted out there before dawn. A very lonely place to die."

Dick flinched. Hoping he was ready to talk, I stopped. I was wrong—Dick didn't say a word. I cursed the stubbornness that runs in our genes and snapped, "The autopsy found semen in her vagina and anus. Have the cops gotten a sample from you for a DNA test?"

"We had sex. For Christ's sake, we were living together. People who live together have sex."

"I don't believe you."

A faint smile of amusement crossed Dick's face. "What—you don't believe we had sex?"

"Not that night. Come on, Dick, if Corrye was raped it could help prove your innocence."

"We had sex."

I still didn't believe him. I also knew he'd continue to lie, so I didn't press him. "What about the argument your neighbors heard earlier that evening? They said it wasn't unusual to hear you two fight."

"Corrye was intense." Dick shook his head and paced from the door to the window and back again. "This is a waste of breath. You don't know anything about an artist's temperament."

I smiled. "I think there's an insult in there somewhere, little brother. I'll let it go—this time. Teach me about an artist's temperament."

"Corrye was working on a new collection of poetry. She was up against a deadline. Corrye was jealous, paranoid, and short-tempered when she was working. And that's when the writing was going good." Dick smiled weakly; I caught a glimpse of the carefree kid I'd grown up with.

"What was Corrye like when she was having difficulty with her poetry?"

"Impossible to live with. I couldn't do anything right. Corrye would lose her temper over the least thing. Thursday night was typical. We fought about beer. I drank the last one. Corrye decided that I'd drunk it just to spite her."

"So you had a loud fight. Loud enough for your neighbors to hear."

Dick laughed. "Blaine, have you seen the houses around here? They're so close together that your neighbors can hear a soft sneeze. After we fought, we made up and went to bed."

"The newspapers say you beat Corrye and raped her. Then you shot her and dumped her on the beach, where she bled to death in the sand. A pair of early-morning beachcombers found her body instead of the treasure they hoped to find."

With a flash of anger, Dick said, "The stories are wrong." He paused. For a brief moment, I saw a trace of something—maybe fear, maybe guilt—in Dick's eyes. He quickly recovered and said, "What's the use? Everyone's decided I'm guilty."

Dick's voice sounded flat and unemotional. And unconvincing. I studied my brother's face. Was I looking at a murderer?

"Then tell me what really happened so we can prove that everyone's wrong."

"We made up and went to bed. We had sex. We fell asleep. I didn't wake up until the cops showed up at our bedroom door."

"One story said you were still drunk."

"Yeah, I was drunk. I'm not proud of that. After we had sex, I passed out. I never heard Corrye leave."

"Passed out and alone. That's not much of an alibi."

"It used to work for you." Dick flushed with indignation. "Don't use that self-righteous tone with me. You may have forgotten about your little drinking problem, but I haven't."

Quickly, before I exploded, I asked, "What bar were you drinking in?"

"I didn't go to a bar. I grabbed a six-pack or two and sat by the water—alone—while I drank. I didn't see anyone. No one saw me."

My stomach sank lower; this time I didn't mention an alibi. "Were there any signs of a break-in at the house?"

"None that I noticed."

"Did Corrye have any enemies?"

Dick couldn't keep his sense of humor buried under his angry pose. He grinned. "Come on, Blaine, how many enemies can a poet have? When the critics hate a poem, they write bad reviews. They don't kill the poet."

"What about you? Do you have any enemies who'd want to set you up for murder?"

"No!" Hostility returned to Dick's voice. "I run a charter fishing boat. No enemies. Just people who want to catch sailfish or tarpon."

"Did Corrye make a habit out of taking late-night walks?"

"Yeah. Corrye always walked the beaches at night. She said she got inspiration from the waves and the moonlight on the water. She never had any trouble."

"Where did you buy the beer?"

"Nowhere. I took it from the refrigerator. That's why Corrye got mad—I didn't leave any for her."

I rested my head in my hands and looked at Dick. He leaned

against the wall, arms rigidly folded across his chest. Despite Dick's belligerent manner, I felt sorry for him. I saw the little boy I'd grown up with—and he was afraid.

"I was hoping for something more. You're not giving me anything to work with."

"That's why you should go home. You can't do anything here." Dick turned and walked out.

If Dick had been a stranger, I would have been gone long before he had the chance to dismiss me. But he was my brother. My brother, the stranger. Guilt overwhelmed me. How easy it had been to let Dick slip from my grasp, to become an outsider, a stranger.

I closed my eyes and remembered roaming the neighborhood with Dick. Two kids, separated by a few years, searching for excitement on a summer afternoon. Two kids who swore they'd always be a team—no matter what. When had the team fallen apart? Had it happened when I dismissed Dick's first job failure as undecided youth? Or had it happened when we allowed birthdays and holidays to slip by without even a card to mark the occasion?

The image of a blond-haired, red-cheeked boy wouldn't leave my mind. I kept hearing Bruce Springsteen's voice: "Now you can't break the ties that bind. You can't forsake the ties that bind." Springsteen was right. I couldn't forsake those ties. Dick might be onerous, he might even be guilty of murder, but he was my brother. This time, Dick couldn't push me away. I'd stay in Key West.

The guard interrupted my melancholy thoughts. He stuck his hand inside the door and shut off the ceiling fan. "Mr. Brown said to tell you he's waiting." Why argue with a guard, when I could argue with the real thing? Instead of saying "Tell Mr. Brown to wait until I'm ready," I got up and slowly made my wobbly legs take me outside.

Even through my sunglasses, the sunlight blinded me. I squinted and saw Brown waiting at the curb. He waved and called, "Come on, time's a-wasting. Let's go. I'll buy you a cup of coffee. There's a place around the corner."

Laska wheeled down the center of the sidewalk, leaving me to follow behind. He called over his shoulder, "You got a place to stay?"

"Not yet. That's next on my list." I lengthened my stride and walked on the grass beside him. "Can you recommend a hotel?"

"Better than that. While you were with your brother, I got you a room at the Seaside House. You'll like it. It's right on the Gulf. You'll get some good views of the sunset. Better take it— everything else is booked. Big fishing tournament happening."

I wanted to say no, I'd stay somewhere else, but common sense kept my mouth closed. I followed Brown around the corner and into a small restaurant. He pointed to a Formica-topped table in the rear. "That'll do. There's enough room for my chair and no one will bother us."

I followed, content to stay in my sheepish mode for a few more minutes. I slid into a chair. Brown pushed the other one away and parked his wheelchair at the table. As the waitress approached, he held up two fingers. "It's not New York City chic, but they make the best *café con leche* in town."

My thoughts were back in the jail, replaying my conversation with Dick. I mumbled, "Great," and rolled the sugar dispenser between my hands.

"Do you believe him?"

"I have to—I'm his sister. Do you?"

"I have to—I'm his attorney."

The waitress arrived at our table. We stopped talking and watched her place steaming mugs of coffee in front of us. The waitress said something in Spanish. Brown laughed and replied. She walked away, still laughing. I swallowed a mouthful of the rich coffee-and-milk mixture. The hot liquid scalded my mouth and lips. I grimaced.

Brown misinterpreted my frown. "She was complimenting me on finally finding a pretty one. We need to establish an alibi for your brother. Dick says Corrye often took long, solitary walks at night. For inspiration." He shook his head. "Don't know what kind of inspiration she found among the drunks that litter the streets. Why don't you concentrate on finding someone who saw her walking to the beach?"

"I'll concentrate where I decide to concentrate. Who's the lead detective on the case? I might want to introduce myself."

Brown didn't attempt to argue; I found myself wondering why he bypassed the opportunity. "Ray Meltzer. He might not be too willing to share information. Ray's a Conch. Corrye was too. They don't like newcomers, especially newcomers who murder one of their own."

"You lost me. What's a Conch?"

Brown muttered a curse about dumb tourists. "Is this really your first time down here?"

"My first, last, and only. I'm trying to make this visit as brief as possible."

"So you don't like our version of paradise. What do you like, Ms. Stewart?"

The earlier sarcastic glitter was gone from Brown's eyes. We had reached the bonding stage of our relationship. I decided to answer his question; maybe it would help. "Oceans never held much attraction for me. I like cities. What about you?"

"My parents named me Reginald. Reggie Brown. I was born in Fairbanks, Alaska. That's why people call me Laska. I hated being cold. I hated wearing parkas, boots, and gloves. In third-grade geography, we studied the South. Right then and there I decided I'd move to Florida. The place where the sun always shines, oranges grow on trees in the backyard, and you never see snow. Here I am. I'll never leave."

Bonding time was over. I shoved the conversation back to business. "What's a Conch?"

Brown sipped his coffee. He narrowed his eyes and stared at me over the rim. "You don't give up, do you? A Conch is a descendant of one of the original settlers. There's always been tension between the old-timers and the newcomers who buy up the property to build condos. Developers versus environmentalists. It's a never-ending battle. This case will inflame sore feelings."

"That's too bad. I'm not interested in soothing hurt feelings. I'm more interested in my brother. Give me your phone number; I'll call you in the morning."

Laska took his wallet out. He pulled out a ten-dollar bill and a business card. I got the business card; the waitress got the money. I also received a lecture. "This is a very small town. It's filled with gossips who have nothing better to do than stir things up. By now everyone knows who you are and why you're here. Be careful."

"Thanks, but I don't need reminders."

The attorney shrugged. "I could say it's your funeral, but I won't. The bail hearing's in the morning. Don't be there." I opened my mouth to argue, but he cut me off. "The courtroom is my show. You follow my house rules. If you show your face, I'll throw you out myself."

The vehemence in Brown's voice stopped me from arguing. "Okay, just remember to follow the same rules when we're talking about my show." My chair scraped on the tile floor as I pushed it back. "I'll call you. Good luck with the judge."

Rape and murder. Rape and murder. Rape and murder. The horrible chant pounded inside my head, keeping pace with my footsteps as I walked to the car.

Laska gave good directions; it didn't take long to find the hotel. I checked in and soon found myself in a desolate hotel room. I dropped my suitcase on the floor and walked out onto the balcony. The sun gleaming on the water and the sounds of laughter from the people eating lunch and drinking on the deck beneath my feet only deepened my depression.

I knew so little about my brother and even less about the dead woman. Who was Corrye Edwards? The poet, the woman my brother swore he loved. If Dick hadn't killed her, who had? I grabbed my wallet, sunglasses, and keys and hurried out of the room.

The store had the musty smell of old books. Books over-flowed the shelves and formed unsteady stacks lining the aisles. I stood in the doorway, uncertain where to begin searching.

A quavery voice called out, "Be right with you," and saved me from picking my way through the crowded aisles. The woman who appeared sounded old enough to be my mother; she looked young enough to be a younger sister. I couldn't de-cide if she had a voice that had prematurely aged or a good plastic surgeon.

The woman wiped her dusty hands on her jeans and pushed

a strand of long blond hair out of her eyes. "Hi. Can I help you find something? Most people need help." She jerked her thumb over her shoulder. "It's a little messy back there."

I grinned. "I won't argue about that. And yes, you can help me. Do you have anything by Corrye Edwards?"

The woman's friendly smile disappeared. "We've been selling a lot of Corrye's books this week. It's too bad."

"Too bad? Shouldn't you be happy to be selling books?"

"Not under these circumstances. I'd prefer having Corrye alive and not have the merely curious buying her poetry. Don't tell me you haven't heard about the murder."

My face reddened with embarrassment. "I have, but I'm not a ghoul—I'm ignorant. I've never read any of Corrye's works."

"That's no surprise. Poets rarely make the best-seller lists. Although Corrye did sell a lot here in Florida after the new governor was inaugurated."

Before I could ask the obvious question, the woman answered it. "She was declared poet laureate of the state. She read a special poem at the inauguration ceremony. The furor died down after a few months. But Corrye was still a local hero. A lovely woman, even after she won the big prize. Now, which book would you like?"

"How about all of them? Did you know Corrye?"

The woman walked down an aisle and pulled a half-dozen paperbacks from a shelf. "My family's owned this store for forty years; I grew up here. You probably won't believe this, but Corrye used to be my baby-sitter." She came back and dropped the books on the counter in front of the cash register. "Anything else?"

Small towns where everyone knows everyone else can be great places to run an investigation. "No, that should take care of my reading needs. So Corrye was your baby-sitter. What was she like?"

"Sixty-five ninety-five." The woman took my credit card and started working on the slip. She wrinkled her forehead. "I don't remember too much. I was about six or seven. Corrye was fifteen, maybe sixteen. She used to read a lot. She carried a notebook and was always scribbling things in it."

"Any boyfriends?"

"Hey, how would I know? Corrye would make me take a bath, then she'd make up a bedtime story and put me to bed. She went away to college, I remember hearing some fuss about that—she didn't want to go. When she graduated, she came back here and went to work in her daddy's office. It's a good thing he had a business, because Corrye couldn't hold a job. Too flighty people said, always spacing out as she thought about a new poem."

"What kind of business did Corrye's father own?"

"Real estate. The Edwards family owned half of Key West at one time. They made a fortune selling it off bit by bit and building houses on the rest. They'd rent or sell the houses. You know, that's how Corrye met her husband."

"Her husband—wasn't he a famous painter?"

The woman nodded and gave me the credit card slip. "Just sign on the dotted line. Augustin Mendieta. Only he didn't get famous until after he died."

I signed the receipt and asked, "How did they meet? Did he come in to buy a house?"

"God no. Gus never had any money. Corrye's dad hired him to do odd jobs. You know, painting, cutting grass, stuff like that. Corrye was a senior when she first met Gus." She sighed. "It was love at first sight. I remember the wedding. They waited until Corrye graduated. They were a beautiful couple. He was tall, dark, and handsome—just like in the story books. Corrye looked like a princess. She was so tan and beautiful."

"And they lived happily ever after?"

"For some years, at least. Corrye started getting published. Gus had a big show in Manhattan and started selling some pictures. Then he committed suicide."

"What about Corrye? What did she do after her husband died?"

"It was so sad. Corrye became Key West's version of Emily Dickinson. Rarely left her house. She started seeing somebody not too long ago, but I don't know anything about him." Tears glistened in her eyes. "I only know what I saw in the papers. They say he raped and murdered her."

My throat tightened; I lost all interest in asking questions. I grabbed the sack of books, managed to say thanks, and walked out of the store.

Rape and murder. The chant started inside my head the moment I walked out of the store. *Rape and murder.* I stayed calm until I got behind the closed door of my hotel room. Once I was safely alone, I did two things. I called the office. Eileen was in a meeting; I breathed a sigh of relief and left my phone number. Then I threw myself on the bed, buried my head in my arms, and cried.

The telephone rang. My first impulse was to ignore it, but I can never ignore a ringing telephone. I picked up the receiver and tried to sound cheerful when I said hello.

Dennis's deep voice greeted me. "I called your office just as you were hanging up. Jona gave me your number." I tried to muffle a sniffle. Dennis's ears weren't fooled. "What's wrong?"

"I spent an hour with my brother this afternoon." I inhaled a shaky, ragged breath and admitted the truth. "It's worse than I imagined."

"Do you think Dick killed her?" Dennis carefully kept his voice neutral.

I didn't repeat the line about having to believe Dick because he was my brother. Tears rolled down my cheeks. I let my fears out in the empty room. "He says he's innocent. You don't know how much I want to believe him. . . ."

"But you can't. Why not?"

"When we talk about Corrye, he's fine. But the second I ask about his life or the murder, he stops talking. Dick's scared, but he won't talk. Dennis, he keeps telling me to go home. That I can't help him. Does that sound like an innocent man? If I were wrongly accused of murder, I'd be screaming for help. I wouldn't push it away."

Dennis laughed. "Poor Dick—he's going to be disappointed when he realizes you won't leave just because he said so. If that worked, I'd be repeating 'Go home' over and over again."

"I miss you too. I'd love to be on the next flight out of here, but—"

Dennis heard the tears clog my throat. He quickly asked, "What's your next step?"

I cleared my throat and said, "I don't know. I really haven't thought about it. I'm going to visit the cops tomorrow. Dick's attorney officially hired me; I'm hoping that will make the police cooperative. I want to see the autopsy. I want to find out exactly what Dick is supposed to have done."

The list-making process calmed me. Talking more to myself than to Dennis, I said, "I need to talk to Eileen. I want to know more about this guy who's representing Dick. I—"

Dennis broke in. "Do me a favor, will you? Don't do anything tonight. Don't call anyone. No one. Not even Eileen. Take the evening off. Have a nice dinner. Read a book. Go to bed early."

I reluctantly said, "Okay, but I hate making promises like that. They always seem to get broken."

"Try, will you? I'll feel better if you get a night's sleep before you jump into this. Don't even go out for dinner. Hang up and call room service."

"You're pushy for a guy who's so far away."

"Just looking out for my wife's best interests. I wish—"

"I do too, Dennis. Please, don't say it. If you do, I'll be wanting to book the next flight home."

"And you can't do that. Go have dinner. I'll call you in the morning."

Disappointed, I said, "In the morning—not later?"

"Sorry, dear. I love you, but I'm working. Don't know where I'll be later, or how late I'll be. Dinner and bed—promise?"

I promised and told him I loved him. I hung up the phone and listened to my stomach rumble. It had been a long time since I'd wolfed down a bagel at JFK. Following Dennis's advice, I called room service and ordered a cheeseburger. Quickly, before I added a six-pack of beer to the order, I asked for a pitcher of iced tea. Instead of drinking myself into a stupor, I'd drink myself into a sleepless night.

When the waiter arrived, pushing a cart of food, he offered to set up the table on the balcony. "You'll be able to watch the sun go down. Should be good tonight. On a really good night you can see a flash of green when the sun goes down—that's really special."

Eating outside seemed like a good idea, so I agreed. I grabbed a slim volume of Corrye's poetry and went outside.

The balcony overlooked a large wooden deck. Round tables, protected by colorful beach umbrellas, dotted the area. Every chair was filled with people drinking and waiting for the nature show. Margaritas, piña coladas, daiquiris, beer, and other drinks I couldn't identify from my perch, but I could taste the alcohol in each and every drink.

My appetite disappeared. I nibbled on the burger, played with the fries, and drank a half gallon of tea. Finally, I gave up making believe I was eating and opened the book. I flipped through the pages and glanced at the poems. The ending verses of the last poem in the book caught my eye:

> *Nothing can touch me*
> *until the harsh daylight shines again.*

> *I call to the night:*
> *Protect me from the reality of your love.*

I let the book rest in my lap and stared out at the setting sun. These words weren't the work of a woman in love. Had Corrye's poetry changed after she met my brother?

Chapter 4

I read until it was too dark to see the print. After I closed the book, I couldn't remember a single word. I went inside and dropped the volume of poetry on the bed. With my promise to Dennis ringing in my ears and a stack of messages from Eileen sitting next to the phone where I'd dropped them, I sat on the edge of the bed and dialed Eileen's number.

The sound of an answering machine clicking on brought a smile to my face—I'd keep my promise to Dennis. I left a message telling Eileen I'd call in the morning. I hung up and paced around the room, trying to chase away the uneasy feeling in my stomach.

Key West is a party town—not a great place for an alcoholic. I didn't want to stay in the room, but I was afraid to go outside, where I'd be able to step into a bar without any thought. Going to bed could have been a good option, if it had been earlier than ten o'clock.

I decided to run away from my restlessness, the bars, and the clubs. To the south side of the island. I ran through the quiet residential streets, past the high school and the marshes. As I knew it would when I stepped out the door, my run led me to Smathers Beach.

Every time I thought of Dick, I moved faster. My breathing became labored. Perspiration soaked my shirt and rolled down my face by the time I reached the long, narrow beach. The sweat dripping down my face gave me a perfect excuse to stop running and stick my feet in the water.

The beach wasn't completely deserted. I circled around a couple making love in the sand, pulled off my sneakers and socks, and waded into the water until it lapped at my knees. I stopped wading and faced the ocean.

The water and sky welded together, forming a black hole that threatened to swallow anyone who dared to walk too far. Key West, the end of the world. The place where my brother had decided to step off. Could I pull him back, or was he falling too fast to be saved?

Despite the warmth of the water, I shivered. I splashed back to shore, picked up my running shoes and damp socks, and slowly walked along the water's edge in the direction of the airport. After a few hundred yards, I abruptly veered away from the water, drawn inland by an eerie glow shining beneath a solitary palm tree near the center of the beach.

A lantern, its lens covered with red plastic, had been wedged against the tree's base. I knelt in the sand for a closer look. Distraught fans had set up a shrine. Flowers, pictures, copies of Corrye's poems, notes, and wreaths were laid in a semicircle around the tree.

A voice spoke from the darkness behind me. "Are you a fan?"

I hate being surprised. I spun around. A tall, slender man stood in front of me. He wore shorts and a loose-fitting golf shirt. The darkness hid his face and the tiny lines and wrinkles that give away your age.

"I'm sorry, I didn't mean to startle you." He held out a hand and pulled me to my feet. "I asked if you were a fan. It's been like an all-night prayer vigil around here. There's always a fan or two, sometimes half a dozen, gathered around this tree. They talk, cry, and recite Corrye's poetry. They leave things. The city removes it. The fans bring new stuff as fast as the city takes it away. It's kinda nice, don't you think?"

"Nice, but sad." Even though I knew the answer, I asked, "Why this tree?"

"It's where I found her."

My heart pounded. I'd stumbled across more than a grieving fan. I switched my gaze to his face and tried to see his eyes. The thick lenses in his aviator glasses absorbed the faint light from the quarter moon.

"That must have been awful. And when you found out who it was . . ." Memories of corpses floated through my mind. I shuddered.

"Is that all you're going to say? No questions? Most people have questions."

I responded to the challenge in his voice. "If I ask questions, will you answer them?"

"Try me."

"When did you find her? Did you see anyone near the body? Do you know if the autopsy has been completed? I wonder if there was water in her lungs."

He folded his arms across his chest, always a bad sign. "Who are you? Fans don't ask questions like that. Are you a reporter or something?"

The contempt in his voice suggested that he classified reporters as a very low form of life. Wondering where private investigators fell on his list, I said, "I'm not a fan. But don't worry, I'm not a reporter either."

He growled, "Then what are you?"

I hesitated, balancing the desire to stay undercover with the reality of small-town gossip. Key West is a small town and Corrye's murder was a high-profile story. News of my arrival had probably already spread through town. I decided to tell the truth. "My name's Blaine Stewart. I'm Dick Aldridge's sister. I'm also a private investigator."

"Do you really think he's innocent?"

I answered in a voice harsher than his, "I don't know. I'm going to find out."

I walked away. Some guys never get the message. He trotted after me. "Hey, I didn't see a car in the lot. Did you walk? Do you want a ride back to your hotel?"

"No thanks. My parents always told us not to take rides from strangers."

"What did your parents say about the cops? Is it okay to ride with them?"

He pulled a leather billfold from his hip pocket and flipped it open. Moonlight flashed on a metal badge.

"Right now my parents would probably tell me to keep out of cop cars. One family member in the hands of the police is enough."

"Don't you worry that your personal feelings about your brother will cloud your professional judgment?"

"Nope. Do you?"

"You've got me wrong, lady. I don't have any feelings for your brother."

"I'm not talking about my brother. I'm talking about Corrye Edwards. What kind of feelings did you have for her?"

My blind guess shook him. He flinched. After a moment's hesitation, he whispered, " 'Midnight encounters on a beach . . .' "

Words I had read less than an hour ago popped into my head. " '. . . pleasurable interludes in the night. Your words have no meaning. Your lips bruise—' "

"Okay, so you've read her poetry. Corrye recited that poem to me the night she wrote it." He pointed to the palm tree. "We used to sit right there. Right under the same tree where I found her body. Corrye recited the poem. She had a soft voice—I had trouble hearing her over the noise from the planes landing at the airport."

"Were you in the habit of meeting Corrye here in the middle of the night?"

"I know what you're thinking—and you're wrong. Corrye and I were friends. Key West doesn't have many beaches, and Corrye liked to walk along the water. When I first joined the force, I had the midnight-to-seven tour. We used to meet here."

Headlights from a passing car swept over us and broke the mood. He shook his head to clear away the memories. "Why am I telling you this?"

I shrugged. "Midnight encounters on a beach. There's no telling what can happen. Isn't that the point of the poem?"

"Come with me. I want to show you something."

The urgency in his voice convinced me. He led me to an unmarked patrol car and held the door open for me. I slid inside and looked at the equipment while I waited for the cop to return. The logs, radio, and assorted memos printed on Key West letterhead reassured me—I hadn't gotten into a madman's car.

The overhead light gave me a brief moment to examine my companion. His tan face was lined and years older than his voice. The light shone on thick silver hair. He slammed the door and started the engine in one smooth movement.

"Seen enough?"

I buckled my seat belt and ignored his question. "Do you have a name? Or should I just call you Mr. Policeman?"

"Raymond. Ray Meltzer."

One nice thing about a small town, it's easy to run into people you want to meet. "Where are we going?"

Ray jerked the car into reverse and pulled out on the road. He swung the car around in a wide U-turn and headed back to the center of town. Meltzer repeated, "I want to show you something. Then I'll drop you off at your hotel."

An uneasy silence filled the car. Ray concentrated on driving. I stared out the window, trying to pick out the few landmarks I recognized. We didn't talk until we reached our destination: the Key West police station.

Ray parked at the curb and half-turned in his seat to look at me. "Wait here. I'll be right back."

I watched Ray disappear inside the building and wished for a cigarette. After less than five minutes, Ray strode down the sidewalk, casually swinging a manila envelope in his hand. He got in and dropped the envelope on the seat between us. "You're staying at the Seaside House, right?"

I nodded. "Word gets around fast. How do people in this town have time to work? They seem to spend all their time keeping track of me."

Ray grunted and pulled away. He drove along Duval Street to the hotel. Our progress was slowed by the people spilling out of the bars, clogging the sidewalks and the street.

Meltzer finally tired of fighting the human traffic. He pulled into a bank's empty parking lot and let the engine idle. After turning on the interior light, he took a plastic evidence bag from the envelope and handed it to me. "I found this in Corrye's pocket. It's her last poem."

The dim light and splatters of blood on the paper made the reading difficult. I held the paper inches from the light and read:

Prelude to Death

There was no warning,
No trumpet blare, no neon sign,
No yellow balloon.

Only a whisper,
Loons on the lake, crying in the fog.
A look in my lover's green eyes.

I turned away, not believing.
Love's savage pain forces me back.
My heart beats a song of betrayal.

A prelude to my death.

Chapter 5

"What color are your brother's eyes?"

"Green." My temper flared. "Is that the extent of your case against my brother? He has green eyes, therefore he's guilty. You're convicting him on the basis of a line in a poem. I wonder what the judge will think about your case."

Meltzer grabbed the evidence bag from my hand. I was happy to let it go. I scraped my fingers against the vinyl upholstery, trying to wipe away the horror that seeped through the plastic and stained my skin.

He thrust the envelope at me. "Here, take this. Read it all. Then tell me you think your brother's innocent."

I didn't move. Meltzer shook the envelope in front of my face. "Take it. It has copies of our reports, the photos, your brother's statement. All you'll need to see why we arrested your dear brother. Keep it. His attorney is going to want this stuff. Maybe he can plead insanity and keep your precious brother out of the chair." Ray took a deep breath and tried to control his outburst; his chest shook with the effort.

He snapped the light off, leaving the car in darkness. "Not all cops are bad. I feel sorry for you. It must hurt like hell. I know you don't want to think that your brother could murder someone, but he did. Believe me, we arrested the right man. Take these reports and read them. Read them like a professional, not a member of the family. You'll agree with us."

I took the envelope. Before Ray could slip the transmission into drive, I opened the door. "Thanks, but I'll walk home from here. You've done enough for me tonight."

Papers and photos spilled out on the table. I rapidly flipped through the pages and turned them facedown on the table—my stomach wasn't strong enough for me to look at them. I couldn't force myself to read the reports. After one pass through the contents of the envelope, I gave up and thought of the detective's words. My personal feelings were clouding my judgment.

I stuffed the papers into the envelope and decided to go to bed. Maybe the professional would return in the morning.

When I woke up, bright sunlight filled the room. I rolled over and grabbed my watch from the nightstand. Nine forty-five. I groaned. So much for the professional side—the lazy side was stronger. At least Laska Brown's insistence that I keep away from Dick's arraignment worked in my favor.

Room service delivered my breakfast moments after I stepped out of the shower. I signed the bill and felt guilty. I didn't have a wealthy client to bill for room-service meals in expensive hotels. I took the tray out to the balcony. The envelope was still waiting, right where I'd tossed it before ordering the coffee that would sour my stomach and the toast I wouldn't be able to swallow. The manila envelope glowed in the sunshine. It was hot to the touch, or maybe it was only my imagination that burned my fingers when I touched the flap.

I poured a cup of coffee and shook the papers out. They scattered across the top of the table. Hurricane season was three months away; the gust of wind I prayed for didn't arrive and sweep everything into the Gulf.

To take the first shot, the photographer had stood at Corrye's feet and snapped the shutter. The body filled the entire frame of the grainy black-and-white print.

Corrye was sprawled on her back, eyes closed. Her matted hair glistened as if still wet from a late-night swim. The sleeve of her University of Havana sweatshirt had been torn. Her frayed shorts appeared to be intact. Corrye's hands were clenched at her sides. Her legs were straight, ankles touching.

The second picture focused on Corrye's face and neck. Large, dark bruises disfigured her face. She'd been beaten before she died. I went inside the room and grabbed a book of Corrye's poetry from the floor next to the bed and went back to the balcony. The picture on the back of the book showed a woman entering her fifties with a broad smile and proud, defiant eyes.

The rest of the pictures, six of them, showed the body and the bare ground surrounding the tree from various angles. I hurriedly flipped through them and picked up my brother's statement.

Written in dry police language, the two pages contained the same story Dick had told me the day before. Corrye was working, Dick took the beer and sat by the ocean to drink. When he went home, he and Corrye fought. They made up, had sex, and Dick passed out. Ray's report was also sketchy. It described finding the body, the trail of the killer who'd dumped the body, and left, confronting Dick, and the arrest—once again, nothing I didn't already know. Disgusted, I stuffed everything back in the envelope and went to call Eileen.

I didn't talk to Eileen; she was in court. Eileen's secretary transferred me to Brad Carlson, my second-in-command. Brad and I grew up together. From kindergarten to the end of high school, Brad and I were nearly inseparable, until college. When Brad went to Penn State on a football scholarship, I stayed in Manhattan and went to NYU.

Brad graduated and made it to the pros. I graduated and made it to the NYPD. After a number of horrible jobs, Eileen and I became partners. An injury ended Brad's pro football career just days after we had decided to expand our staff. When I heard the news, I didn't hesitate. I called Brad and offered him a job. He took it, despite misgivings about having no experience as an investigator.

"Hey, Babe, Eileen told me you wanted a rundown on a Reginald 'Laska' Brown. Got it. B.A. from Yale. He graduated the year before your brother. Maybe they knew each other."

"Maybe. Was Brown really born in Alaska?"

"Yep, he comes from Fairbanks. His family is in the oil business. Of course, just about everybody in Fairbanks is in oil. Anyway, Brown didn't follow in the family footsteps. Soon as he could, he got out of Alaska."

"When did he get to Florida?"

"Brown had a full ROTC scholarship. Graduated and spent graduation week drinking. Drove his car into a tree and never walked again. Brown spent almost every day of the next two years getting drunk. Then he dried up, got into the University of Miami, and did law school. Admitted to the Florida bar four years ago. He's a member of the Association of Trial Lawyers of America, National Association of Criminal Defense Lawyers, the Trial Bar, the American Bar Association—"

I interrupted. "Enough with the memberships. Tell me about Brown's firm."

"Rodríguez, Brown, González, and Greenspan. Offices in Miami and Key West. They specialize in criminal and civil law. They have a full-page advertisement in the phone book. It says they practice in all state and federal courts. Brown has a reputation for taking flashy criminal and family law cases."

I sighed. "That doesn't help me."

"Babe, if you give me a clue about what I'm supposed to find, I'll look for it. But as far as I can tell, everything's kosher. Brown's a respected attorney." He laughed. "If there is such a thing—my present company excepted, of course. Brown, his firm, and his partners are well thought of in this country and Cuba—that's where Rodríguez and González are from. They got out when people could still get out. No ghosts. No skeletons."

When I didn't respond, Brad gently said, "Babe, you told Eileen you don't like this guy. Are you hoping I'll find something to justify your bad blood?"

"Mr. Morality. Are you sure you didn't miss something?"

Brad's role as corporate conscience can be a difficult one, but he never gives it up. "Just say the word and I'll look clear down to Brown's underwear. I only want you to think about what you're doing and why. Let's not waste resources where we don't have to. Couldn't I be doing something else to help Dick?"

I talked as I thought. "You're right—I don't like this guy. Take another look at Brown."

"Okay, Babe, you're the boss. If there's dirty underwear, I'll find it."

I should have felt better, but I didn't. I said goodbye and hung up. The phone rang before the receiver had a chance to settle in the cradle.

"Hope I'm not interrupting your beauty sleep, or your sun-tan time—"

"Cut the bullshit. How did you do in court, Mr. Brown?"

"Look down from your balcony. I snagged us a table by the water. I'll meet you there in five minutes." The phone clicked in my ear before I had a chance to repeat my question.

Chapter 6

"No bail."

I swept the coffee cups to the edge of the table—I wanted to sweep them off the table—and leaned forward. "What do you mean, no bail? I thought you knew this judge. You said that because Dick didn't have any priors—"

"For Christ's sake, keep your voice down. Cause a scene here and it'll be all over the front page of tomorrow's paper. The prosecutor wants to make a point with this case, and the judge let him. Another hearing is scheduled for the end of the week. I'll get your brother out then. Speaking of getting out, Dick says he wants you off the case and out of town."

"It's time Dick learned he can't always get what he wants. You're his attorney—what do you say?"

"I say you stay. At least that's what I told Dick." My mouth dropped open; Brown noticed. "You had time to check my background. You know I win my cases. I don't win them alone. I checked your credentials—they're adequate."

"Does that mean I can use you as a reference? Prospective clients will be happy to hear that I'm adequate." Without giving Brown time to respond, I quickly asked, "Where did my brother and Corrye live? I want to look around."

"I don't want to tell you how to do your job, but—don't you think you should spend your time looking for someone who saw

Corrye on the beach? That would be more productive than snooping around in your brother's drawers. We need a witness. We don't need to satisfy your curiosity about your brother's sex life."

"I don't give a damn about what you think I should be doing."

Brown leaned back in his chair. Realizing he thought I'd physically attack him, I leaned forward until my nose was inches from his face. "I asked for directions—not advice. Directions and keys, that's all. I can't ever imagine asking you for advice."

The attorney stared into my eyes. I glared back. He broke eye contact and glanced around the tiny café to see if anyone was listening. "Don't fuck with me—you'll be sorry. I might not be able to chase you down, but I have friends who can."

"Try another line, Mr. Brown. I'm not quivering with fear. I've been threatened by bigger, better, and meaner bastards."

"You don't know me, Ms. Stewart. If you did, you'd understand that I don't make meaningless threats."

"I'm still not quivering. Where does my brother live? Do you have a key?"

Laska obviously felt we had reached some sort of understanding. He relaxed and pulled a key ring from his jacket pocket. Laska was the first man I'd seen wearing a suit jacket that morning. He'd also shaved and washed and trimmed his hair. Apparently the judge hadn't been impressed.

Brown swung the ring in a short arc over the table. The gold keys shone in the sunlight. "It's at the Southernmost Point— can't get any farther south and still be on the U.S. continent. You can't miss the house. It's on the corner where Whitehead meets South Street, right next to a pink house. The place looks like a wreck because it's built from wrecks—shipwrecks. Corrye's great-grandfather salvaged shipwrecks. That's how people built their houses. They used whatever they could get from the ships before they sunk. People made fortunes with salvage. Stories say some people used to lure ships on the reef so they'd sink."

I snatched the key ring from his finger. "Thanks for the history lesson. Have the cops been through the house?"

"Now that's a really stupid question. Of course they've searched the house. What makes you think you'll find anything that can help your brother?"

"Because I'm good and I'm smart. Maybe the cops weren't looking hard enough. I know how cops think. They already have their man. No sense wasting time looking for something that might prove him innocent."

"It's your brother's time you're wasting. If you want to waste it . . ." Brown shrugged. "You know, I have a defense to plan. When are you going to fill me in on what you're doing to help the cause?"

"I'll fill you in when I have something worth talking about. In the meantime, why don't you do your job? Get my brother out of jail."

I got up and walked away from the table, leaving Brown to pay the bill. I asked the cashier for directions to Whitehead Street. She grabbed a thin magazine from a rack behind the cash register and slid it across the counter. "Map's inside. It's got all kinds of stuff about what's happening in town. There's coupons for diving and booze cruises, and other stuff."

Out of the corner of my eye I saw Laska approaching. I thanked the woman and hurried out. The bumper-to-bumper traffic and mopeds whizzing by convinced me to leave my rented car in the hotel parking lot. I walked around the corner, hid in the shade of a bar's awning, and opened the visitor's guide to the map in the centerfold.

According to the map, Whitehead was a block away. The walk to Corrye's house would have been interesting, if I were a tourist. I crossed the street, dodging a tram filled with tourists. The car pulling it had been made up to look like a locomotive. I walked down the narrow sidewalk, keeping pace with the tourist train, and listened to the conductor's bad jokes and stories about the town.

I walked past the aquarium, the Audubon House, and the house where Hemingway wrote *A Farewell to Arms* and *For Whom the Bell Tolls*. I listened to stories about the gingerbread patterns in the woodwork, the outlandish inscriptions on the tombstones in the cemetery, and the tamarind trees that are called tourist trees because the bark turns pink and peels just like a sunburned tourist. I ignored the sign outside the Key West Lighthouse that invited me to climb to the top to see the view of the island and the surrounding waters. The train finally turned off in search of additional landmarks; I kept walking on Whitehead Street.

When I reached the squat concrete pillar that was painted in black, red, and yellow stripes, I stopped. If I stepped off into the water and swam ninety miles, I'd land in Cuba. Since Castro had no reason to welcome me with open arms, I retraced my steps to Corrye's house.

The house didn't look different from the other houses. In any other neighborhood the bright turquoise paint would have been outrageous. Here it was normal. The house on the right was sky blue, the one across the street was bright pink with blue shutters.

A black van was parked in front of the house. Bold yellow lettering on the van's doors advertised *Island Reptiles & Tropical Birds*, followed by a telephone number. A man sat behind the wheel. His eyes followed me as I walked through the gate and up the stairs. When I turned to look at him, he started the engine and abruptly pulled away. I watched him leave and resolved to make sure all the doors were tightly locked when I left.

I stood on the porch and felt a strange quiver in my stomach. The house had already begun to take on a run-down air, or maybe it always looked that way. Boards sagged underfoot. Soggy newspapers, two rusty bikes with high-rise handlebars, and empty beer bottles littered the porch.

I picked up the mail and shuffled through the envelopes. Bills, junk mail, coupons, no personal letters—nothing unusual. I unlocked the door, pushed it open, and stepped inside.

The hot, moist air inside the house barely stirred. A parrot squawked from somewhere in the back of the house. I followed the noise through a maze of rooms cluttered with furniture to a small study. Bookshelves that started at the floor and ended at the ceiling lined the room. The only break in the rows and rows of books came from a large window that looked out to the back-yard. The view reminded me of pictures of tropical rain forests.

The bird, an emerald-green parrot, screamed at me in Spanish. I couldn't tell if the words were pleas for food and water; they sounded like curses to me. I opened the cage and grabbed the empty containers. The bird nipped at my fingers and tried to escape. I slammed the door before it could fly out.

Using my great investigative skills, I found the kitchen, the water faucet, and the birdseed. I refilled the water bottle and feed tray and put them back in the cage. The bird rewarded my humanitarian efforts by trying to remove a chunk of flesh from my hand.

Animal-keeping chores done, I sat at the desk and felt a slight pang of disappointment. I had expected more from a Pulitzer prize winner than a metal desk painted battleship gray. The desk looked more like a castoff from the local high school than the place where so many wonderful poems had been written.

If Corrye had a filing system, it wasn't readily apparent. Small piles of paper covered the top of the desk. The tiny papers were covered with cramped handwritten fragments of poems, ideas for poems, and reminders to buy skim milk and nonfat yogurt.

The lack of organization carried over to the drawers. I riffled through the files but couldn't find anything but more notes, fan letters, and royalty statements. I slammed the drawer shut and prowled around the house, idly looking at the antiques in the rooms and walking off nervous energy.

Rows and rows of paintings hung on the walls. Every painting had the same confident signature: Mendieta.

The paintings on the ground floor were traditional seascapes and small dusty villages. As I moved up the stairs to the second floor, the canvases grew larger, more abstract, more threatening. The masterpiece hung in the center of the second-floor hallway, directly beneath a skylight.

The canvas was huge, six feet by six feet. A large orange eagle, talons outstretched, hovered in the air above a line of workers trudging through a field. Bales of sugarcane were slung over their shoulders. In the background, other workers hacked at the cane with glittering machetes.

The sun shone on the bird, creating a halo around its head,

as it prepared to dive from the sky and swoop down on the workers. The vivid colors, the terror on the faces of the field hands, and the menacing open beak of the bird held me in front of the painting; I waited for the attack.

I stepped back and noticed the faint outline of a missing picture on the wall to the right of the bird. Retracing my steps, I went down the stairs and walked back, slowly counting. Twenty-one paintings on the wall. Traces of ten that had been removed.

I found one more curiosity in the house: separate bedrooms. The two bedrooms were very lived-in. Beds were unmade, dirty clothes filled the hampers, shoes were haphazardly kicked under the beds. Fan letters addressed to Corrye were in one room; bills for Dick in the other.

I spent two more hours in the house, examining everything. Dick and Corrye didn't eat meat, but they drank a lot of beer. Corrye smoked unfiltered cigarettes and used No. 2 pencils to write her poems on unlined white paper. Dick kept his fishing poles on the dusty floor beneath his bed.

Along with separate bedrooms, they kept separate checkbooks. I took both down to Corrye's study. The bird cursed at me while I sat at Corrye's desk to study the registers.

The poetry business was lucrative—Corrye's checkbook showed periodic deposits of ten or fifteen thousand dollars. When routine bills drew the balance down to less than a thousand dollars, another large deposit brought it up. Dick's account was overdrawn by $28.75. I sat at Corrye's desk with both checkbooks open and wondered about Corrye's will.

Chapter 7

The bird sensed it was about to be left alone again. Raucous calls followed me out the door. As I stepped out on the porch and locked the door, the cries grew louder. I vowed my first call would be to find someone to take care of the bird.

After walking half a block, I stopped and pulled my little guidebook from my pocket to find a different way to the police station—one that had a lot of shade. Duval Street, one block away, seemed to be the most direct path. The residential atmosphere slowly gave way to laundromats, bodegas, small restaurants, and assorted stores. Waves of heat rose from the sidewalk, slowing my progress.

A blast of cool air rushed through the open door of an art gallery. The sun was too hot and the invitation too tempting to ignore. Even though I'd be late for the meeting I'd scheduled with Ray, my friendly cop, I walked inside. My body temperature immediately dropped back to normal ranges.

No one else had fallen for the air-conditioning ruse. The large open room was empty; not even a salesperson was in sight. Paintings seemed to float in the air, suspended by thin wires running down from the ceiling. I stood in the center of the room and slowly turned in a circle.

My untrained eyes couldn't tell one painter from another— until I spotted the eagle. It was the mate to the hovering eagle in Corrye's house.

In this painting, the eagle had finished its attack. Crimson blood dripped from its talons. Workers were scattered facedown in the field. The rows of sugarcane were flattened under their bodies.

From the center of the room, the scene was almost dreamlike. When I stepped closer, the hatred burning in the eagle's eyes frightened me.

"Powerful, isn't it?"

The voice startled me. I jumped, pulled back from the field to the art gallery.

The man standing at my side wore white. White tennis shorts, white shirt, white socks, white sneakers. His pasty skin matched his clothes. Instead of asking who won the tennis tournament, I asked, "Is that an authentic Mendieta? It's my understanding that his works are rarely seen on the market."

Interest lightened the man's eyes. "That's a very astute observation. Are you a collector?"

God forgive me for the lies I tell. I nodded. "My friends call me a collector. It's not large, but I'm working to expand it. Tell me about this painting."

"It is a Mendieta. Augustin, Gus, painted it in the sixties, shortly after he arrived in this country. We've been handling his work ever since he got here. Mendieta was born and raised in Cuba. He got out just before Castro took control. Gus's family was very political, very anti-Castro. His mom and dad disappeared just before he escaped. They were never seen again."

Taking a guess, I said, "I thought Mendieta's wife wouldn't part with her husband's work. How did this painting come on the market?"

"Poets, even prizewinning poets, don't make a lot of money. Corrye began selling selected works about eighteen months ago."

"I thought Corrye's family was wealthy."

"They were, but Corrye was a soft touch. She had a bad habit of contributing to every cause that came her way. When Gus was alive, she supported his anti-Castro work. After Gus died, Corrye went overboard. She blamed Castro for her husband's suicide; she said he was despondent because conditions in his homeland were getting worse. In the past year or two, she was very vocal about her support. Judging from the number of canvases we sold, Corrye was giving a lot of money to the cause."

The man hesitated, seemingly unwilling to introduce bad news. "I'm sure you're aware that Corrye was killed recently. Tragic. In fact, she brought this canvas in on the very day she died. It could be quite some time before another Mendieta comes on the market."

I rewarded his salesmanship with a smile. "That's an interesting thought. What's the price?"

"Seventy-five thousand dollars." I grimaced; his voice quickly lost its casual tone. "We sold several smaller Mendieta works earlier this year for ten to fifteen thousand dollars each. As you can see, this is one of his larger works. This painting is the second in a series of three on Cuba. Unfortunately, Gus never completed the final work in the series."

"I'm just a beginner. Seventy-five thousand dollars is well beyond the limits of my meager budget."

His lips narrowed. I fell into the category of time-waster. I said, "However, I would be very interested if a smaller, less important Mendieta became available." Years of running after subways and buses got me out of the gallery before the owner could ask for my name or a place where he could contact me.

I found Ray patiently sitting on a bench in front of the police station. When I approached, he rose to his feet and held out his hand. I shook it and apologized. "Sorry, I got sidetracked. I hope you weren't waiting too long."

"That's okay." He gestured at his bare legs. "I took advantage of the sunshine to work on my tan. My legs are so skinny. Without a tan, they look like strands of spaghetti. Do you want to sit here, or would you rather go inside to the air conditioning?"

I squinted at the sun and said, "Let's sit out here." Baking in the sunshine was better than sitting inside surrounded by cops and only a few feet away from Dick's cell.

Ray gallantly waited until I was comfortably seated before taking his place on the bench. After a group of bicycling sight-seers rode past, Ray cleared his throat.

"Did you look through the material I gave you? I know it's brutal, but I hope you understand why I gave it to you."

"There are a few things I don't understand. Why was my brother charged with murder? Your envelope didn't contain a single thing that implicated Dick."

Ray stretched his legs out and examined his tan. "Come on, you said you're in the business. Then you know most homicides are committed by someone the victim knows."

"Are you telling me Dick is the only person in Key West who knew Corrye?" I shook my head. "I don't think so. I'm surprised the judge didn't throw the charges out."

"The judge agrees with us. He refused to set bail."

"I understand that had more to do with politics and family connections than guilt or innocence. Where's your proof? It certainly wasn't in your envelope."

Ray patiently explained, "Lovers have been known to kill their beloved in a fit of jealous rage. Your brother and Corrye were having loud, violent arguments. The neighbors, and our records of the times we sent someone out to break them up, will attest to the frequency and viciousness of the battles. Corrye wanted your brother out of the house. Your brother didn't want to leave—he had a good thing going."

Dick's overdrawn checking account came to mind. I heatedly asked, "What's that supposed to mean?"

"Rumor says your brother's fishing business was going belly up. Corrye paid all the bills. Your brother was nothing more than a gigolo. When Corrye tried to throw him out, he killed her." Ray wiped his hands. "That's it. Case closed."

"Case closed? What about some evidence? How about a murder weapon?"

"We'll find it."

"It's a stretch to go from loud arguments and a failing business to murder. A stretch a jury might not make. I hate to be repetitive, but you don't have any proof."

"Don't worry. We'll get it."

His smug attitude irritated me. I'd seen it happen too many times before. The cops knew who was guilty. They'd find the proof—even if it didn't exist. That's how innocent people wind up on death row.

Chapter 8

Ray told me to have a nice day and left me sitting on the bench. He ambled into the station. Feeling like an old, arthritic lady, I put my hands on the wooden bench and pushed myself to my feet. I trudged up the walk to the police station.

Dick was waiting in the same room as the day before. His cheeks were hollow, his eyes empty. Could he have lost ten or fifteen pounds in the hours since I'd last seen him? In the brief moment when Dick dared to look directly at me, I saw a flicker of anxiety.

"Look, Blaine, I made a big mistake when I called you. I shouldn't have dragged you into this mess. Go home, please."

"You're more afraid of having me here than you are of being found guilty of murder. Why?"

Dick's eyes flashed with anger. "You're nuts. Coming down here like some kind of savior—"

"Don't blame me for being here. I came at your invitation. I was perfectly happy in bed with my husband when you called."

The metal chair screeched across the tile floor when I pushed it back from the table. I stood up, walked over to Dick, and put my hand on his arm. "You can make my job more difficult by not cooperating, but you can't send me away. I'm not leaving."

Dick wouldn't look up from the floor. Without giving him a chance to tell me to go away again, I asked, "Why did you and Corrye have separate bedrooms?"

"You've been in the house?" Dick swore under his breath. "Corrye didn't like to be touched. She never let anyone sleep in her bed. Said it made her feel vulnerable and exposed. When Corrye goes—I mean went—for walks at night, I wouldn't hear her leave the house."

"How did you and Corrye meet? I can't picture you hanging out in coffeehouses hitting on poets."

"I don't want to talk about it. I want you to leave." Dick pleaded with me. "Please, Blaine, listen to me. Go home before it's too late."

"Too late for what?"

"Just too late, okay? Take my word for it—go home."

"Corrye was selling her husband's paintings. Why?"

Dick looked at me with respect. "You've only been here for a day. How did you know that?"

"Just doing my job. Corrye delivered another painting to the gallery on the day she was murdered. Was she donating money to her causes or to your business?"

"You're a heartless bitch."

Dick's attempt to make me angry didn't work—I'd used the same tactic too many times to fall for it. I smiled and quietly said, "And you're an accused murderer. Do you want to spend the afternoon shouting insults at each other? Just remember, when we're done I can walk out of here and go wherever I want. You can't."

Dick shrugged. "That's fine with me. I've been telling you to get out of here. So go. Go home with a clear conscience."

I started asking questions. Dick hunched over in the chair, cradled his head in his hands, and ignored me. I'm stubborn, not stupid. I gave up and left Dick slumped in the chair.

The bench in front of the building was still empty. I sat and painstakingly reviewed my time with Dick. The bright sunlight and the carefree faces of the people walking by depressed me. Imitating Dick's bad posture, I slumped down and stared at the grass breaking through the concrete.

My investigation had reached the sorry point where my best informant was the cop who had arrested my brother. I slumped down even lower and thought about Dick. The haggard look on his face haunted me. Was it guilt or fear that burned in his eyes? Why was he trying to send me away?

The sun became unpleasantly hot; I felt my skin beginning to burn. I got up and plodded back to the hotel. I'd continue my search for Corrye's killer from inside my air-conditioned car.

The Seaside House is a beautiful hotel with one major drawback: there's only one way to get to your room. You have to walk through the lobby and join the crowd that's always gathered in front of the slow, unsteady elevator. No one can sneak past the vigilant clerk at the front desk. I know; I tried.

The center of the lobby is filled with a palm tree that brushes the top of the twenty-foot-high ceiling. Wicker chairs, occupied by impatient husbands waiting for their wives, surrounded the tree.

The woman at the desk nodded as I walked past. I nodded back. From the corner of my eye, I saw a flash of orange; I turned and watched an overweight man struggle out of a chair. He grabbed the armrests and pushed himself up. The wicker wobbled. The buttons of his fluorescent island shirt strained to stay fastened. I lost interest and turned to jab the elevator button.

The man churned his short legs and arrived at my side before the elevator touched down, but not before three other people joined the line. If the elevator had been faster I would have been impressed.

He touched my arm. "Pardon me for bothering you, miss. Are you Blaine Stewart?"

His head was level with my shoulder. I looked down on a full head of curly hair and said, "I'm sorry. I really don't have time—"

"Hear me out. I think you'll make time. I was told I'd find you here. I've been sitting in this damn lobby all morning, collecting dust and waiting. Cost me ten bucks to get that cow of a clerk to point you out to me."

"That's too bad. You wasted your time and your money."

The elevator finally arrived. I let the other people go past, then stepped inside. The little man stuck his meaty thigh against the door so it wouldn't close. I snapped, "Get out of the way."

"Look, miss, I'm trying to be helpful. Come on, won't you give a working guy a break? Listen to me for a minute or two. I ain't trying to pull a scam. I swear."

Sometimes it's easier to give in—especially when the other occupants of the elevator start grumbling. I stepped out before the impatient people pushed me out and said, "People who swear they aren't pulling a scam are usually in the middle of one. You have my complete attention—until that elevator comes back, and then I'm gone. What do you want?"

"I won't be wasting your time. I got some great stuff for you." He touched my elbow. "Come on, this place has a pretty good bar. Let's go grab a brew."

"Let's not. I don't drink with strangers. We can talk here, Mr.—"

"Oh my God, I'm being rude. You can call me Al. Al Tooney."

He held out his hand. I shook it. My hand nearly slid out of the grasp of his sweaty palm. I slipped my hand free and inconspicuously wiped it dry on the back of my shorts.

While I was drying my hand, Al fumbled with his wallet. He managed to shake a business card loose from between two credit cards and held it out. I took the wrinkled, damp card and looked at it.

Albert Tooney, Licensed Private Investigator, Your Path to Justice.

"Your path to justice. . . ."

Al smiled. His eyes nearly disappeared behind his upturned cheeks. "Thought of it myself. What do you think of it?"

"Catchy."

"I understand you're in the business too. You use a slogan?"

"No."

"Hey, you oughta try one. My clients love it."

My temper flared. "I'm not interested in your marketing ideas. You said you have information. What is it?"

"So you don't want a beer."

I wanted to strangle him. I jammed my hands in my pockets

before they wrapped themselves around his throat. Through clenched teeth, I said, "Your information?"

"See, it's like this." He touched my arm and made a second attempt to walk me to the lobby. Tooney's fingers left a moist stain on my skin.

I dug my heels into the carpet and refused to move. "You have ten seconds to say something that interests me."

"How about somebody who spotted Corrye Edwards on the beach the night she was killed? Would you be interested in that?"

"Maybe." The greedy sparkle in his eyes betrayed the reason for his offer. I leaned against the wall and crossed my arms. "How much will it take to make this phantom witness appear?"

"Ah, I'm glad we're finally on the same wavelength. You understand how things work in the real world."

"How expensive is this wavelength we're on?"

Al didn't understand body language. He thought I agreed with his request. "You know, it's a pleasure doing business with a professional. My client has numerous expenses and fears about her safety. A token payment would convince my client that you share my concerns."

"How much?"

"Ten thousand."

I couldn't stop myself. I laughed. More proof of too much sun softening the brain. "Mr. Tooney—"

"Please, call me Al."

"Mr. Tooney, you're wasting my time and trying to extort—"

"That's a harsh word."

"For a harsh situation. Let's not even discuss what would happen to your license if the right people heard about this. Professional courtesy, I won't make threats against your license. You haven't shown me anything worth ten dollars, much less ten thousand dollars."

Tooney's smile collapsed. "You're making a big mistake. Ask your brother to talk to you about the fish he was catching with his boat. Then call me." He turned, took two steps away, and called over his shoulder, "Don't wait too long, honey. If my client gets nervous, there's no telling what might happen."

I grabbed Tooney's arm and yanked him around to face me. "You tell your client I'm not falling for a shakedown attempt by a small-town loser. I'll pay for legitimate information. But don't go on a shopping spree. To get ten grand, you'd have to bring me the murderer and enough evidence to make the charge stick."

"But you'd pay? You're on the level? Ten grand for the murderer?"

Tooney's smile repulsed me. I stepped away and jabbed the elevator button a few times, trying to speed its arrival. Convinced there was no way this clown could deliver, I said the only thing that would get rid of him. "You bring me the killer. I'll write you a check."

Chapter 9

Wednesday morning started with a disaster. The telephone woke me—that alone is enough to ruin my day. I answered the phone, expecting to hear Dennis's voice. My stomach dropped when I heard Ray's voice. He didn't waste any time saying hello.

"I thought you'd want to hear it from me and not read the story in the paper. We found the murder weapon. A nine-millimeter automatic. It matches the bullets we recovered from Corrye's body. I'm waiting on the fingerprints. Want to bet we find Dick's prints all over it?"

The quiet triumph in the detective's voice angered me. "Is this more small-town speculation? Where did you find this murder weapon?"

"Now, Blaine, I understand how upsetting this is for you, so I'm not gonna get mad. I'm just trying—"

"I know, you're trying to help. Where did you find it?"

"The judge gave us a search warrant for your brother's boat. I found the gun in a storage compartment, buried under a load of fishing gear."

"*You* found the gun?"

"Sure did. This has been my case from the beginning. I'm going to see it through to the end."

"Were you . . ." I wanted to ask Ray if he'd been alone when he searched the boat, but caught myself. That question would end Ray's cooperative mood. "Did you find anything else?"

"Nope. I didn't need to look for much else. Seems like we got just everything we need to make our case stick."

"Don't you think Dick's too smart to hide the murder weapon on his boat? Don't you think he would have tossed it into the ocean? That is, if he killed Corrye Edwards."

"Your brother's a bright guy." The detective chuckled. "Even bright guys make mistakes. Maybe he thought he'd get away with murder. I don't know why your brother stashed the gun on his boat. Why don't you ask him?"

Good question, but Dick would never answer it. After delivering all his bad news, Ray cheerfully told me to have a nice day and hung up. I dropped the receiver back into its cradle and tried to find the energy to get out of bed. I wanted to bury myself under the sheets and stay there. Before I gave in to the urge to hide, I rolled out of bed to take a shower. As I walked past the television, I pushed the power button.

When I'm at home, I never watch the morning news shows; I'm too busy rushing to get out of the house. I avoid the evening news too; I prefer to get my daily dose of bad news from the papers. It's different when I travel. I always turn on the *Today* show. Not because I'm a fan. I don't care about the news or the weather. I wait for the glimpses of Manhattan that flash on the screen before the commercials start. I get lonesome for home when I'm away. The brief spots are my way of keeping an eye on my city.

The screen instantly filled with the anchorwoman's face. She shook her head and said my brother's name. I sat on the edge of the bed and watched.

"More details are emerging in a shocking story coming out of Key West. As we reported yesterday, Corrye Edwards, re-nowned poet and only the ninth woman to win the Pulitzer prize in literature, died late Friday evening. Authorities first reported that her death resulted from a late-night boating accident. This morning, however, in a surprising development Key West offi-cials have revealed that Edwards was murdered, allegedly by her live-in lover, Richard Aldridge. Authorities, who kept details se-cret to allow the police investigation to proceed, went on to say that the alleged killer is in custody—"

I slapped the television with the palm of my hand, and the

reporter's earnest face disappeared. Dick had finally made the national news.

My secret rules for private investigators include one that says if no one's bleeding, brush your teeth and take a shower before you get to work because you don't know when you'll get another chance. The telephone rang while I was brushing my teeth. Since the hotel is thoughtful enough to put an extension in the bathroom, I couldn't ignore the ringing. I rinsed my mouth and answered the phone.

"Did I wake you?"

"No, Eileen, I'm wide awake. If you're calling about the news, I just saw it. There's more." I sat on the edge of the tub and told her about the call from Ray.

Eileen listened without interrupting. When I finished, she quietly said, "I think we have another problem."

"Mom? How's she reacting to all this? I've been afraid to call her."

An edge appeared in Eileen's voice. "Don't bother. I'm handling it. She wanted to fly down there and hold Dick's hand. I convinced her that would be the worst thing she could do. We agreed to let you do your job without parental interference. She's counting on us."

My sister and I have an unspoken agreement not to discuss the emotional aspects of a case until it's over. Sometimes we follow the agreement; most times we don't. Eileen sounded too tight, too controlled, to break the rule. Instead of asking what was wrong, I asked, "What's the problem I don't know about?"

"I asked Brad to put together a dossier on Dick. I knew you'd need one, so I thought I'd save some time. Blaine, I'm worried. Really worried."

Eileen's voice worried me. I asked, "Why? What did Brad come up with?"

"The report's been sitting on my desk since Brad gave it to me yesterday afternoon. Either Brad has lost his touch or there's something very wrong with our little brother."

My seat on the bathtub was getting uncomfortably hard. I stood up and paced as far as the short cord allowed. "Eileen, just tell me what's in the report."

"Nothing. That's the problem, Blaine. According to this report, Dick hasn't held a job since he left college. Brad couldn't even come up with a simple credit report on Dick."

"That's ridiculous. I'll talk to Brad. There must be a simple explanation."

"Such as?"

"I don't know. Maybe he's using the wrong social security number. Maybe he spelled Dick's name wrong. Eileen, you're getting excited about nothing. Do me a favor—don't blow up at Brad. Let me talk to him. He's used to me yelling and carrying on. You might scare him."

"Blaine, this isn't funny."

I thought of the envelope full of crime scene photos that was in my suitcase and agreed. "Nothing's funny anymore. I'm sitting on the edge of a tub in a hotel bathroom. My hair's sticking up in little red spikes and I can't get into the shower because people keep calling me with bad news. I agree, Eileen. Nothing's funny. Terrorize your own staff. Leave mine alone."

Chapter 10

After Eileen hung up, I left the bathroom to make my next call from a more comfortable spot. My shower would have to wait a few more minutes. I stretched out on the bed, pulled the telephone to the edge of the nightstand, and dialed.

I set a first for my young marriage: I woke my husband up. Dennis, a notorious early riser, sounded half asleep when he answered the phone. "Blaine." He yawned and tried to cover it. "You're up early. What's wrong?" He yawned again. "What time is it?"

"Seven-thirty. Not so early, especially for you. Why are you still in bed?"

"Sleepless nights, missing my wife. When are you coming home?"

I pictured Dennis lying in bed with his hair rumpled and the covers pulled up to his chin. "Soon, I hope."

"Not soon enough. I'm turning into a nervous wreck."

I laughed. "Dennis, please control yourself for a few minutes. I have a professional question. What if you attempted a background check on someone and couldn't find anything?"

"Simple. You screwed up. Start all over. Did—"

"We did. Brad ran the check, and he's too good to leave out a step. Did you ever hear of a person wiping his record clean? Clean like he never existed. Wouldn't he need help to do that? Government help?"

"Are you asking me to find out if your brother was getting government assistance to disappear? Say through something like the Witness Protection Program? It doesn't work that way, Blaine. Don't go looking for a government plot to make excuses for your brother."

"Well, you know I hate conspiracy theories, but . . ." When Dennis didn't laugh, I said, "Don't be mad, please. I'm not asking you to do anything unethical. I'm not trying to abuse my position as the spouse of a federal agent to get information." I scratched a mosquito bite on my ankle and watched it swell. "Although I wouldn't be upset if you did."

Dennis didn't have to tell me he was angry, I heard it through the phone. The silence smoked and burned in my ear.

"Dennis?" More silence. "Okay, I'm sorry. Forget it." I almost muttered something about marrying a Boy Scout, but caught myself. I'm learning to not blurt out every insult that comes to mind. "Let's not fight. I don't enjoy long-distance fighting. It's much more fun in person. Besides, I don't want to fight with you."

Dennis graciously accepted my apology without saying if he would help. We hung up. I took a quick shower, then dressed and left without bothering to dry my hair. The sun would take care of that.

I walked along Caroline Street, searching for a place where I could eat breakfast without interruption. I reached the end of Caroline Street and the opposite side of the island before I found a restaurant that appeared to be isolated enough for me. So isolated that it didn't have a name. From the outside, the restaurant looked like an abandoned fishing shack that would blow over in a strong wind—just the place for a peaceful breakfast.

The booths lining the walls of the dim bar were empty. A waitress, who was much too cheerful for eight o'clock in the morning, pointed to a side door. "It's nicer outside on the patio. Take any table you want. I'll bring coffee in a sec."

The outside was a pleasant surprise. A tree grew in the center of the floor; vines meshed overhead to form a green roof. Tables and chairs were scattered around, just far enough away from each other to ensure a peaceful meal. A small bar took up one corner, the six stools were already occupied by beer drinkers.

I sat at the most isolated table and opened my newspaper. The waitress delivered a carafe of coffee. I ordered fruit and toast and pretended to read the local paper while I waited. I flipped through the *Key West Citizen* and thought about my brother.

What did I know about Dick? Not much. He's nine years younger, the baby of the family. Athletic and bright, Dick's school years were filled with success after success. It all ended when Dick graduated from Yale. A degree from an Ivy League school didn't bring the high-paying, easygoing job Dick thought he deserved. The one that he bragged his school connections would secure. Swallowing his disappointment and never talking about it, Dick drifted around the country, floating from one dead-end job to another, always talking about the big deal that was just around the corner.

No one in the family ever said anything, but faint gleams of disappointment flickered in veiled eyes when Dick glossed over his latest fiasco. I poured another cup of coffee and wondered if I should have spoken up. If I had sat Dick down and said, "What are you doing?" would his future have been different?

Dick gradually withdrew—and no one chased him. Every six or seven months, someone would receive a postcard from Dick's latest home. Once a year, on Christmas Eve, he'd make a telephone call to Arizona. "Your brother called. He said he's fine," was my mother's only comment after her annual conversation with Dick.

The waitress delivered my breakfast. Al Tooney followed close behind her. He wore the same floral-print shirt as the day before; a few grease stains had been added.

"Is it okay if I sit, honey? I have to talk to you."

I glared at him. "Don't call me honey. You know I'm not paying, so why bother?"

Tooney grabbed a chair from the table behind him and dragged it to my side. He straddled the chair; the polyester slacks strained to hold his meaty thighs. Tooney rested his chin on the backrest and said, "That's no way to talk. Don't be so suspicious. I'm trying to be your friend."

I banged the mug down on the table and opened my mouth. Tooney held up a pudgy warning hand. "Now don't try to scare me away by yelling. Lots of curious locals hang out here. Some people got nothing better to do than gossip about what they see here." He tapped his index finger on the paper. "Today's fight is tomorrow's headline."

I glanced at the bar. Two people were openly watching us. Two others nonchalantly leaned in our direction, hoping to overhear something interesting. The rest were buried in their beers.

"Okay, Tooney, you win. What do you want?"

"I'd like to know if you're interested in the business proposition we discussed yesterday."

"There's nothing to discuss. I'm not negotiating any deal with you. So don't waste your time trying."

"That's precisely why I'm here. To show you that I'm not trying to waste your time. I've come with a free pass, a show of good faith. Just so you'll understand that I'm not jerking you around. My client is concerned that your brother is getting shafted."

"Who's your client?"

"Tsk, tsk." Tooney waggled a finger in the air. "And you call yourself a professional. Don't you know I can't reveal my client's name? You know, that old confidentiality dodge. . . ."

I wiped my hands on the napkin and tossed it on the table. "Al, just being around you makes me feel dirty."

"It's a dirty business we're in. There's only one type of business I can think of that's dirtier." He paused; this was my cue to ask, What business is that, Al? I didn't.

My lack of cooperation didn't stop Tooney. He shook his head mournfully. "Government work. Dirty, stinking, covert government work. Makes us look like saints. We're ninety miles from Cuba. Go take a look at your brother's boat, then give me a call. I think you'll want to talk."

"Tooney, what—"

"Nope, Tooney's done talking for free. Got expenses to cover. Next time we talk, the meter's going to be running." He stood up. The orange shirt slid out of his pants, exposing a vast hairy belly. With a dignified tug on his shirttail, Tooney covered his stomach and bowed slightly.

It wouldn't be fair to say Tooney waddled to the door. He didn't really waddle; he rocked from side to side.

A man's voice sounded behind me. "Don't get involved with that guy. He's a real scumbag." I looked over my shoulder. A man with a bushy white beard that made him look like Santa Claus in shorts stood behind me waving a beer mug in the air.

He took a step closer and lowered his voice so the people at the bar had to lean toward us to eavesdrop. "There's hardly a man, woman, or child alive in this town who hasn't been fucked by that scum. Take my advice—keep a close hand on your wallet when he's around. Count your change before he leaves. Now that's a hard word to put out against a man, but it's true. You watch yourself around that one. I'm only telling you 'cause you're new around here."

The man didn't look drunk. He didn't sound drunk, but it's hard to tell sometimes. Keeping my voice low, I said, "You sound like you've had firsthand experience with Tooney."

"Indeed I have. Indeed I have." He sat in the chair Tooney had just left. I smelled fish, salt water, and wind when he moved past me. It wasn't unpleasant—he smelled like the ocean.

"Been living here all my life. Seen 'em come. Seen 'em go." He held out a calloused hand for me to shake. "My name's Tab. Tab Dixon."

I shook his hand and neglected to mention my name. "So, you know Al Tooney."

"Known him a dozen years. I was one of the first people he fleeced when he hit this town. Cops should have run him off the Key years ago, but they say he hasn't broken any laws. Not so they can prove."

"What's his con?"

His eyes sparkled with curiosity. I was dealing with more than a drunken old man. "What's your interest?"

"The man's trying to sell me something. I'm wondering if it's worth buying."

Tab snorted. Specks of beer flew from his beard and landed

on the table. A waitress noticed the spray and hurried over to wipe it away with a damp towel.

Moments after she disappeared into the kitchen, the bartender appeared. He gently lifted Tab from his seat and said, "That's enough, old boy. Time for you to go home and sleep it off."

The routine had been played out many times before. Tab didn't protest. He solemnly saluted me and walked away, his shoulders squared in a dignified set. The bartender followed to be sure Tab didn't run into a detour on his way to the door.

After watching Tab leave, the waitress came back to the table. "I'm really sorry about that. Tab's harmless. He usually doesn't bother people. I don't know why he decided to pick on you."

"He wasn't really bothering me. But thanks, I appreciate your looking out for me." I smiled, but inside I was seething. Tab had been a bonus; now he was gone.

I left ten dollars on the table and went out to the bright sunlight. In a perfect world, Tab Dixon would have been waiting for me, ready to whisper his information in a beery voice. Key West wasn't part of the perfect world—the street was empty.

Chapter 11

"I'm sorry, Mr. Brown is in court. May I help you with something?" The secretary's coolness evaporated when I told her my name; friendliness sparkled in her voice. "Laska said you might call. I'm Carol, his assistant. What can I do for you?"

"I want to look over my brother's boat. Do you have any idea where it's docked? I don't want to visit every boatyard on Key West."

She laughed. "We do have a lot of boats around here. You could waste a few weeks doing that. Hang on—let me see if I can find anything in Laska's file."

Carol dropped the receiver on the desk. I listened to the sounds of footsteps and fantasized about smoking a cigarette. She came back a few minutes later. "Sorry, I had to search to find a file. Mr. Brown isn't always the neatest. Files all over the place. Let me see what I can find." I listened to a few moments of silence before Carol triumphantly said, "The boat's called the *Argo*."

The *Argo*? The ship Jason sailed to Colchis to find the Golden Fleece. Was Dick searching for his own golden fleece, or had he become a Greek freak just like Eileen? Eileen's love of Greek mythology started in grammar school. Against the advice of a well-meaning librarian who underestimated the abilities of the little kid standing in front of the counter, Eileen checked out a thick encyclopedia filled with Greek stories. A passion was born. Eileen had a Greek for every situation; maybe Dick had caught the same obsession.

"Laska's notes don't say where the boat's moored, but try the Roosevelt Marina. It's on the north end of town. Most of the charter boats tie up there, because it opens up into the Gulf. Let me tell you how to get there. . . ."

I scribbled directions on a pad. "Thanks. One more thing. There's a very hungry bird at Corrye's house. Can you arrange a bird-sitter?"

"A bird-sitter? Sure, I guess." Her voice sounded less assured than before. "That shouldn't be too hard. I'll tell Laska. Anything else?"

I said no. She told me to have a great day and hung up.

The traffic would be stop-and-go, but I didn't care. I'd rather stare at the traffic from the inside of an air-conditioned car than sweat it out on the streets. I grabbed the keys from the top of the television set and left.

My car crunched over the gravel in the marina's parking lot and left a cloud of dust hanging in the air behind it. Most of the parking spaces were taken. I squeezed the car into a space next to a silver mobile home with New Jersey plates and got out to look around. My search for the *Argo* wouldn't take long; most of the boat slips were empty. I locked the car and started down the shaky wooden ramp to the piers.

A woman wearing a shocking pink body suit, matching sandals, and a large straw hat, sat at the gateway to the docks. As I passed her, she grabbed the hem of my shirt and pulled me back. "Fleet's out, honey."

"Excuse me?"

Her voice rose with the impatience that comes from speaking to a person who needs a hearing aid. "I said the fleet's out. If you're looking for a boat, you'll have to wait. It'll be another hour before they get back. Then another hour for lunch before they go out with the afternoon shift."

I mumbled a polite, noncommittal answer and tugged my shirttail from her hand. The woman lowered her voice and leaned forward to share her secret. "Of course, if you want to catch anything, you should wait till morning. Otherwise, you'll be wasting your money. Fish don't bite in the afternoon."

"Thanks, but I'm not interested in fishing."

The woman nodded; she'd found a compatriot. "Ah, you're waiting for the boats. That's why I'm here. I'm waiting for Captain Bob—he's the best."

I'm usually very good at understanding the things people tell me, but the tropical heat had melted my brain. For the second time in our brief conversation, I said, "Excuse me?"

"The fish, girl. I'm waiting for the fish. Why do you think I'm sitting here? Not so I can be a sitting duck for stupid tourist questions. 'Where's the Little White House? Is Jimmy Buffett playing tonight? What happened to the Bottle Wall?' Well, the Bottle Wall's gone, and I ain't answering if you ask a stupid question."

"Fine with me. I'm not upset."

The woman scowled. "Haven't you ever heard of buying fish off the tourists when their boats land? They just want to catch 'em, they don't care about eating 'em. . . ."

Her words blew away on the Gulf wind that whipped around the marina; I didn't ask her to repeat them. The woman was still talking as I walked down the ramp to the docks.

I didn't get very far. This time, my interrupter was male. Dressed in a nautical theme—captain's hat, fishing vest, Day-Glo shorts, and a T-shirt advertising a long-forgotten tournament— he carried two long fishing poles to complete the outfit. I tried to walk by; his poles blocked my way.

I politely asked the man to move. He smiled at me and said, "Don't take her to heart. Sally's nuts, you know. I haven't seen you around here before. You need help with something?"

I didn't return his smile. "Thanks for the offer, but I've had enough help for one day. I don't need any more."

Since I'd already been polite, I didn't feel it was necessary to ask him to move. I pushed the fishing poles aside and walked down the dock, checking the names painted on the back of the boats. Since most of the boats were gone, I spent most of my time looking at the water. It was clean, not at all like the East River.

My new friend followed behind me, continuing to offer assistance. When I abruptly stopped to look at a boat, he stepped on my heels. I whirled around to snap at him.

The man tipped his hat apologetically and backed away, waving his hands in the air. "I'm sorry. I'm sorry. I'm only trying to help. Is that what you've been looking for? That boat?"

"Yeah. Do you know anything about it?"

"Maybe. You here to repossess it?"

"Maybe I just want to go fishing."

"Not in that boat." He laughed. "You couldn't catch a cold on that boat. The guy that runs that boat don't know shit about fish. Now if you want to be catching something other than fish, this would be your boat. But you don't look like you run with that kind of crowd."

"And what kind of crowd would that be?"

"Now I ain't one to make idle gossip about my fellow man. So let's just forget I said anything."

The expectant gleam in his eyes couldn't be misread. I pulled a twenty from my pocket and dangled it in the air. He grabbed the bill and rubbed it between his fingers.

Andrew Jackson's power amazes me. The feel of the crisp paper against the man's skin overpowered his distaste for gossip.

"I've been sitting on this dock for years. Ever since the war ended. The Korean War. 'Course, you're too young to remember Korea."

"Korea doesn't interest me. This boat does."

"Boats go out. Most boats have people on them, people who want to catch fish. Boats come in. Most of the people on those boats have fish. Not the *Argo*. Boat goes out, no people. Boat comes in, no fish."

My stomach sank. There was only one way my brother could afford a charter boat that never had any passengers: drugs.

I tried to keep my voice steady even though I wanted to scream and asked, "What comes in? Cocaine? Marijuana?"

Instead of sounding cool, I was too sharp, too quick. My staccato questions turned off the information flow. My new friend backed away, eager to put some distance between us.

"I don't know. You shouldn't worry about it either. Fella that owns this boat mixes with a rough crowd. Fact is, he's in jail even as we speak. In jail for killing somebody. No telling what might happen to a nosy body. Take your money back. It's not worth it." He thrust the bill at me.

An informant's offer of a refund is usually a sign that more money is needed to keep the conversation flowing. I ignored his outstretched hand. "If the owner's in jail, who's taking care of the boat?"

"Don't know. Don't care. You shouldn't either."

Thinking another twenty would buy more cooperation, I slipped my hand into my pocket. The man put a weathered hand on my arm and said, "You can pull out a thick roll of hundred-dollar bills and it won't do a thing 'cept make me envious. Let me give you some friendly advice—for free. Swimming in bilgewater is dangerous. Watch yourself."

He tipped his hat, then hurried away before someone spotted him talking to me. I turned to examine Dick's boat.

The *Argo* was about forty-five feet long. The white hull and decks gleamed in the sun. I climbed over the stainless-steel railing, put my foot down on the *Argo*'s deck, and realized an awful truth about myself: I'm a landlubber.

Being off the solid, unmoving ground made me nervous. When the boat rocked underfoot, I judged the distance to the dock—just in case I had to jump. Then I laughed at my foolishness. The *Argo* seemed capable of staying afloat in even the roughest seas. The stability didn't comfort me. As I explored the boat I kept a close eye on land.

Beneath the deck, I found two staterooms, a bathroom, a kitchen, and a large open room. Some people might call the space cramped, but I'm from Manhattan—a lot of my friends have smaller apartments.

Unlike Dick's bedroom, the staterooms were spotless. I didn't see any signs of the search that Ray Meltzer said he had made. Cops don't care about leaving a mess behind. Was Ray obsessively neat? Or was he so obsessive about proving my brother guilty that he'd manufacture a murder weapon?

I climbed from the galley to the top of the bridge, examining everything. I looked at the fancy electronic equipment set in the dashboard and tried to guess what each piece did. I opened and closed the doors to every compartment I found. I rummaged through the fishing equipment and flipped through the navigation charts that had been crammed in a plastic envelope.

What did I accomplish? Nothing. I climbed back to solid ground.

There was a long wooden building at the end of the T-shaped dock. The sign on the roof promised boaters would find food, bait, beer, gas, rentals, and sales inside. How could I resist? I walked down the dock.

The screen door squeaked when I opened it and loudly slammed behind me. Inside I found a combination general store, diner, and bait shop. The cash register sat on top of a glass counter near the door. Hooks, rolls of fishing line, and lures were strewn on the shelves.

No one sat at the tiny lunch counter. No shoppers loitered in the narrow aisles. I didn't see anyone except a kid, not more than fifteen years old, sitting behind a battered metal desk, beneath a sign that said *Sales*.

The kid didn't see me approach; he was too busy drooling over the centerfold. The look on his face was one usually associated with *Playboy* centerfolds, but he was staring at the picture of a thin red boat bouncing across the ocean. I didn't want to interrupt his fantasy. But I did.

"Excuse me." I looked at the name stitched over his shirt pocket. "Ken, can I ask you a few questions about a boat?"

He reluctantly pulled his eyes away from the magazine and smiled. "Hi—you want to buy one?"

I laughed. "The direct approach. I like that in a salesman. Does it work?"

He blushed and attempted to joke about his embarrassment. "Not very often. My dad tells me I have to be a little cooler. Are you interested in a boat?"

"Yes, I am. But don't get too excited—I'm not interested in buying one. I just want some information. I get the feeling that you know a lot about boats. Do you mind if I ask you a few questions?"

"Naw." He closed the magazine and shoved it into the top drawer of the desk. "I don't mind. At least I can tell my dad I had a prospect today. What do you want to know?"

"I want to know more about a boat that's moored in the marina. The *Argo*. What do you know about it?"

"She's a beauty." Suspicion tightened his face. "Are you a reporter? My dad said I shouldn't talk to reporters. He says they don't care about the truth. They make up stories to sell papers. We don't need the publicity."

I held the palms of my hands out for him to examine. "Look, no hidden tape recorders. I'm not a reporter. I'm a private investigator."

He didn't look convinced. I laid a business card on the desk in front of him. "Don't worry, you won't get in trouble with your dad—I don't like publicity either."

"I don't know. My dad might get mad if I talk about the *Argo*. He told me not to."

"Then we won't talk about the *Argo*. Let's talk about a boat just like the *Argo*. Could I take it out in the ocean?"

"Oh sure, that's an oceangoing vessel. Sleeps six. Cruises at twenty knots. Diesel engines. Custom-built. 'Course, it was used when he bought it. I know, 'cause my dad sold it to the guy."

"How much does a boat like that cost?"

He tried to sound nonchalant, but his voice quivered from the thrill of letting the figure slip from his mouth. "For a boat like the *Argo*? 'Bout two forty-five."

I whistled. "How do people come up with that kind of money? What do they do, get a mortgage or something?"

"Sometimes. Sometimes they walk in and drop a bunch of cash on the desk. Couldn't believe it the first time I saw it happen. But it does."

"And the *Argo*? Was that one of those times?"

The boy's face reddened. "There's nothing illegal about paying cash. I don't know why people think we're doing something illegal. I know you're supposed to file some papers when somebody moves more than ten thousand bucks in cash. My dad files all the paperwork the government says he has to."

"Does he? I wonder. Two hundred and forty-five thousand dollars dropped on the desk might be too much temptation. I'd think twice about screwing up a cash deal just because the government says I need to drop a form on a bureaucrat's desk."

The boy opened the drawer and pulled the magazine out

again. It fell open to the centerfold. He bent his head to study the picture and mumbled, "My dad didn't do nothing wrong."

The kid's chin quivered. Feeling ashamed of myself for upsetting the boy, I patted his shoulder and tried to steady him. "I'm sorry, Ken. I'm sure your dad didn't do anything wrong. You've been a great help. When I'm ready to buy a boat, I'll come back to you."

The hotel thoughtfully equipped the telephones with extra-long cords—long enough to reach the balcony. I sat in one of the two chairs, dialed the office, and watched a sailboat glide into the Gulf.

Marcella, our receptionist, loves to fill me in on the latest office gossip. When that's dull, she fills in with the latest Hollywood tales. This time she didn't waste any time on gossip, she immediately connected me to Brad's office.

Brad answered on the first ring. His voice sounded unnaturally subdued. "Hey, Babe. What's up?"

"Don't sound so crestfallen, Brad. I'm not calling to chew you out. I hear Eileen's been taking care of that. Sorry—since I'm away, she doesn't have anyone else to yell at."

"Your sister hasn't come close to the awful things I've been thinking about myself. I haven't been doing a very good job, Babe. Not for you. Not for Eileen. Not for Dick."

"Why should you be any different from the rest of us? No one's doing a very good job with this one, Brad."

Brad sighed.

I briskly said, "Before you fall into a catatonic depression, could you do me one quick favor? Go have a drink with your best credit bureau friends. Dick had a credit card." I pulled out the statement I'd taken from Dick's room and read the numbers to Brad.

"They should have something on him—this bill's six weeks overdue. Dick has a very expensive boat and no money in the bank. I'd like to know who was stupid enough to lend money to him."

Brad mumbled okay. I twisted the cord around my finger and slumped down in the chair. "Don't worry about Eileen. She's worried, not mad. I'll call you tomorrow."

"Wait a sec, Babe. Don't hang up on me. Some guy called you early this morning before anyone else was in. I picked it up. At first I thought the guy was a crank, but something in his voice made me think he was legit. He said you knew him from Anmac."

"Anmac?"

"Yeah. He said to meet him on Thursday at the usual time in the usual place. When I asked him what this was about, he said, 'It's about a prelude to death.' Babe, does this make any sense?"

"Yes."

"Want to tell me about it?"

"No. Anmac was way before your time. It has nothing to do with anything. That guy was probably a nut case who's been reading a history book. I'm going to be busy the next day or two. I'll call when I get a chance. Tell Eileen not to worry."

"Babe, I'll be waiting to hear from you. Call me at home if you have to. You know, you should get a beeper and a cellular phone. Get on the information highway and stay in touch with your loved ones—and your office."

"I have a beeper, Brad."

He laughed. "And I've heard your complaints about electronic tethers. Where is that beeper of yours?"

"In my desk, I think." I stared at the name I'd scribbled on the sheet of hotel stationery I'd taken from the desk and started worrying about who might be listening to our conversation.

"I don't like cellular phones. You know how easy it is for people to eavesdrop when you're talking cellular."

"Okay, Blaine, I understand your paranoid streak." Brad understood my unspoken message. When Brad starts calling me Blaine, it means the message got through. Brad would follow our prearranged plan and enforce tight security in the office. If people were listening, they wouldn't hear anything interesting.

During our brief conversation, my hotel room lost its aura of safety. I paced around the tiny balcony and tried to make sense of Brad's message.

Anmac had been a Silicon Valley leader, until it claimed that millions of dollars of computers and software had been stolen from its warehouse.

Continental Insurance Group, Anmac's insurance company, wasn't happy about the prospect of a multimillion-dollar claim. Before settling, Continental hired my firm to investigate.

I took off for what I thought would be a quick visit to sunny California and found myself mired in a swamp of lying, cover-ups, and treason. Anmac had developed an elaborate scheme. It would mark its supercomputers up to a hundred times the list price and sell them to customers who couldn't complain about price gouging. Customers such as terrorists and governments illicitly trying to build atomic bombs.

Anmac, always looking for an opportunity to make more money, reported the equipment as stolen. The company never anticipated questions about its claim.

My investigation was quickly lost in Anmac's labyrinth of deception. Whenever I smacked into a dead end, a phone tip, smudged copies of an Anmac memo, or an unsigned note would mysteriously appear and put me back on track. During one of my countless trips to Washington, I met my informant: Calton Wolff, my very own Deep Throat.

Cal was one of the CIA's rising stars in the counterterrorism unit of its national intelligence office. Cal never explained why he leaked information to me. I accepted what he offered with cynical disbelief that faded as each tip proved to be true.

Even though I hadn't heard from Cal for nearly six years, I didn't hesitate. "Prelude to death"—Corrye's last poem. The message was clear enough to send me flying to Washington.

Chapter 12

Flying into Washington's National Airport always leaves me breathless. The views of the Washington Monument, the Capitol, the White House, and the rest of the town are fantastic, but I never pay attention to the scenery. I'm too busy holding my breath and praying that the pilot will successfully guide the plane between the monuments to the runways on the banks of the Potomac River.

The plane landed without any problem. I didn't waste time breathing sighs of relief or congratulating the pilot. I grabbed my small suitcase and hurried to rent a car.

Our usual meeting place was at a sculpture called *The Awakening* that's at the tip of the West Potomac Park, a park that's directly across the river from the airport. A canoe would have been the quickest way to get to the park, but I didn't have a canoe. I had to drive into town, past the Jefferson Memorial, around the Tidal Basin, and back down along the Potomac to the end—Haines Point.

I drove down the one-way street that leads through the park to Haines Point and thought of the first time I met Cal.

I had been in Washington on another fruitless trip to try to untangle Anmac's lies. A note slipped under the door of my hotel room promised answers—if I showed up at something called *The Awakening* at a place called Haines Point, at midnight.

I don't usually follow anonymous tips without backup, especially tips requiring midnight rendezvous. But even then, Cal's message was too authoritative to ignore. My desperation was also too great to ignore.

A thick fog cut visibility to a few feet ahead of my car's nose. I crept along the unfamiliar road with my hands gripping the steering wheel and leaning forward to peer through the windshield.

I regretted being alone, regretted that my gun was locked away in Manhattan, and regretted the hope that a note slipped under the door of my hotel room could lead to a break in the Anmac case.

At the end of the park, the road curved in a narrow semicircle and turned back toward the entrance. As the headlights swept around the curve, they flashed on a giant green hand breaking through the ground. I threw the car into park and jumped out. I squinted through the fog and saw an arm, a knee, a foot, and a giant head struggling to break through the soil.

Even though this time I expected to see the giant, it startled me. As usual, Cal was waiting. I parked the car at the curb and hurried to the statue.

Cal smiled gravely as he shook my hand. "You married again. Your husband, the FBI agent, is very well thought of by his superiors."

I stared at Cal. His hair still had thick waves, but they had gone from coal black to gray. His green eyes hadn't lost any of their luster. "I know I shouldn't be surprised by anything you say, but I am."

Cal smiled, showing wide, sparkling white teeth. "When I saw the reports, I did some checking to be sure it was the same Blaine Stewart. Is it?"

I sat in the palm of one of the hands breaking through the ground. "The same, but with a lot less patience than before. What's this about, Cal? Are you still working in counterterrorism? Is that where my name showed up?"

Cal squeezed my shoulder and smiled again. "Patience. A virtue that was always in short supply with you. I am glad you responded to my cryptic message."

"I came because I was curious, Cal. I don't remember you being a poetry fan. How did you learn the title of the last poem Corrye Edwards wrote?"

"You came because you know I'm a fan of careful research. I hope you were careful on your way here. We live in precarious times. Caution is imperative."

With any other person, I would have been muttering about wasting time. Cal had the opposite effect on me. I snuggled against the iron fingers of the awakening giant and returned Cal's smile. "It was a long flight, Cal. No one followed me. Although this reunion is sweet, I hope it's going to be worth the trouble."

"Tell me what you know, Blaine. Maybe I can save you some trouble. Do you remember the rules?"

"As if our last meeting was yesterday. No names. Don't be upset if you stop answering questions. I should be happy you're letting me ask questions. Nothing you say is ever on the record. Who would believe a CIA bigwig would feed information to a lowly private investigator?"

He smiled. I paused and remembered the first time I met Cal. That night, the fog hid his sexy smile, the dimples in his cheeks and chin, and the close-cropped hair that gave him a slight military air.

"There is one thing that surprises me. This is the first time in years that I've seen your face in anything but moonlight."

"You're not as hot as you once were." A brief smile flickered across Cal's face. "I mean as far as security matters are concerned. But you are heating up. What have you been doing in Florida?"

My seat in the giant's hand was no longer comfortable. I slid to my feet. "Cal, the old rules might not apply. My family's involved, not a faceless corporation. You know what I'm doing—that's why you called. What can you tell me?"

"What do you know?"

"Corrye Edwards is dead. My brother was arrested. They haven't let him out on bail yet."

"And you're convinced of his innocence. Why?"

I answered slowly, forcing myself to be honest. "I went down to Key West thinking Dick might be guilty. His track record isn't very good."

I kicked at the ground. "I don't have any proof that he's innocent. But I'm not impressed with the cops' proof. Some things don't add up."

"Some things don't add up for me either. When I saw the reports and recognized your name, I made discreet inquiries. There is very-high-level interest in the disposition of this case."

"How high? Why?" As an afterthought, I asked, "And what have you been reading? Why is my name mentioned? Cal, what's going on?"

"We tend to keep a close eye on events in that part of the country. I can't give you any specifics, but you're on the right track."

"Cal, I'm not on any track." I couldn't keep desperation from my voice. "I'm flailing around. You have to give me something to work with."

"Go way back in your brother's life. He's been keeping secrets for a long, long time. Then look at Corrye Edwards. These two lives did not cross by accident."

"Star-crossed lovers? You have turned into a romantic."

Cal shook his head ruefully. "It's too late for me. I'm a hopeless bureaucrat. But not so hopeless that I've lost the belief that our government should adhere to certain moral standards."

"Which standards are being violated?"

A station wagon approached. We stopped talking and watched the car park at the curb. A half-dozen screaming children tumbled out and ran to the statue. As they squealed and climbed around us, Cal patted my arm. The gesture was meant to be comforting. His words weren't.

"I'm acting purely out of friendship. Be careful. I don't want you to go down with your brother."

Chapter 13

The kids spooked Cal. After telling me he'd be in touch—should it become necessary to meet again—Cal walked to a battered Ford pickup truck and drove away. I walked along the river, postponing the trip back to the airport until I knew I'd missed the last flight to Miami. I wanted one night alone, in a place where no one could find me.

I checked into a quiet hotel near the White House. After staring at insipid sitcoms for a few hours, I left an early wake-up call and went to bed. I didn't sleep; I stared at the ceiling and thought. What had my trip accomplished?

By the time dawn broke, I was fuming because I still didn't have an answer to my simple question. The telephone silently accused me of hiding, but I didn't call Eileen. I didn't call Brad. I didn't even call Dennis. What was I going to tell them? That I'd run off to D.C., chasing after—what? Past glory when I was enthralled by Cal's cloak-and-dagger ways?

I slept on the plane. I sleepwalked through the Miami airport to my connecting flight to Key West and slept until that plane landed.

Six messages from Laska were waiting at the hotel desk. I called his office. Ten seconds after the polite secretary put me on hold Laska's voice screamed in my ear.

"Where the fuck have you been? I've been searching all over

this fucking town for you, leaving messages with everyone but your fucking mother! If I had her fucking phone number, I would have called her too!"

When he started wheezing from the effort of nonstop shouting, I cut in. "Well, here I am. Can't I take a day off without causing a world crisis?"

"A day off! You took a fucking day off? What kind of bullshit is that?"

"Calm down, Laska. I was chasing a lead. Unfortunately, nothing came of it."

"Nice story, Stewart. I wish I believed it. Where the fuck did you hide him?"

Laska's voice thundered. I held the phone away from my ear until the angry buzzing stopped, then asked, "What are you talking about? I just got back to town. Who am I supposed to be hiding?"

"Your fucking brother, that's who. He's gone—as if you didn't know. Where the fuck did you manage to hide him? If I lose any fucking money . . ."

"Laska," I shouted above his muttering. Talking fast to overpower the sick feeling rolling through my stomach, I said, "What are you talking about? Where's my brother?"

"You tell me. I felt sorry for that sniveling, cocksucking excuse for a man. So I pleaded with the judge to allow bail. Put my professional reputation on the line. Then, like an asshole, I put up the bail money. Your asshole brother wasn't out for more than three hours before he disappeared."

"When did Dick get out of jail?"

"Ten o'clock yesterday morning. I tried to call you." Accusingly, Laska said, "You said you just got back to town. Where was this hot lead you were tracking down?"

"Doesn't matter. It was a dead end."

"You'll have to come up with a better answer than that."

I looked at my watch and quickly counted. "It's only twenty-eight hours since he got out. What makes you think Dick took off?"

"Jesus Christ, are you as naive as you sound? Your asshole brother was supposed to check in with me twice a day. He missed both check-ins. His boat's gone, too. I made the amazing deduction that he skipped."

"What have you done since your amazing deduction?"

"I gave him the benefit of the doubt—the first time. The second time I called the judge. He issued a bench warrant. Oh yeah, he wants to see you too. ASAP. Meet me at my office in half an hour. I'm going with you."

"So are you representing me too?"

"Not without a retainer. A big one. I've lost enough of my fucking money on your family. Half an hour, Stewart." He slammed the phone down, ending the discussion.

The judge looked hot, even though the air conditioning in his office brought the temperature down to arctic ranges. The judge also looked unhappy, which made me uncomfortable. Unhappy judges can be dangerous.

"Your Honor, this is Richard Aldridge's sister, Blaine Stewart."

The judge didn't attempt to put me at ease. He stared at me; the judicial frown deepened. The judge didn't tell me to sit, so I stood next to Brown's wheelchair.

"As I told you yesterday and again this morning, I was unable to locate her. I subsequently learned that Ms. Stewart has been out of town for the past two days. She arrived back in town less than an hour ago."

The judge waved his hand in the air. "Stop right there, counselor. This is an informal hearing. Let Ms. Stewart explain where she's been. Maybe she can also explain where her brother has gone." He looked at me and said, "Ms. Stewart? I'm waiting."

Being in front of this unforgiving judge's glare made me feel guilty. I cleared my throat and tried to sound innocent. "Your Honor, I have no knowledge of my brother's whereabouts. Up until about an hour ago, I thought he was still in jail. I haven't had any contact with Dick for more than two days now."

The judge leaned back in his worn leather chair and studied my face. "Where did you happen to spend the past two days?"

"Washington, D.C. I have airline tickets and hotel receipts if you'd like to see them."

"That's not necessary—I'm sure the police will ask. Who did you see in Washington?"

The thought of uttering Cal's name never entered my mind. Without hesitation, I said, "No one. I had an appointment. He never showed."

"Let's try this again. Who were you supposed to be visiting in Washington?"

"I'm sorry, Your Honor. I can't tell you his name. I was responding to an anonymous call."

Impatience crept into the judge's voice. "Do you expect me to believe that? Ms. Stewart, your family doesn't have a very good track record with me. I won't be inclined to allow bail if you should wind up in jail."

I bowed my head and waited. Talking would have gotten me into trouble.

"Your Honor." Laska's soothing voice cut through the tension. "I know we got burned by Aldridge, but I'm convinced Ms. Stewart was not party to his disappearance."

"I wish I shared your conviction, Mr. Brown." The judge looked at me over the top of his bifocals. "Young lady, your brother is in serious trouble. As you are if you aided him."

I flushed with anger—at Dick, not the judge. "Your Honor, my brother is in serious trouble with me. For his sake, I hope the police find him before I do."

The judge nodded but refused to smile. "You're not off my legal hook. I'm inclined to order you to stay here in town and keep the court informed of your whereabouts—"

Laska interrupted. "Your Honor, that's—"

The judge quieted Brown with an impatient flick of the wrist. "However, as your attorney was about to point out, I cannot do that. I advise you to cooperate with the police. If you have any contact with your brother, you are to immediately contact them. If you don't, I will find you in contempt of this court. Do you understand?"

I know better than to argue with an angry judge. I meekly said, "Yes, Your Honor, I understand."

He opened up a file and flipped through the papers. When we didn't move, the judge looked up. He snapped, "You can go now."

Laska said, "Thank you, Your Honor." He poked me in the ribs and motioned for me to do the same. I muttered my thanks. The judge grunted and waved his hand to chase us from his office.

I held the door open for Brown and followed him down the hallway. With a quick burst of speed, Brown rolled ahead and coasted to a stop in the lobby. A frown creased his face as he watched me approach. I walked up to him and said, "Now what?"

Laska's frown deepened. "Ms. Stewart, you got off easy. Judge Beyers doesn't like looking foolish. When your brother jumped bail, he made the judge look like an ass."

"We all look like asses at one time or another. The judge will get over it; we all do. Are the cops going to give me the same lecture? If so, why don't you arrange for me to be excused? I'd rather spend my time looking for Dick."

"Forget Dick. It might be best for everyone if your brother stays missing."

Brown's eyes shone with amusement. I leaned down to stare at him eye-to-eye. "Do you know where Dick is? Is this a little charade you designed to keep the cops' questions away from you?"

"Ms. Stewart, I'm shocked that you're asking me such a question. As an officer of the court . . ." He laughed and wheeled away. When Laska reached the door, he pushed it open and called over his shoulder, "Well, come on. Let's get moving. Detective Meltzer is waiting."

Once again, I trailed behind Laska's wheelchair. I didn't hurry to catch up to him. I followed Laska to the police station, where we found Ray Meltzer sitting on the bench at the curb. Meltzer fixed his eyes on me and openly watched every step I took.

Just before we reached the bench, Laska put the brakes on and waited for me to reach his side. He nodded at the detective and said, "You're going to be the safest person in Key West. A cop is going to be watching you from the second you get up to the time you go to bed."

"Can't you stop them? I can't be very effective if I'm leading a parade of cops wherever I go."

"I don't want to be crude, but you haven't been very effective without them."

"You bastard—"

"Oh yeah, your brother had a message for you. He said you should go home. I'm beginning to think he might be right."

"Are you suggesting that I drop the case?"

Brown waved his hands in the air. "Let's be honest. You haven't accomplished a thing since you've been here. It's your call, but I think you're wasting your time. Maybe you should go back home and run that very successful business you boasted about."

The bias Laska had accused me of showing when I first met him stopped me from slapping his face. I stepped around his wheelchair and hurried over to the bench.

Meltzer didn't ask if I'd like to move inside to air conditioning. He curtly ordered me to sit. "Is it really necessary to drag your attorney around behind you wherever you go?"

"Mr. Brown is not my attorney. He's my brother's attorney. Are you suggesting that I need a lawyer?"

"Not yet. But if I find out that you're hiding your brother, you will need an attorney—a good one."

"Thanks for the advice. What do you want?"

"Where have you been since your brother was released from jail? When was the last time you saw him?"

I stretched my legs out and crossed my ankles. "It's been two days since I've seen Dick. I've been in Washington, D.C. Would you care to see my boarding passes and hotel receipts?"

"Yes. Why did you go to Washington?"

I dug the papers out of my purse and held them out to the detective. "I thought I had a meeting. My appointment never showed."

Meltzer glanced at the boarding passes and shoved them in his breast pocket. Then he asked the same questions the judge had. Ray didn't like my answers either.

"You went to Washington for a mystery meeting. How convenient. A nice way to establish an alibi. You know, I tried to help you. And what do I get in return? Lies, nothing but lies."

Laska was quietly sitting next to the bench. I looked at him and said, "Would you like to help me out here?"

"If you insist. You were doing so well on your own, but I'll be happy to intervene here. Ray, you're not listening. The lady was out of town. She has proof from the airlines and the hotel to back up her story."

"Who can confirm her story? Who did she talk to? What did she do?"

I answered, "She spent most of the time walking around the monuments—alone. She ate at Burger King. She didn't talk to anyone who might remember her. She flew back this morning."

"Yeah. It would have been easy to fly back here to help a fugitive escape. I'll check to see if Ms. Stewart took another flight back to Key West. One she neglected to mention."

I sat up, ready to fight. Brown put a warning hand on my arm. "Detective Meltzer, this meeting is over. If you have more questions, call my office. I don't want you harassing her with innuendos about her honesty."

Ray glared at me. When I didn't blink, he swung his glare to the attorney. Laska pushed a strand of greasy hair away from his eyes and smiled. "That's all, folks. Ray, you know my number."

Meltzer was a sore loser. He clenched his fists, and his face turned red. I watched to see if the cop would throw a temper tantrum. Instead of screaming, Ray jumped up and race-walked to the station. Laska's hearty laughter chased him up the sidewalk.

"Well, counselor, I guess you told him. Do you think he'll make my life miserable?"

"Probably. This is a small town. Your brother has insulted it by killing Corrye. Don't yell—I'm not saying Dick killed Corrye, but most people think he did. Then he ran away from the clutches of our cops. You're going to reap the benefits of those insults."

I leaned forward and pushed Laska's sunglasses down so I could see his eyes. "Laska, do you know where Dick is hiding?"

He snapped, "Don't ask me that again. Call me when you decide to go home."

With amazing speed, Laska pushed away from the bench and wheeled down the sidewalk. I watched him go. Was there anyone who didn't want me to leave town?

Chapter 14

I walked across town to the hotel, examining the face of every person that passed me. How could they look so happy?

The woman at the front desk grinned when I walked in the door. Her grin grew larger as I approached. I ignored the woman's smile and asked, "Do you have any messages for me?"

She pointed at a large white box sitting on the counter. "No messages, but that came about half an hour ago. If I had to guess, I'd say it was filled with roses. It's heavy—must be a couple dozen inside."

"Excuse me?"

My snippy New York voice cleared the smirk from the woman's face. Flustered, she tried to explain. "I mean, you just got in town a few days ago and you're getting flowers. You know, I've lived here for eight years now and I never get flowers." She slid the box across the counter and asked, "New boyfriend?"

Guilt for my short temper softened my response. "New husband waiting at home is more like it. He must be getting impatient."

A broad green ribbon encircled the box. A small envelope was tucked under the ribbon. Expecting a sexy message from Dennis, I tore it open. I glanced at the note and swore under my breath. The blood drained from my face. "Who delivered this? How long ago did it get here?"

The smile dropped from the woman's face. "A kid delivered it. Why?"

"A kid? Do you know who he was?"

She stammered, "I don't know. Just a kid. A lot of them have summer jobs delivering flowers, and groceries, and other stuff. I dunno, he was here a while ago. Things have been busy—I kinda lost track of time."

Before the clerk could ask what was wrong, I grabbed the box, spun around, and hurried away.

I don't know how the registration clerk thought roses were in the box. It was heavy, much heavier than a dozen roses, and a few inches longer than a typical florist's box.

I crowded in the elevator with a group of tourists and listened to their excited chattering about their plans to fly to Fort Jefferson early the next morning. Cradling the box in my arms, I pushed to the back of the elevator as far away as possible from stray arms and elbows that might knock it from my grasp.

No one paid any attention to me. I made it to my room without trouble. With a sigh of relief, I locked the door and sat on the edge of the bed with the box resting in my lap. I looked at the card again. It wasn't signed, but a signature wasn't necessary. I recognized Dick's sloppy handwriting.

Blaine, if you won't take my advice and go home, take this. You'll need help. Don't worry—it's clean.

I slid the ribbon off the box. A wide band of clear tape secured the lid. I broke the tape, and a fingernail, and tossed the lid on the floor. I moved the green tissue paper aside, and my fingers touched metal. A blue-gray AK-47 was nestled in the paper.

The Soviet Union built the first AK-47s in 1947. Since then, it's become the favorite weapon of guerrilla fighters and terrorists. With the stock folded, the rifle was about two feet long—not much longer than a long-stemmed rose.

I picked it up and unfolded the stock. It was an evil-looking weapon, capable of firing bursts of ninety to a hundred rounds a minute.

Dick's little present could have come from any of the dozen or more countries that manufacture their own version of the

AK-47. The serial number had been roughly scratched off with a file.

I dug to the bottom of the reinforced box and uncovered a dozen magazines of ammunition—enough to defeat a battalion of heavily armed Marines. *What kind of trouble had my brother gotten himself into?*

Leaving the rifle on the bed, I dragged the telephone out onto the balcony and dialed Dennis's office. I wanted solace.

Our conversation started off pleasantly, but quickly deteriorated. After saying he missed me, Dennis asked, "Just what have you been doing down there?"

"Why are you asking? You know what I'm doing. Dennis, what's wrong?"

"I spent the last hour being asked a number of very unpleasant questions about you. I had to listen to a number of very unpleasant insinuations."

I tried to get the alarm I was feeling from my voice. "What kind of questions? What kind of insinuations?"

Dennis didn't answer my questions. Instead, he said, "I got pulled off all my cases this morning. They said conflicts of interest have arisen. Blaine, I'm doing desk duty. For God's sake, they're making me talk to a junior high school assembly this afternoon. What are you doing?"

"Why are you blaming me? What were you working on? Maybe you pissed somebody off and I'm just an excuse to discipline you."

Dennis sounded as if he was speaking from behind clenched teeth. "I was working on illegal immigrants. Believe me, this isn't about me, Blaine. It's about you. Whose toes are you stomping on?"

"I honestly don't know." I stared at the rifle on the bed and wished we could openly talk about it. "Do you want me to come home?"

"What good would that do? You've pissed off somebody important enough to make my life miserable. So—"

"Dennis, let's not fight about this, especially over the phone. Take a few days off from your desk duty and fly down here." *Please*, I silently pleaded, *I need you.*

My message didn't get through. Dennis said no. "This isn't a good time for me to take off. If I go away I might not have a job when I come back."

"Are you asking me to ease up on my investigation?"

"Are you trying to start an argument? Blaine, don't make it worse by putting words in my mouth. I'm not asking you to back off your investigation. I can tough it out until you're done."

The steely edge in Dennis's voice couldn't be missed. Trying to keep my own voice gentle, I asked, "Can you? You don't sound very certain."

"Will you stop? Please? There's nothing to discuss."

I was afraid Dennis would hang up. But he surprised me. I didn't hear the click of the receiver hitting the cradle; I heard Dennis's soft breathing. The silence built until I couldn't stand it any longer.

"Dennis, I'm going to get the first flight out of here tomorrow. I'll be home in time for dinner."

"Don't run out on your brother."

"Why not? He's—" Paranoia struck. I stopped in midsentence. "Dick's being a pain in the ass. Nothing's going right. Believe me, Dennis, I don't know who I've insulted or why they're taking it out on you." My voice faded as I thought of contacting Cal.

"It's done." Dennis sounded as if he didn't have a single friend in the world. I wished I could crawl through the wires and appear at his side.

Dennis didn't give me a chance to tell him how I felt. He said, "Blaine, you won't accomplish a thing by running back here." His voice changed to an official pitch. "Somebody's lurking outside. I'll call you tonight."

Quickly, before he hung up, I said, "Dennis, wait."

"What? I don't have time to rehash this."

"I love you."

"I know." Then he hung up.

I leaned against the railing and watched the scene below me. The tables on the patio below started to fill with early-afternoon drinkers. Seagulls swooped down searching for scraps of food. My head spun. How could everything seem so normal?

The AK-47 gleamed in the sunlight. My mind spun off in a different direction. What should I do with the assault rifle?

My mind raced with a thousand ridiculous possibilities. I could leave it under the bed for the housekeeper to find. I could start a revolution. I could take it to sunset at Mallory Square.

I decided to find a deserted beach and toss the rifle into the ocean. As soon as I thought of that solution, I changed my mind. That rifle might come in handy. I decided to put it in the most obvious place: Corrye's house.

I went inside, dug my backpack out of the closet, and dumped my running clothes on the floor. I lined the bottom with the ammo rounds and wiped the rifle clean with a towel, wrapped the rifle in an old T-shirt, and jammed it in on top. It was a tight fit, but the AK-47 and ammo fit. I rocked back on my heels and stared at the bag.

The knapsack would pass casual inspection, but anyone who touched the thin material would instantly feel the rifle. Before I could have second thoughts, I found my keys and left.

I kept a careful eye on the rearview mirror as I drove across town. If Ray Meltzer was following, he stayed well hidden. I saw a lot of traffic—mopeds, bicycles with high U-shaped handlebars, gawking tourists, but no police cars.

Corrye's house looked even more run-down than it had on my previous visit. Weeds had sprung from cracks in the sidewalk. The branches on the trees in the front yard drooped and brushed the ground. The floorboards on the porch sagged dangerously when I stepped on them.

When I unlocked the door, the parrot screamed. I fed and watered the bird before walking out the back door to the courtyard behind the house.

At one time the small area might have been carefully manicured, but a jungle had grown in the neglected yard. Palm trees and lush green plants filled the small space. Corrye protected her privacy by enclosing the yard with a towering wooden fence that cut off the view of any nosy neighbors.

I waded through the brush to the densest vegetation lining the back section of the fence. I buried the rifle under a stack of palm fronds.

I wrapped the ammunition magazines in a plastic bag I found wedged under the fence and buried that package under a different pile of leaves. I stepped back to examine my work. The leaves quickly sprang back up—my hiding place wouldn't be spotted.

I went back inside the house and climbed the stairs to Dick's bedroom. I stood in the doorway, mouth open.

All traces of Dick had been removed. Dick's clothes and every scrap of paper that had been scattered on the floor were gone. The dresser drawers and closets were empty too. Everything, except the furniture and dust balls, was gone. Even the sheets and pillowcases were missing.

Chapter 15

A police car was parked at the curb. Ray Meltzer waved. I turned to lock the door, then trotted down the stairs and walked to my car. Meltzer honked the car's horn. I ignored him and slid behind the wheel.

Ray pulled his car next to mine and expertly blocked me at the curb. I rolled the window down and turned to him. "What?"

He faked a friendly smile. "How'd it go? Did you find anything inside?"

"Nothing but a hungry bird. Would you move? I have things to do."

Ray mockingly craned his neck to look inside my car. "What's that in the backseat? It's not your brother, is it?"

I squeezed the steering wheel and stared out the windshield. Ray laughed. "So now you're not talking. That fits the family profile."

His sneering laughter set my temper flaring. I turned to Ray and asked, "What do you want from me?"

"Hey, don't get mad. I'm trying to help. You're wasting my time by trying to hide your brother. You're wasting your time too, because we'll find him."

"Thank you, Mr. Time Management. I appreciate the tip." I turned the ignition key, tapped the accelerator, and let the engine roar.

Meltzer yelled so I could hear him over the noise. "We've got the Coast Guard out searching for his boat. We're also putting helicopters and planes in the air. We'll find him. Why don't you save us a lot of time and money? Tell me where your brother's hiding."

I lifted my foot from the gas. "You spend too much time in the sun with nothing on your head. Those ultraviolet rays are dangerous, you know. I don't know where Dick is. If you want to waste your time following me around, go ahead."

I abruptly switched the engine off and opened the door. "Better yet, why don't I ride with you? That way you won't suffer the embarrassment of losing me."

Ray did a great imitation of a traffic cop. He held up his hand and said, "Whoa, now let's not rush into a confrontation."

"Too late. You started it, detective. How are you going to end it?"

Raw horsepower was Ray's solution. I leaned against my car and watched Meltzer speed out of sight. Once Meltzer's car disappeared, I got into my rental car and chugged across town on four cylinders—I missed my Porsche.

I walked around the marina, sweating in the hot sun and trying to ignore the smell of diesel fuel and dead fish. I talked to the kid at the gas pumps, the bartender in the bar, and the clerk at the bait shop. No one had seen Dick climb aboard the *Argo*.

The clerk's answer was the same as the others. "I didn't pay any attention. If I stopped to watch every boat come in and go out, I'd never get the shelves stocked." I thanked him and bought a soda.

I sat on the edge of the bulkhead and let my legs dangle out over the water. Another dead end. Meltzer was right. I was wasting my time.

I finished the soda and tossed the empty at the trash can a few feet behind me. It missed—a sign that it was time to start moving.

I decided to start with Al "Your Path to Justice" Tooney. I pulled Tooney's card from my wallet. Eaton Street, not too far from the hotel. After retrieving my soda can and throwing it away, I drove to Tooney's office. Maybe I could brighten his day by offering him a few bucks.

Number 40 Eaton Street was a tiny storefront stuck between the only working cigar factory in Key West (or so the sign on the canopy said) and a fast-food stand specializing in conch fritters. Window-shoppers glanced at the closed venetian blinds in the window of Tooney's office and kept walking.

I tried the door. It wasn't locked, so I opened it and went inside. A foul odor—the smell of dead flesh—filled the air.

I hardly noticed the new, sleek furniture, or the expensive computers sitting on a table near the door, or the modern art—the real thing, not reproductions—hanging on the walls of the large room. My eyes were drawn to the mahogany desk in the center of the room.

Al Tooney sat behind the desk in a high-backed black leather chair. He was wearing the same orange shirt he had had on when I first met him. He was slumped over, face down on the desk.

I didn't go near the body. From the moment I set foot in the room, I knew I'd be looking at a corpse.

I wanted to search the office before calling the police, but couldn't. The foul smell of decomposing flesh made me gag. I ran out to the sunshine and hot, clean air, slamming the door behind me.

There was a telephone booth at the end of the block. Rudely pushing through the strollers, I hurried to it and dropped a quarter in the slot.

The coin clanked down. The dial tone sounded and brought me to my senses. How could I call the cops? Once they arrived on the scene, I'd be shut out. If Tooney had any useful information, I'd never see it.

Swallowing hard at the thought of going back inside that room, I slammed the receiver down and walked away. I had more quarters—maybe a kid would find the coin I'd left in the phone and feel lucky. Someone should feel lucky; I didn't.

Even though I was prepared for the smell, my stomach rolled, and pitched, and dove when I walked in the door. It's hard to ignore a corpse, especially when it's sitting in the middle of a room, but I tried.

This time I carefully examined the expensive furnishings and the fancy computers that still had the plastic wrapped around the monitors. Everything looked as if it had just been unloaded from a delivery truck. Had Tooney suddenly come into money?

I took a few short, quick breaths through my mouth and walked around the office. I found several boxes filled with lamps, vases, statues, and other accessories. I found an ivy plant, a small pine tree, and some other plants. I didn't find any signs of a struggle. Tooney's filing cabinets were stuck in a small closet next to the bathroom.

I pulled open the top drawer and hoped for another surprise. Maybe I'd find neatly organized files with the answers to all my questions. Two cops, guns drawn as if they were rushing a dangerous criminal, burst in. Sounding like actors on a TV show, they yelled, "Freeze. Put your hands in the air."

Never argue with people who are pointing a gun at you—it's a good rule I try to follow. I slowly raised my hands and said, "It's okay, I don't have a gun or anything."

The two cops were a few inches taller than me, which put them well over six feet tall. They wore dark sunglasses that hid their eyes. I didn't need to see their eyes; their stern voices and steady guns didn't invite disagreement.

One cop kept his gun aimed at me while his partner pressed a finger against Tooney's neck. He shook his head. "This guy's had it."

"You have the right to remain silent . . ."

I closed my eyes and let the policeman's voice drone over me. No matter how innocent you might be, the sound of handcuffs closing around your wrists raises feelings of guilt and hopelessness. You start believing yourself guilty of anything.

". . . do you understand?"

I opened my eyes and turned around to face the policeman. "Yes, I want an attorney—"

"Later." The older one, the one in charge, took my arm and led me to the door. "You'll have time to make your call when you get to the station."

I dragged my feet, reluctant to leave Tooney's office. I'd had too many bad experiences with the police to believe I'd be safe in their hands.

Bad news travels fast everywhere, and Key West was no exception. A small crowd had already gathered on the sidewalk, attracted by the police car's flashing lights. The crowd parted to let us through and watched with unabashed curiosity.

I shuffled along, eyes focused on the ground, because I didn't want to meet the curious stares. I usually hate the newspaper reporters and hungry photographers who hover around crime scenes. This time, I hoped someone was taking my picture. I didn't want to be taken away without any record left behind.

I got pushed into the backseat of the patrol car, and we drove away. The only sound in the car during the short ride to the police station came from the air conditioning. Even though the car was cool, sweat dripped down my forehead and into my eyes. I concentrated on taking slow, deep breaths.

The cops pulled into the police station's parking lot, hauled me out of the car, and took me through the back door. My nerves jumped when we walked past the booking room to a corridor lined with empty cells.

I dragged my feet on the worn concrete, looking for an anchor. "Wait a second. What's going on here? Why are you arresting me? I want an attorney."

"Later." My resistance was easily overcome. They dragged me along and stopped in front of a cell at the far end of the hallway. They took the handcuffs off and pushed me inside. I sat on the cot and buried my head in my hands; I didn't want to see the cell door close. The sound was scary enough.

I didn't have much time to worry. After a few minutes, the steel door at the end of the hallway opened. Ray Meltzer paused in the doorway, then slowly walked toward me. I sat back, casually crossed my legs, and rubbed my wrists to get the blood pumping again.

Meltzer stopped in front of the cell. He was smiling. "You and your brother seem to have trouble staying away from dead people. Maybe I can get you a special family rate."

"Only if it includes a telephone call to my attorney."

Meltzer's temper flared. "Don't tell me how to do my job."

"Then do it." I kept my temper under control—barely. "How did you manage to get me arrested?"

"No need to manage anything. We got a call about suspicious activity at Tooney's place. Our officers found you ransacking his office. And with poor Tooney sitting dead in his chair. We caught you red-handed."

"Your boys caught me looking through Al's files. Not murdering him."

"Give me time. I'll make the connection."

"I'm sure you will, just like you connected my brother to Corrye's murder. What are you going to do, plant another murder weapon?"

Ray flushed, and his voice rose. "Don't make me out to be the guilty party. Your brother's the one who did the murdering—not me. I didn't commit any crimes."

"So you say. What magic evidence are you going to find to prove I killed Tooney? Did you get a special price for weapons to plant as evidence?"

It was the wrong thing to say. Meltzer spun around and quickly walked away. I called after him, "Hey, where are you going? You can't just leave me here."

Meltzer stopped and turned to me. In a low voice he said, "Yes, I can." Then he walked away.

I sat on the cot, waiting for Meltzer to return and let me loose. At ten o'clock the overhead light clicked off. Only the dim light outside the cell stayed on.

I stretched out, stared at the bars, and tried to keep my mind away from Florida's death penalty. I tried to fight the claustrophobic feeling that comes with being helplessly locked inside a six-by-six room. I eventually fell asleep.

Twisted bits of conversations and shadowy figures filled my dreams. Everything was striped by the shadows of the bars.

I woke up in the middle of the night, choking, disturbed by dreams of Mendieta's paintings.

Like most Americans, I knew little of life in Cuba. I saw occasional photos of Fidel Castro or news stories of people who risked their lives to flee their homeland in leaky, overcrowded boats or inner tubes strung together with ropes.

What would force me to tie two, three, or four inner tubes together and set out over miles of open sea? I made a list of the horrors of the voyage: sharks, storms, relentless sun, seasickness; the list went on and on. When I fell asleep again, I dreamed Augustin Mendieta's eagle hovered overhead, preparing to attack.

Chapter 16

A loud, obnoxious, and very welcome voice woke me from my uncomfortable sleep. "Hey, Stewart, look alive. I've arrived to spring you. Set you loose. Liberate you from the evil clutches of Key West's storm troopers."

My stiff bones and the shaky cot creaked as I stood up. Laska Brown wheeled himself down the corridor, calling out as he moved. He was alone.

I smiled and grabbed the bars. "Hey, counselor, am I happy to see you. It took you long enough to get here."

Brown let the chair glide to a halt in front of the cell. He picked a key from the breast pocket of his shirt and swung it in the air. "Don't bust my chops. It would be a damn shame if I lost this pretty little key."

"It's a damn shame that you're the only honest person in this pitiful town."

Brown unlocked the door and swung it open. "As much as I'd like to accept your grudging compliment, I can't. There are a few other honest people around here. Some are cops. Some are people who considered your brother a friend. About an hour ago, one of those friends rousted me from my comfortable bed. I came down here and raised hell. I'm surprised you slept through it. I made a lot of noise."

I stepped out of the cell and made an exaggerated motion of

breathing free air. "Come on, let's get out of here. Where's Meltzer?"

"Hiding. Everybody's trying to avoid me and any discussion of false-arrest suits. Meltzer said you stubbornly refused his offer to let you call me. Is that true?"

I stopped walking and looked at Brown. "What do you think?"

"Pretty weak. That's what I told Ray. Do you want me to go after him?"

"I prefer to get my revenge outside court. It's more satisfying than a judicial slap on the wrist. Would going to court do any good?"

Brown cheerfully answered, "Nope. Except next time they arrest you, they'll find a charge that sticks. Even our own crooked Dick Tracy couldn't prove you killed Tooney. They tried. They even pushed the local medical examiner to do an examination. The preliminary reports point the finger at Burger King and Ronald McDonald. Too many cheeseburgers. Al clogged himself up until his heart couldn't force another drop of blood through his arteries."

"So this"—I waved my hand at the empty cells—"was a warning."

"Yeah. Did it make a lasting impression?"

"What do you think?"

The attorney glanced at me. "I think we should get out of here before those guys change their minds and stick both of us in a cell."

It sounded like good advice. I quickened my pace to keep up with Brown. We didn't speak until we stepped outside. The hot air took away the chill that had settled into me during the long, lonely night. I closed my eyes and tilted my face upward to catch the full force of the sun.

Brown touched my arm. "This rescue mission is on the house. But your family has used up all its credit. Next time, I'm gonna bill you. Double if I get dragged out of bed again. I'd love to stay and chat, but I have work to do. Why don't you go take a shower or something? You look like shit."

After telling me his car was around the corner, but not offering me a ride to the hotel, Brown waved and wheeled down the walk. He stopped, looked over his shoulder at me, and called, "Try to stay out of trouble, will you?"

It wasn't even six-thirty in the morning. No one, except the crew emptying the trash cans, was out. I walked along White-head Street to the hotel, feeling dirty, sweaty, and tired. But not confused.

A night in jail had had the effect Ray Meltzer desired. I decided to get out of town.

After a quick shower, I dumped clothes into the suitcase and checked out. It only took a few minutes to get to the airport, and not much longer to return the rental car.

Last-minute fliers can't always get the direct flights. I spent the day flying. From Key West to Miami. From Miami to Atlanta. From Atlanta to JFK. I caught a taxi at the airport—just in time to get caught in rush-hour traffic. By the time the cab pulled up in front of the house, I'd been traveling for nearly ten hours.

Stiff from airplane and taxi seats, I struggled up the stairs and into a quiet, empty house. I dropped my keys on the small table in the hallway that's used for keys and mail, and turned on the small lamp.

I walked around the house, calling Dennis's name without getting an answer. Had his desk duty turned into overtime?

I called his office and listened to the telephone ring twenty times. My wandering led me to the kitchen. My new marriage had one great advantage I hadn't expected: we always have food in the house. I made a sandwich and took it to the living room, where I stood in front of the window, watching for Dennis as I ate. When I finished, Dennis still wasn't home. After leaving the dish in the sink, I went upstairs and fell into bed.

I woke the next morning with my face buried in the pillow, my outstretched arm touching the empty space beside me. I had vague memories of feeling Dennis next to me in the middle of the night. Or was it a dream?

Yawning, I pulled on a robe and went downstairs to look for my husband. I couldn't find him. I called his office and listened to the telephone ring five, ten, fifteen times before slamming the receiver down. Where was Dennis?

Concerned, I called my office and listened to the same empty ringing. That's when I realized it was Saturday morning. Too early for the procrastinators who straggle in on weekends to catch up on paperwork. No one would be in for another hour or two.

Saturday morning also meant Dennis was at the gym, trying to stick to his new exercise routine. After a week of room-service meals and restaurants, I enjoyed the chore of making coffee. The *Times* was sitting on the kitchen table. I took it and a mug of coffee to the living room and made myself comfortable on the sofa. I tried to read the paper, but found myself watching the door, waiting for Dennis.

Most people come home from the gym looking a little tired, a little sweaty. Not Dennis. His brown hair was dry and neatly combed. His suit and shirt were crisp and wrinkle-free. Only his dark brown eyes looked tired.

We kissed, with all the passion of two distant cousins meeting at a distant relative's funeral. I pulled my legs up to make room for Dennis on the sofa and asked, "When did you get in last night? Why didn't you wake me?"

"I tried. You wouldn't cooperate. Every time I prodded you, you mumbled that I should leave you alone. So I gave up. If you'd given me some warning, I would have been here when you got in."

"I made a quick decision to leave Key West. Rushing to make connecting flights didn't leave me much time to make telephone calls."

I leaned forward to kiss him. "I missed you. Nice suit. Is that the latest in gym wear?"

"Gym wear?" Dennis fingered his silk tie and slowly loosened the knot. "I skipped my workout. I had a meeting."

"On Saturday? I thought you were stuck behind a desk. What was your meeting about?"

"You."

My stomach sank. I sat up and leaned against the armrest.

Dennis stared at the tips of his shiny shoes. Anger slipped into my voice. "Are we back on the 'Blaine, what are you doing to ruin my career' argument?"

"We never got off it. Speaking of ruining things, should I ruin your happy homecoming now or later?"

"Now." I sighed and put the coffee mug on the floor. "What happened?"

"I've been suspended pending the outcome of an investigation into this conflict of interest I'm supposed to be having between my wife and my job. Thirteen years, Blaine. I put thirteen years of my life into this job."

I felt as if I'd been punched. I could only imagine what Dennis was feeling.

I wrapped my hands around his and said, "Those have been thirteen spotless years, filled with commendations. They can't overlook that. You said you've been working on illegal immigrants. How can that possibly be a conflict of interest with my brother's case? He's accused of murdering a poet, for God's sake. How could Dick murder Corrye and still have time to sneak illegals into the country?"

Dennis pulled his hands away and got up. He paced in front of the sofa. "At least I haven't been fired—yet. Blaine, we need to talk. Seriously."

I sat up even straighter. I wanted to look into Dennis's eyes, but found it easier to look away. "I'm listening. What is it?"

"I want out."

My breath caught in my throat. I whispered, "You want a separation. Why? Because of this problem with your job?"

"A separation?" A puzzled look came over Dennis's face. He stopped walking and stared at me. "Blaine, what are you talking about? I want out of my job. Not our marriage."

"You want to quit your job?" I started laughing and crying at the same time. "Is that all? When I came home last night and you weren't here . . . Then I woke up this morning and you were gone. You didn't even leave a note."

Dennis knelt in front of me and cupped his hands around my face. He gently turned my head so I had to look in his eyes. "So you've been sitting here letting your imagination convince you that I want a divorce." He kissed me. With his lips pressed against mine, he mumbled, "You have to stop imagining crazy things."

I promised. Kissing and making up took the rest of the morning and part of the afternoon.

Chapter 17

"I'm glad you didn't open the curtains this morning. We'd get arrested for indecent exposure." Dennis kissed my shoulder, then shifted to find a more comfortable position.

I wrapped my arms around Dennis's chest so he couldn't get away from me. "What kind of job are you going to look for?"

"I don't know. How about selling computers? I think I'd be good at sales."

"How about encyclopedias? The kids would love you."

"How about shoes? I like feet."

"How about—"

The phone rang, interrupting our career-counseling session. Dennis said, "Who's going to get up? Me or you?"

"You. It can't be for me. No one knows I'm here."

Dennis groaned, but he got up to answer the phone. I grinned and watched him, admiring the way his calf muscles stretched and contracted as he walked. He grabbed the phone and said hello.

I rolled on my back and listened. "As a matter of fact, I do. She's right here, stretched out on the sofa. No, she's awake. She's just being lazy. So lazy that she never did put any clothes on today."

He laughed and walked back to the sofa with the phone. "Nope, you're not interrupting anything. Now, if you had called about fifteen or twenty minutes ago . . ."

Dennis laughed again, then held the phone out to me. "It's Eileen."

"Hi. I was going to call."

Eileen chuckled. "Dennis told me you've been busy since you got back. I didn't mean to interrupt anything. I was getting worried. It's been a few days since we talked."

Eileen still sounded worried, but she tried to hide it. "I didn't expect to find you back in the city."

"I'm taking a little R and R. After spending Thursday night in jail, I decided to get out of Key West for a few days."

Eileen's voice rose. "Jail?"

Dennis said, "You didn't tell me that," and sat beside me.

Answering both of them, I said, "It's a long story. Too long to go into over the phone. Eileen, why don't you come over for dinner? I can fill both of you in. Maybe I can even charm Dennis into cooking something." He nodded. I smiled my thanks. "My charm worked again. Come around seven."

Eileen agreed, then hung up. Dennis took the phone from my hands and balanced it on the armrest. He put his arms around me. "Tell me the whole story. Why did you come home? What's this about jail?"

I rested my head against Dennis's chest and closed my eyes. "I'm running away. But you'll hear all that at dinner. Why do you want to quit the FBI?"

"It could be that I'm running away too."

Dennis bent forward to kiss me, but I refused to be distracted. I opened my eyes and moved away from him. "Running away from what?"

"You first. Why are you running away from Key West?"

"Because I was—am—afraid. I need to get back on solid ground, if only for a few days, to regain my footing. My confidence too. Your turn."

"Same problem. Fears. Shaky legs. Shaky confidence."

"What's given you trembly legs?" I reached down and ran my hand along his calf. "Feels pretty solid to me."

Dennis grabbed my hand and pulled it away from his leg. Without letting go, he said, "No fair. I thought this was a serious conversation. It's your turn again. What happened to your confidence?"

"My brother. The cops. The government. An assault rifle. A putrid corpse." I stopped and wrinkled my forehead. "Let's see, am I leaving anything out?"

Dennis prompted me with a kiss. "How about missing your incredibly sexy husband? Wasn't that enough reason to come home?"

I laughed. "Oh, that's it. I missed my incredibly sexy husband to whom I've been married for three and a half months." I sighed. "That and I felt like I was riding a waterspout in Key West. Getting too dizzy to hang on. Your turn."

"Time out. Let's back up to your list for a minute."

"Back to my incredibly sexy husband?"

"No. Back to the government and the assault rifle. What are you talking about?"

"Do we have to talk about this now?" I kissed Dennis's hand. "I'd rather talk about the sexy husband business."

The playfulness disappeared from Dennis's voice. "Yes, we do have to talk about this now. Trust me."

I shifted to get a clear view of Dennis's face. "I have this friend who works with the government. After years of silence, my friend called me the other day. He told me the government is interested in Dick's case."

"The government is always interested in the murder of one of its citizens."

"I'm not talking about philosophical interest. My friend works in Washington. He's very high up. Very well connected."

Dennis's eyes narrowed. I put my index finger against his lips and said, "Don't ask. Trust me. Even Brad doesn't know my friend's name, and you know I tell Brad everything that's business-related. Then Dick disappeared and an AK-47 showed up at my hotel. Complete with a note from my baby brother saying I might need a friend.

"Then I found the body of a sleazy private investigator who'd been trying to sell me information. The cops didn't believe that I merely found the body. Going on the theory that murder runs in the family, they decided I'd killed the guy. So I had a free night in jail while they tried to find evidence to put me away for murder.

"That's when I decided to get out of town." I took my finger away from Dennis's mouth. "What do you think?"

"Is your friend reliable?"

"Completely. In a sad, sick way the assault rifle made me feel better about Dick. I was afraid he was running drugs into Florida. All the classic symptoms are there: no visible income, big flashy fishing boat that never has any customers, living in prime smuggling waters. Maybe he started out that way, but I think Dick moved on to guns. That boat of his is within cruising distance of Cuba—maybe he's supplying the revolutionaries."

I sat up. My head barely missed Dennis's chin. "Cuba. That's the connection to Cuba. Her husband was a Cuban expatriate who hated Castro."

My excitement almost propelled me from the sofa, but Dennis held me back. "Whoa—you're not going to skip out so fast. That's an imaginative, but untested, theory. Are you going back to Key West to bounce it off every person you meet?"

I settled back against Dennis's chest. "It's worked in the past. Do you have a better idea?"

"I might. Ask me a question."

"You said you were working on illegal immigrants. Why was the FBI interested? Isn't that an INS problem?"

"Not this time."

"But you can't talk about it, right?"

"Right." Dennis kissed me, then said, "Blaine, you asked the wrong question."

"What's the question I should have asked?"

"Is it possible that your brother killed Corrye?"

"Dennis, I don't want to ask that question. I don't want to believe Dick could have murdered anyone."

"I abused my position and made a few telephone calls. They found your brother's fingerprints on it. Ballistics tests say it's the gun that killed Corrye. . . ."

Tears filled my eyes. I rubbed them away with the back of my hand and cursed Dick. "Damn him. Why the hell did he bother to call me with a pitiful story?"

"Momentary remorse. Pulling one last big con on his family.

I don't know. Guys like your brother have a million reasons for the things they do. Unfortunately, none of them come close to the truth."

Dennis wrapped his arms around me. I clutched them so he couldn't let go. I broke the silence by asking the question Dennis had been avoiding. "Why do you want to quit?"

"I've had too much. Too many scenes like this one."

His answer sounded too rehearsed for me to believe it. Carefully skirting conversations neither one of us wanted to have, I pinched Dennis's arm. "Hey, what's for dinner?"

"I don't know the answer to that question either. Want to try another?"

"Eileen's going to be hungry, you know. She won't be happy with pizza."

"Well, then it's time to get moving." Dennis gently pushed my arms aside and stood up. "Come on, let's get dressed. If you expect me to make dinner for your big sister, we have to go shopping."

Dennis left me and walked upstairs. I followed, stopping only to pick up his suit and my robe from the floor.

Dennis and I strolled across town from my brownstone in the Village to the Union Square Farmer's Market, trying to act like a normal couple out on a sunny Saturday afternoon. When we arrived at the farmers' stalls lining the northern end of the park, I hung back and watched Dennis hunt for the perfect tomato, fresh fish, and home-baked pies. I dutifully held the bags while Dennis haggled over the price of corn.

When I got tired of shoving through the crowds of Saturday shoppers, I found a shady spot beneath a tree where I could sit, eat an ice cream cone, and watch the people. After Key West, the people walking past seemed almost dull.

Dennis found me there nearly an hour later, flushed with success and carrying a colorful spray of flowers. He waded through the shopping bags that surrounded me, handed me the flowers, and helped me to my feet. We took a cab home. It had been a perfectly normal afternoon.

Eileen arrived on time, holding a bottle of red wine in one

hand, white in the other. I stared at the bottles, unable to move. Eileen watched me with an uncertain look on her face.

We try to keep my drinking from disrupting our lives—it did that for too many years. Having alcohol in the house or being around people who are drinking doesn't usually bother me. Except every so often, it hits without warning . . . then the world stops spinning. The only thing that matters is a drink. Those feelings were hitting more often than any time since I stopped.

Dennis came out of the kitchen to greet Eileen and quickly took in the situation. He kissed Eileen's cheek and smoothly plucked the bottles from her hands. "Dinner's in half an hour, give or take a few minutes. Why don't you two catch up while I finish my creation du jour?"

Eileen hugged me before stepping back to examine my face. "You don't look very tan."

"I haven't had much time to soak up the rays. Besides, if I had sat in the sun, I'd be lobster red, not tan. You tan, Eileen, I burn. The sun doesn't like my red hair and fair skin."

Eileen smiled, but the questioning look didn't leave her eyes. I blushed and pushed her in the direction of the kitchen. I didn't want to be alone with Eileen; she'd ask questions I didn't want to think about.

"Let's go see what Dennis is cooking. You guys can drink your wine and ask me as many questions as you'd like."

Instead of moving, Eileen asked her favorite question. "Are you okay?"

I tried to laugh. From the suspicious look on Eileen's face, I guessed she didn't believe the shaky sound.

"It's been weeks since you asked me that. Why drag it out now?"

"Because when you left, you were okay. You don't look very okay now."

"I'm not drinking."

"I didn't ask if you were drinking. I asked if you were okay."

" 'Okay' is your code word for sober." I mimicked Eileen's voice. "Are you okay, Blaine? Translation: Are you sober, Blaine?"

Dennis came out of the kitchen and stood behind me. He

rested his hands on my shoulders and said, "An argument, and it only took two minutes. I think you guys just set a record. Congratulations. The happy homecoming is complete. I missed the sound of two sisters fighting."

I looked at Eileen, who looked ashamed. I laughed. "He's right. You should have brought boxing gloves, not wine."

Dennis continued acting as peacemaker. He linked arms with me and Eileen and walked us to the kitchen. "We will have a nice quiet dinner—even if I have to make you two sit in different rooms."

I blushed, and Eileen did too. Dennis smiled but didn't loosen his grip.

"Hey, lighten up. I'm going to get a black-and-blue mark." I pulled Dennis's thumb back until he let go. "We're not going to punch each other." I leaned forward to look at Eileen. "Are we?"

Eileen smiled. "No, not even if you start—sorry. I take that back. Dennis, we're done fighting. Blaine, I'm glad you're back. I missed you and I was worried."

Dennis walked us into the kitchen. He pointed to the chairs and ordered us to sit. Dennis poured a glass of wine and put it in front of Eileen. I got seltzer. The thick wedge of lemon floating among the bubbles didn't make it any more appealing.

Eileen twirled the glass in her hands and stared at the swirls of red wine. "I had a phone call this afternoon."

That's Eileen's lead-in to really bad news. I swallowed a mouthful of water and wished it were wine. "Who called?"

"Dick."

Chapter 18

Dennis banged a pot down on the stove and cursed as he burned his hand. The noise barely registered; I couldn't take my eyes from Eileen's face. "When did he call you?"

"This morning."

Dennis held his singed finger under cold water and asked, "Eileen, did your brother call you at home or at the office?"

"Home. I didn't go to the office today. Why?"

We exchanged glances over Eileen's head. Maybe the government hadn't gotten around to taps on Eileen's home phone. Maybe I was being too paranoid.

"What did he say?"

Eileen noticed, but didn't comment. "Dick said you had disappeared. He called because he was worried. So am I. What's going on down there?"

"Where was he calling from?"

Eileen can be a very stubborn person. She leaned back in her chair and stretched her legs out. "I'm not saying another word until you answer my question. What's going on?"

I can be stubborn too. Instead of answering Eileen's question, I asked one of my own. "Did he say where he's hiding?"

"Hiding. What do you mean by hiding?" A puzzled frown settled on Eileen's face.

"I mean hiding. Dick's attorney got him out on bail. As a thank you, Dick skipped a few hours later."

"What can he be thinking? If he's innocent, why did he run away? I'm sorry to say this, but . . ."

"Don't. Eileen, I'm having enough trouble believing Dick. I don't want to hear your doubts too."

As Dennis sliced, diced, sautéed, and served dinner, I told them about my adventures in Key West and Washington. The shopping trip Dennis and I had made to Union Square had been a waste of time—I didn't taste a thing. I chewed, swallowed, and talked.

I pushed my plate to the center of the table and absentmindedly patted my pockets in search of cigarettes. "That's all I have to report. Eileen, exactly what did Dick say to you?"

"He certainly didn't say he'd skipped bail. He said Cal is bullshitting you and you shouldn't believe anything that creep tells you. Who's Cal?"

The blood drained from my face. Dennis put his fork down and gently touched my hand. "Blaine, what's wrong?"

"Nothing." I stood up and took a handful of dirty plates to the sink to cover my confusion. *How had Dick learned about my meeting with Cal?* "What else did Dick say?"

"That was it. I asked him if he wanted me to go down to Key West to help with his case. He said no. He told me you should stay away too."

Dennis, the FBI agent who wasn't quite ready to quit his job, appeared. He asked, "Did you hear any noises in the background? Was there anything that might give a clue to where he was calling from? I don't suppose he called collect."

"No, for once it wasn't a collect call. No background noise. I've been replaying that call in my mind ever since Blaine told me Dick was AWOL. There isn't anything that stands out." Eileen shifted in her seat to look at me. "Blaine, what are you planning to do next?"

I turned to face her and leaned against the sink. "I don't have a real plan. I am going back to Key West."

Dennis shook his head but didn't say anything. Eileen protested. "I don't like it. Dick's gone. The police down there have already shown a complete disregard for proper procedure. What can you possibly accomplish down there, except getting into more trouble? I know I'm being overprotective again, but—"

Dennis calmly interrupted. "But you are. Leave her alone, Eileen. Blaine has to run her investigation as she sees fit."

While I nodded agreement, Dennis said, "Blaine, we're past keeping secrets about this case. Is Cal your source in Washington?"

I nodded miserably. "I can't imagine how Dick came up with that name. Promise me that your inquiring minds won't start to wonder about Cal."

"Only if you promise to check in regularly. No more hiding to play games with your spymaster friend."

I felt as if I'd been put on a leash, but I didn't argue. I mumbled, "Okay, Dennis," and ran water over my dirty dish.

Desperately trying to find normal ground, which is why I'd fled Key West, I asked Eileen, "How's Don? Is he flying this weekend? Where's Sandy—what did you do with her? I thought she'd be anxious to see her Aunt B."

Eileen briefly smiled at the thought of her daughter. "Sandy wanted to come, but I got a sitter. I thought we'd have too many adult things to talk about." She hesitated, then quietly added, "I don't know where Don is tonight."

I waited. Eileen doesn't like to be pushed. Dennis didn't move either. A quiet nervous tension filled the kitchen.

Eileen quietly spoke the words I'd been unable to voice earlier about my own marriage. "We separated. We've been having too many fights in front of Sandy. We decided to take a break. Don's staying with one of his pilot friends."

"You separated?"

Eileen nodded. "Ten years of marriage and it ends with Don sacking out on a friend's sofa bed. Sandy's used to Don being away on trips, so we haven't said anything. No sense in her being upset too."

"And you? How upset are you?"

Eileen shrugged and bit her lower lip. "I'm dealing with it. Look, Blaine, I don't want sympathy. I'm only telling you this so you'll know what's going on. Forgive me for being short-tempered." She folded her arms across her chest and defiantly stared at me.

I walked over to Eileen and hugged her. "If you need anything . . ."

"Don't worry, I can take care of myself. You have your hands full with Dick."

And Dennis, I thought. I looked across the table. He winked. I smiled; maybe I wouldn't have to worry about Dennis.

After Eileen left, Dennis and I retreated into our individual, secretive worlds. We stuffed the dishwasher with the dinner plates, put leftovers in the refrigerator, and made small talk about nothing. Even when we went to bed and joylessly made love the distance remained.

I spent Sunday in the office. Dennis grumbled when I told him my plans, but not as loud as Brad grumbled when I suggested he skip brunch with his latest woman and meet me at the office.

Several neat stacks of papers covered my desk, according to the system Jona, my secretary, had developed over the years. A legal pad with important notes sat in the center, where I couldn't ignore it. Phone messages that required a return call were piled in the far right corner of the desk. The stack in the far left corner contained other phone messages, no response necessary. Mail, opened and filed according to importance, occupied the near right corner. Field reports took up the left corner.

It's a great system that works—sometimes. I tossed my briefcase on the desk; papers scattered and fluttered to the carpet. I popped open the can of seltzer I'd gotten from the small refrigerator in our pantry and settled down to catch up.

Brad lumbered in an hour later, half an hour later than he'd promised.

"Hi, Babe. Welcome home. Sorry I'm late."

I looked at Brad's sleepy eyes, his rumpled hair, wrinkled shorts and polo shirt, and laughed. "You look like a walking hangover. I hope you had some fun last night. Sorry. I didn't realize eleven a.m. would be cramping your style."

Brad dropped into a chair. I cringed, expecting it to fold under the bulk of the muscles left over from his days as a pro linebacker.

He shook his head. "You've been married too long. You forget how wild a Saturday night should be."

"For God's sake, Brad, we went to kindergarten together—and I remember how long ago that was. Don't you think it's time to give up the all-night orgies?"

"Nope. I hate lectures from jealous married women. Did you drag me in on a Sunday morning to discuss my lifestyle?"

"Nope. Let my vivid imagination fill in the details. What did you find out about my brother?"

Brad tossed the file he was holding on my desk. "It's all here. Let me sum it up so you don't waste time like I did. I didn't find a goddam thing."

I rubbed my forehead in an unsuccessful attempt to chase away the headache that was starting to pound. "Dick's thirty years old. There must be some record of a job, a car loan, something."

Brad shook his head. "Nope. Nothing."

"What the hell is going on here?"

My question had been asked with desperation, not the expectation of an answer. Brad attempted to answer anyway. He clasped his hands behind his head and stared at the ceiling.

"Dick has some powerful friends—or enemies. I thought it might be interesting to know how he got them. So I started to do a little snooping."

"And?"

"Dead ends. His fast track ended after college."

"Tell me something I don't know. I lived through it, remember?"

"My latest woman, as you so gracefully phrased it, is a Wall Street investment banker. Coincidentally, she's a Yalie. Graduated in your brother's class."

"Did you find that out before or after you started sleeping with her?"

"Babe, that's a very rude question; I won't dignify it with an answer. Would your filthy little mind like to hear what my friend told me?"

I impatiently tapped a pencil on the blotter. "Only the parts that relate to my brother. Please skip the pillow talk."

"I'm sorry the time away hasn't improved your disposition. Dick was a member of a very exclusive club, the Snakes and Vipers."

I shook my head. "Is that supposed to mean something? If so, I'm sorry, because I've never heard of it."

"You've heard of the Skull and Bones, haven't you?"

"Sure, the infamous secret club that's not very secret. Presidents, soldiers, cabinet members, top executives have all been members. But no one will talk. The folklore says the connections last long past college. Some of the best conspiracy buffs blame Skull and Bones for a lot of corruption and behind-the-scenes maneuvering in this country. A weird club."

"With a lot of power. Snakes and Vipers is even more secret, and supposedly more powerful. Dick was one of the twenty Yale boys inducted at the end of their junior year. Guess who recommended him for membership? Reginald H. Brown."

"That sneaky bastard. I knew he was hiding something." I tossed the pencil on the desk; it rolled to the floor. Instead of retrieving the pencil, I opened the file folder and scanned the mostly blank pages. "How come none of this is in your report?"

"I didn't think it was wise to put it in writing. Before you ask, yes, I've been sweeping for bugs. Nothing yet."

"What about today?"

Brad faked a hurt look. "Come on, Babe, give me credit for picking up a few tricks of the trade in the years that I've been following your illustrious footsteps. I swept this place this morning. That's why I was late—I was returning the equipment to my buddy.

"I also had somebody watching to be sure we didn't have any early-morning visitors. Didn't you see the guy polishing the hallway? That's Darryl. You know, Darryl, the new guy. The guy you hired before you took off for Key West. He's pretty good."

I shook my head. I'd been too busy worrying about Dick, Eileen, and Dennis to take notice of a new face. I had fallen into the trap of not noticing the janitors, the cleaning ladies, the deliverymen. The people who have keys to our offices; the people we allow inside without a second thought.

"Sorry—if I thought before I snapped at you I wouldn't have to do so much apologizing. Give Darryl my compliments." I ruined the apology by adding a suspicious afterthought. "Is your lover a Snake and Viper? Are you sure you're not being fed false information?"

"Snakes and Vipers are the most conservative of the old-liners. No women, no Jews, no blacks, no gays. There's a code of silence, but people who feel they've been harmed by a club that sets its own rules are often willing to talk. My lady friend has too much money to be scared by a pack of grown-up boys playing power trips."

"Then she's naive."

"I went to a lot of trouble to cultivate this source. I believe she's genuine."

"Okay, your intuition is usually on target. That still leaves us at a dead end."

"Not really. I'm going up to New Haven this week to see if I can track down some other Snakes and Vipers. It might be nice to know who Dick's playmates are."

"Do you believe all these stories about how powerful groups like Skull and Bones or the Snakes and Vipers are?"

Brad stretched his legs out until they grazed the bottom of my desk. His nonchalant pose couldn't hide the worry in his eyes.

"I've done a lot of research in the past few days. A number of high-ranking people in the government and private industry have been members of these secret societies. George Bush was a member of Skull and Bones. He directed the CIA before he became president. Who knows how many old Bones were in his closet when he moved into the White House?"

"What does your friend say about Snakes and Vipers?"

The worry lines on Brad's forehead grew more pronounced. "They don't claim to have ex-presidents as members. Even worse, they have a lot of the president's men. Including the CIA and the FBI."

The pit got deeper and deeper.

Chapter 19

Brad's not the only person with Yale connections. My small circle of friends includes a few Yale graduates and two professors. After Brad left to revive his romance, I started making calls. Keeping my address book up to date paid off.

All of my conversations got off to a bad start. I woke people up, interrupted breakfast with the kids, or caught a family rushing out to church.

Two people abruptly hung up when I mentioned Snakes and Vipers. Two others politely confessed ignorance—then hung up. The fifth, Marc, an assistant professor in the humanities department, didn't hang up.

After a few pleasantries, I asked about the Snakes and Vipers and waited to hear the click of a receiver being dropped into the cradle.

Marc surprised me. He thought for a few moments then said, "Blaine, that's a tough question. Officially, these clubs, or whatever you want to call them, don't exist."

"What about unofficially?"

"You're not taping this, are you?"

"No tapes, no notes. Marc, as far as I'm concerned, this call never happened. I don't even know you."

"We did meet once at a wedding, remember. I can't forget speaking to you."

I remembered dancing with him at Ashley's wedding. I also remembered thinking about more than dancing. "Oh, did we meet? I'd forgotten."

I heard the low, soft rumble of a laugh. "I bet you have. When are you coming to visit? You never followed up on my invitation. It still stands, you know."

"That was at least a half-dozen years ago, Marc. I'm a happily married woman now."

"Yeah, and Ashley and Judd are long since divorced. A man needs to keep his dreams alive."

"Keep your dreams, Marc. I want to talk about nightmares. What about these secret groups?"

"Your call comes at an interesting time. I'm just finishing a novel about Yale's secret underworld."

"Isn't that a dangerous undertaking? If these stories are true, couldn't you find yourself out of a job?"

"Not really, Blaine. My advance will carry me through my next novel and beyond. But it is nice of you to worry. If the book doesn't sell, I'll move to New York City. Would you take me in?"

Marc's teasing tempted me at a time when I didn't want to wonder about what might have been—or what could be. I quickly changed the subject. "Snakes and Vipers. What did your research turn up?"

Marc lectured. I took notes.

"There are eight secret societies on campus. Most of them started in the early 1830s. Only juniors are inducted into the clubs. Each club takes in ten to twenty members each year. Fifteen a year times one hundred and sixty-three years. That's almost twenty-five hundred members. Multiply that by eight groups."

I'd been following Marc's calculation on the legal pad. "And you get twenty thousand. That's quite a network. I assume many of the members have attained powerful positions."

"Yes, in business and government. Some, like Snakes and Vipers, recruit other members from other schools. The networks stay strong and secret. Members won't admit to being members. If you mention Skull and Bones, Snakes and Vipers, Wolf's

Head, or any of the other groups in a room where members are present, they'll walk out. The ban on talking about the groups lasts forever. And that's not all—"

I interrupted. "Let's go back to the beginning, Marc. How did these groups start?"

"There are a number of theories. Some trace the groups back to German society. The Freemasons, Hitler, and the John Birch Society also get the blame. None of these theories give the groups a beneficial origin. They were not formed out of a Christian desire to form a new, charitable world. Some say George Bush's New World Order is derived from Skull and Bones doctrine."

I laughed nervously. "Marc, that's hard to believe. You're saying a president of the United States was—"

"That's why I'm calling my book fiction. No one believes it could be true. Blaine, I've spent too much time on this to call it playacting, posturing by boys who believe themselves more important than they are, or foolish tall tales spun by the envious. It's like UFOs. No one believes in them—until one hovers in the sky above his head."

"Why does someone get tapped for membership? It's got to be more than fraternity-brother charisma."

"Groups like the Snakes and Vipers want the future leaders, the behind-the-scenes power brokers. The incoming freshman class is scrutinized for potential candidates. A close eye is kept on their politics, grades, activities, and friends. Even their sex and drinking habits are tracked over the years. The potential for mutual blackmail forms strong loyal bonds."

"Marc, one last question. Someone mentioned that these groups have CIA connections. Is there any truth to that?"

A tone of suspicion entered Marc's voice. "I'm going to ask a question I should have asked sooner. I don't suppose I was the first thing on your mind when you woke up this morning. Why are you calling early on a Sunday morning to chat about Snakes and Vipers?"

I spun my chair around and looked out at the normal, sunny morning sky. "Marc, I'd be lying if I said I called after all these years because I missed the sound of your voice—although now that I hear it, I'm sorry I haven't called sooner. I need information from a trustworthy source. I hope I haven't imposed."

Marc mumbled, "Of course not."

I quickly prompted him to continue. "The CIA?"

"I don't feel comfortable with this discussion. I never feel comfortable speculating about the CIA."

"But since I asked . . ."

"But since you asked, I will. Let me tell you a story. It's all unsubstantiated, of course. The story says Bush was the first CIA director in twenty years who wasn't in power because of the Snakes and Vipers. He was Skull and Bones. The trend ended with him. Snakes and Vipers have been in control since Bush left. Be careful, Blaine. This spider web has spread over the entire country."

I tried to laugh; Marc cut me off. "I'm telling you what I've learned through years of careful research. You may not believe it, Blaine, but I'm convinced. I'm not a lunatic. I'm a scholar, trained to investigate the facts. If you don't want to listen, that's your choice. That's it. I don't have anything else to say on the subject."

Our attempts to turn the conversation back to its earlier bantering tone failed. After a few brief, awkward moments, Marc wished me well, invited me to visit him on campus, and hung up.

I dropped the receiver in my lap and stared out the window. For the hundredth time, I asked myself, *What kind of trouble has my brother gotten himself into?*

After dinner, I went upstairs to pack. Dennis followed and stood in the doorway watching. I tossed the suitcase on the bed, clicked the hasps open, and turned to the closet to find clean clothes.

I threw a pair of shorts into the suitcase and looked at Dennis. He stood in the doorway, back rigid, hands stuffed in the pockets of his shorts. "So what are you trying to tell me, Dennis?"

"I'm not telling you anything. While you were at the office, I spent the day thinking. I'm asking you to drop it. Your brother's gone. He doesn't care what happens. Why should you?"

Dennis raised his voice. "Blaine, your goddam brother is ruining my career. I'm going to get fired before I can decide if I want to quit. He's going to ruin our marriage if we're not careful. Don't you care?"

I threw a T-shirt in on top of the shorts. In a low, calm voice, I said, "Of course I care about what Dick is doing to us. I can't give up now. I'm going back to Key West in the morning. I trust our marriage will survive until I get back."

"And what if I get fired?"

Despite the stormy gleam in Dennis's eyes, I laughed. "You can come work with me. Eileen would love to have you on staff. We can share my office. Besides, haven't you been talking about quitting?"

Dennis didn't laugh. He turned and stomped down the stairs. I nearly followed but didn't. I didn't want to fight, I wanted everything to be the way it had been before Dick called me. I finished packing and went to bed. Alone.

The sinking of the mattress under the weight of Dennis's body woke me from an uneasy sleep. I touched his back. He rolled over and took my hand. He whispered, "Sorry, I didn't mean to wake you. I didn't mean to yell either."

I kissed his hand. "I was only half asleep. I was afraid you were going to spend the night on the sofa."

"I tried. It's not very comfortable. Maybe we should get a new one."

"So you can sleep on it when you're mad at me? No, let's keep that lumpy old sofa. Is that the only reason why you decided to come to bed?"

Dennis answered through what sounded like clenched teeth. "I said I was sorry."

I dropped his hand and rolled onto my back. "Dennis, I'm not asking for an apology. I don't blame you for being mad. Hell, I'd love to strangle Dick as payment for the messes he left behind."

Dennis didn't answer. I folded my hands under my head and counted his soft intakes of breath. When I reached ten, I said, "Help me out, Dennis. I've run out of ideas. I have to go back."

"Would you like to kiss and make up before you leave?"

"Would you?"

Dennis kissed my shoulder, then my cheek. He murmured, "Yes," as his lips touched mine.

Monday morning came too soon. Dennis went back to work. I went back to the airport. With my promise to keep in touch ringing in my ears, I bought a ticket to Washington. A ticket I didn't tell either Dennis or Eileen I was going to buy.

As the plane flew south, I stared out the window and let my mind roam. Unfortunately, it roamed in a large, confused circle. I was involved in something I didn't really understand. As I got in deeper and deeper, I understood less and less.

Cal wasn't happy to hear my voice. "How did you get my home phone number? I thought you understood that you would never contact me. Never. Not at home. Not in the office. Never."

I glanced around the phone booth. A few tourists wandered by. It was getting harder and harder to shake off feelings of paranoid conspiracy. No one seemed to be paying attention, but the good ones always look disinterested.

"That's what you get for sleeping late on a Monday morning, Cal. I called your office, and they said you hadn't arrived yet. So I decided to interrupt your beauty sleep. I haven't been sleeping lately. Why should you? I have a few friends who are very good at finding phone numbers. They said getting yours was a challenge. They love challenges."

"You called my office!" Cal's voice rose. "Whatever possessed you to be so reckless?"

"Don't worry, I didn't leave my name. I'm standing in a phone booth at the foot of the Washington Monument. Unless your pals have tapped every public phone on the Mall, I'm not worried. Are you worried that your home phone is tapped? If so, all the more reason to meet me. You wouldn't want anybody to hear what I have to say."

Cal snapped, "Since you have lost control of your senses, I have no choice but to humor you. Where shall we meet?"

"Not the same place as last time. I'll give you half an hour to meet me in the other place. Cal, I have a roll of quarters in my pocket. If you don't show up, I'll spend them on phone calls to people who'll be interested in ancient history."

Cal sputtered. I slammed the phone down before he could form a sentence.

The "other place" was the top floor of the Air and Space Museum, eye level with the wheels of Lindbergh's plane, *The Spirit of St. Louis*. After forty minutes of sitting on the edge of the seat, carefully scrutinizing everyone who approached, I spotted Cal climbing the stairs. He looked older than he had at our last meeting. Older and angrier.

My intuition was right. Cal's temper hadn't cooled. He dropped onto the bench next to me and heatedly said, "I don't like threats, especially from people I've gone out of my way to help. I hope this game is important enough to justify the risk."

"It is, Cal. I'm not playing games. I'm not making idle threats. You're fucking with my brother's life, my husband's life, and my life. I want to know why."

Cal's loose grip on his temper snapped. "Do you think you're special? That you're above all the rest? Who do you think you are, summoning me like some servant?" Cal moved to rise to his feet.

"Wait a second." I put my hand on Cal's thigh and anchored him to the bench. "You didn't do me any favors. Your leaks benefited you more than me. I didn't get a great promotion and hefty raise when my superiors were forced out. You did."

Cal flushed. "How dare you? You've been spying on me."

"Not spying, Cal. You're the expert at that. I checked up on your career. I thought it only fair—you've been keeping track of me."

His shoulders slumped in surrender. I was alarmed; I'd never seen such a defeated look on Cal's face before. I found myself apologizing.

Cal coldly brushed my sympathy aside. "We can talk. But the old rules still apply."

"Do we have to continue playing games? I have too much at stake to waste time playing guessing games."

"It's my way or no way. Make up your mind." He stood and beckoned me to follow. "Well, come. We can't talk here."

We walked down the stairs and out the front door without speaking. As soon as we stepped onto the sidewalk, Cal took a crumpled pack of Salems from his jacket pocket and offered me a bent, slightly flattened cigarette. Even though I desperately wanted it, I said no.

Cal lit the cigarette and took a deep drag. "You haven't become one of those politically correct nonsmokers, have you?"

"Nonsmoker, yes. Politically correct? Never."

I thought of the reasons why I'd stopped smoking and shuddered. The fear of a disease coursing through my blood, a fear developed during my last case, was still strong enough to make me forget my nicotine cravings.

"But I have gotten unbearably grouchy since I stopped. Grouchy enough to blow the whistle on the whole damn government, if necessary. I'll start with you."

Cal took my arm and led me across the street. We walked along the Mall in the direction of the Washington Monument.

"When the monument opened, it was the tallest building in the world. That's still the tallest building in the city. You know, the government wanted to build a lavish monument. Lack of money stopped it. Like so many government plans, the public never supported it."

"How many times does the government go ahead with its plans despite public opinion?"

Cal flicked the half-smoked cigarette into the gutter. "You've gotten smarter, or better connected. I'm only sorry you're wasting your talents—and our friendship—on your brother."

"Defending Dick has become a full-time job. Why are the high and mighty powers taking such an interest in my fuckup brother?"

"My dear, you are being dragged into an unfortunate affair that becomes more and more unfortunate with each passing day. Frankly, I don't understand why you persist."

"Man turns his back on his family, well he just ain't no good." Cal's face was blank as he tried to make sense of my quote. I didn't feel like explaining the Bruce Springsteen lyrics to him, so I just shook my head and said, "Forget it."

"Well, Blaine, now that I have gotten over my anger, I must admit I am glad you telephoned me. God bless modern technology, especially car phones. While I was rushing to answer your impertinent summons, I made a number of telephone calls."

Cal wrapped his fist around my hand; the skin felt calloused from yard work. "I am prepared to offer a solution to your family's discomfort."

I tried to pull my hand away, but Cal tightened his grip. "I'm disappointed. I never expected you to play deal-maker."

"Another harsh, harsh word. I'm an emissary. A peace-maker."

"Cal, there has never been a declaration of war. So why are you offering peace? Who are you representing?"

"Myself. You have my complete reassurance that I can mend all these broken relationships. That is, if you offer some reassurances in return."

"I don't have anything to deal."

"Your brother does."

"That's a problem. As I'm sure you know, Dick is among the missing."

"My dear, I have great faith in your abilities. You're smart. You're persistent. You'll find him."

I pulled my hand away with a force that surprised both of us. "Do you think I'm going to look for Dick when your people are following behind? As far as I'm concerned, Dick can stay missing. That's better than leading you to him."

"You have my word of honor—"

"Cut the bullshit, Cal. No one in your business has any honor."

"You try my patience. You cannot afford to try my patience. I am one of the few willing to negotiate with you."

We were nearing the monument. I stopped walking and pointed to a bench. "Let's sit. It's time for you to tell me a story." When Cal didn't move, I said, "My first requirement for a settlement is a story. A story about why and how this mess came about. Why are you so concerned about my brother?"

Cal mournfully shook his head. "It pains me to say this. I am afraid we have reached the end of our journey together. I cannot betray—"

"You've done it before. Why is it different this time?"

"Blaine, you have an unnerving habit of interrupting. I'm sorry; I cannot help you. I will give you a very serious warning that you should not disregard: be careful. Do not try to contact me again. I am sorry, but not surprised. Too many of these relationships end in disappointment for both parties."

Cal turned and walked away. He didn't slouch away in defeat. His shoulders were square. I swear he was whistling under his breath as he walked across the Mall. I watched until he disappeared in a crowd of tourists, then turned to find a cab to the airport.

Chapter 20

On the flight south, I was too restless to sleep, too worried to stare out the window and let the clouds lull me into relaxation. The closer the tiny Gulfstream got to Key West, the more restless I became.

Finally, in desperation, I dug into my bag and pulled out a thin, worn paperback. *Tropical Heat*, Corrye's first book of poetry. Dennis, claiming he'd found it in the dollar bins of used books at the Strand bookstore, had given it to me before I left home.

The poems dated back to the early sixties. I flipped through the book, reading two or three lines of a poem before impatiently skipping to the next one. The last poem in the collection caught my attention; it was dedicated to Ray Meltzer. I closed the book and went back to staring out the window. As the plane made a wobbly landing at the Key West airport, I decided on a new plan.

The registration clerk at the hotel was happy to see me return. The fishing tournament had departed, searching for bigger fish in other waters. I had my choice of rooms and settled for 4B, the same room I'd had when I first checked in. I tossed my suitcase on the bed and put on the lightest pair of shorts and T-shirt I had. Then I grabbed my sunblock, a hat, and a towel and headed for the beach.

Late June is the off-season in Key West. The locals who have the time and money head for cooler climates to recover from the tourist crush; the rest seek air-conditioned comfort.

At two-thirty in the afternoon of a hot weekday, Smathers Beach was nearly deserted. A few swimmers were in the water; vans renting beach chairs and selling cold drinks lined the road.

I parked the car and sat against Corrye's palm tree. From my seat beneath the tree, I could watch the water and see the road. Traffic was light. I spotted the black reptile van again and counted the mopeds that passed. I reached 177 before a familiar unmarked police car pulled into an empty spot at the curb.

Ray Meltzer climbed out of the car and walked across the sand to Corrye's shrine. The good-natured smile fell from his face when he recognized me. I smiled, stood, and held out my hand. "Ray, I came to apologize, not fight."

He limply shook my hand and dropped it as if he feared contamination. "That's really nice of you, but I'm the one who needs to do some apologizing. Things got out of hand the other day. I am sorry."

"Done and forgotten."

"When did you get back in town? Brown told me you'd taken off."

"I've been back for a few hours. Ray, I need your help." I watched a deep frown crease his face and quickly said, "Now don't accuse me of meddling in police business. I've been sitting here all afternoon, because I knew you couldn't let a day go by without coming here. You didn't meet Corrye here on the beach like you told me the night I first met you. You knew each other for years. You were in love with Corrye, weren't you?" I almost blurted out, "Why did you lie?" but caught myself.

"Now you are meddling. Why should I tell you a thing? It's your brother—"

"I don't want to talk about my brother. I want to talk about you and Corrye. This morning on the plane I read Corrye's poetry again. Do you remember the poem 'Another Love'? How could you forget? She dedicated it to you. Did Corrye give you up for another love? Did you ever forgive her for leaving you?"

"It's none of your business. I don't know why I should listen to your crap."

"Because I know what it's like to try to keep living when someone you love has been killed."

"Do you? I wonder." Unable to match my steady gaze, Ray looked away and addressed the ocean. The water was calm, protected by an offshore reef.

"In a way, you remind me of Corrye. At least your temper does. Hers would flash and flare just like a match. Then it would go out. Yours does the same."

I gently asked, "When did you and Corrye first meet?"

"Probably in kindergarten. Corrye and I were born and raised here in Key West. We're Conchs. They call us that because the conchs are so common around here. They became a major part of our diet. Conch fritters, conch chowder . . .

"You won't find many Conchs left in this town. The taxes are too high. The houses are too expensive. Nowadays, the people moving in have money to buy our old houses and fix them up like they used to be when we made money from the sea."

"So you and Corrye grew up together."

"Yeah. We went to school together. Dated. We did everything together. Some folks bet that we'd marry. I know my mama wanted us to get married. You see, Corrye's family came from money—they made it selling land and salvaging shipwrecks. My folks were fishing people, pulling their living from the sea. Corrye and I swore we'd never leave. I'll probably die here just like Corrye did."

Ray stopped talking and stared out at the water. Quickly, before he lost his talkative mood, I tried to pull him back. "I know Corrye left Key West to go to college."

"Way back in 'fifty-eight, Corrye went to Vassar. You should have seen the fuss people made. Why, Corrye was even on the front page of the paper. You see, way back then people just didn't go away to college. Especially not such a big, fancy school. God, she was beautiful. She had long, dark hair. Her skin was bronze from the sun. She hated Vassar."

"What do you mean, she hated Vassar? The book jackets say the school had a huge influence on Corrye. It's where she started writing poetry."

"Oh no, the book jackets got that wrong. Corrye wrote poetry from the moment she learned to write. Vassar taught Corrye she didn't ever want to leave the Keys."

Ray started walking along the water. I followed behind, straining to hear his low voice.

"Corrye told me the winters got so cold and so dark that she dreamed she was dead and buried. Corrye stayed there only because her parents said she had to. They threatened to cut her off and not let her back home if she didn't graduate. Her parents wanted to break us up. Once Corrye graduated, she came home and never left Key West for more than three days in a row. Couldn't bear to stay away was what she said."

"Did her parents succeed in breaking you up?"

"Nope. Corrye was stubborn. We wrote, saw each other every time she came home. I broke us up. I was too stupid to realize what I was doing. It wasn't until years later . . ."

Ray smiled. "This sounds like a maudlin conversation between two drunks in a bar. Anyway, I started seeing someone else. Corrye found out; her temper took over. That's it, end of story."

We were slowly walking along the deserted beach, heading away from town and the few sun worshipers who were broiling in the blazing sun. I waded into the water until it lapped at my knees and stood there looking out to sea, giving Ray time to wipe away the tears in his eyes. When he cleared his throat to signal his recovery, I turned back to the beach.

"And then Corrye met Mendieta?"

Ray grimaced. "You don't give up, do you?"

"I'm trying to understand Corrye's life. I'm not asking questions to open old wounds."

"When Corrye graduated from Vassar she came back home and met Mendieta."

I quickly added in my head. "That would have been 1962. Let me see if I remember my history. Castro took over in 1960."

"Actually it was February 1959. And the planning for his overthrow started immediately after that. Mendieta lasted two years or so. He got out of Cuba shortly after the Bay of Pigs invasion, afraid he'd be executed for his part in the debacle."

"Did Mendieta continue his work here in Key West?"

Ray nodded. "Both his painting and his planning. Corrye was attracted to his talent for painting *and* revolution. They lived together for several years, then they got married."

Knowing I was pushing Ray to the breaking point, I quietly asked, "When was that?"

"1967."

"And Mendieta committed suicide ten years later."

Ray took off his baseball cap and wiped his forehead. "I wasn't on the force at that time, but I remember some talk that it wasn't exactly a suicide. You know, they found his body over there, by the salt ponds."

I looked across the street to where Ray pointed. I saw a line of short, dense brush and nothing else. "What's a salt pond?"

"Just what it sounds like. A salty pond. It's protected wetlands back there, all undeveloped land. Gus, or his body, was found just inside that brush. There was a suicide note, but Corrye refused to believe he killed himself."

"Why?"

Ray took his aviator glasses off and slipped on a similar pair with dark lenses. Now I couldn't see his eyes, couldn't judge how much was truth, how much was lies.

"Are you familiar with the term *lancheros*?"

I shook my head. "I cheated my way through high school Spanish. I only picked up the basics, and I've forgotten most of them."

"*Lancheros* are boatmen, usually Cuban expatriates, who go back and forth between Key West and Cuba or Miami and Cuba. They run goods through the embargo, run people out. Sometimes they run drugs out too. Next time you see your brother, ask him. I'm sure he's familiar with the term."

Ray turned to walk back to what I'll always think of as Corrye's tree. I put a hand on his arm and held him back.

"Wait a second. Are you suggesting Dick's a *lanchero*? That he was running drugs?" I thought of the gun planted in Corrye's backyard and wondered how far Ray was from the truth.

He shrugged. "Now you're jumping to conclusions. But it's not a bad conclusion. Dick's Spanish is good—it's obvious he didn't cheat in high school. He also has a big, oceangoing boat.

"When we talked to the other captains on Charter Row, they didn't have much to say about your brother's fishing abilities. They had plenty to say about an empty boat coming and going. My conclusion, Blaine? Not very far from your own."

Ray's voice was heated. Trying to cut off the argument he hoped to start, I said, "You're losing me. Before we fight about my brother, let's go back to Mendieta. What connection do these *lancheros* have with his death?"

"Boats would go in filled with guns and leave filled with people or drugs. Mendieta was the local coordinator. Of course, there was never any concrete proof. Those Cubans are awfully closed-mouthed. Castro didn't appreciate the pipeline. Rumor says El Señor put an end to it."

"Wait a second. Are you saying Castro engineered Mendieta's death? And then he managed to make it look like suicide?"

"Blaine, we're only ninety miles away from Cuba. Don't be so naive. Mendieta's actions were threatening the government of a hostile country. What do you think happened?"

I shook my head. "I don't know. Living ninety miles from Cuba must give you a different perspective. I'm not used to conspiracy theories involving foreign nations. I'm more accustomed to conspiracies designed by our own country. What did Corrye think about all this?"

"Oh, she was in complete agreement. She was convinced her husband had been murdered. Of course, no one would listen to Corrye. She was written off as a crazed widow, a crank."

Pieces of the jigsaw puzzle were coming together—at least in my mind. "Don't you think it's ironic that Corrye's body was found near the spot where her husband's body was found?"

"No, I don't. I think Corrye was murdered by a jealous lover. Your brother doesn't have a political bone in his body. But he's got plenty of jealous ones."

I didn't know why Ray was cooperating with me, but I didn't want to risk ending it. I let the attack on my brother pass without comment. "Did Corrye continue her husband's anti-Castro work?"

Ray nodded. "Of course. Corrye was just as committed as

her husband had been. Corrye didn't have a voice as a leader, but I think she gave a lot of money to support the effort."

A lot of money would explain the empty spaces on the walls of Corrye's house. "What groups?"

"I don't know. I told you, the Cubans keep to themselves. They have a healthy mistrust for any government."

For the first time, I suspected Ray of not telling the truth. He looked at his watch and said, "Look, Blaine, I'm out of time. I'm supposed to be on duty in five minutes. I told you all this because I don't want you to think I've got it in for your brother. I truly believe he's guilty."

I didn't want to believe Ray. I couldn't.

"Before you run off, let me ask you one last question. Where was Corrye killed? Was it in the house or on the boat?"

Ray tried to look in my eyes, but lost the battle and stared out at the ocean. "Not in the house. Not here. My money's on the boat."

"You don't know where Corrye was killed." My voice rose slightly at the end, turning the sentence into a question.

Meltzer shook his head. "Now, you've got me on that. You see, somebody forgot to give the order to check the boat for bloodstains, so no one did. By the time we realized our mistake, it was too late. The boat and your brother were gone. Sorry, Blaine."

The detective patted my arm, then hurried away. As he got into his car, I thought about how deftly he'd turned the conversation away from his feelings for Corrye Edwards. Had she been killed by a jealous lover? Was Ray Meltzer that jealous lover?

Chapter 21

I leaned against Corrye's tree and watched Meltzer drive away. Had Ray supplied me with a lead, a motive, or a convenient detour from the truth? I slowly trudged across the hot sand to my car.

While Dennis had been searching the bookstore for Corrye's poetry, I had spent my time, and money, in the travel section. I sat in the car with the air conditioning on high and flipped to the index of my new Key West guide book. Under the listing for Cuba, I found "land owned by," "Missile Crisis," and "refugees in Key West."

The passage on "refugees in Key West" contained a reference to the José Martí Cultural Institute on Duval Street. Sometimes you follow a careful plan. Sometimes you do things just because you don't have any plan at all. This was one of those times; I drove off to find the institute.

Even though chips of concrete were missing from the building's facade and the paint on the walls had been bleached to the color of the sand on Smathers Beach, the José Martí Cultural Institute had an air of elegance.

The entrance was beneath a towering arched portico. A mosaic of the sun rising over the ocean was laid in the floor. Delicate wrought-iron grillwork protected the door and windows. My eyes were immediately drawn to a mural beneath one of the arches flanking the door.

A tall palm tree filled the foreground. A listing fishing boat fought to reach an island that was barely visible on the horizon. My sensitized eyes recognized the bold style of Augustin Mendieta.

I tried the door. It was locked. I pushed the bell and kept pushing it until a woman appeared and waved at me to stop. I didn't take my finger away from the bell until she took a ring of keys from her pocket and unlocked the door.

The woman, who was about my age, looked up at me with impatient eyes. She didn't mention my rudeness. "*Buenas tardes.* I am sorry to disappoint you, but we are not open for visitors who do not have appointments."

"I am sorry. I hope you will forgive my intrusion. I'm doing research on the life Cuban refugees have built for themselves in Key West. I was hoping someone at the institute could aid my efforts."

I looked over the woman's head without any difficulty—she was only about five feet tall, almost a foot shorter than me—and pointed to the wall over her head. "Was that mural also painted by Augustin Mendieta? I recognize the one out here as his work."

"Yes. Both are early works, done years before he gained fame. Augustin was a tireless supporter of the institute."

I'm a wizard at pushing my way inside places where I haven't been invited. I smoothly wedged my foot in the door. Sometimes your toes get crushed, but it usually works. "Can I get a closer look? That is, if it's not an intrusion. I don't want to take you away from your work."

I leaned against the door and bet the woman would be too polite to turn me away. She hesitated. I smiled and leaned against the door a little harder. I won.

"Okay, but only for a few minutes. Many duties require my attention."

The woman stiffly moved away from the door. I stepped in before she changed her mind and held out my hand. "My name is Blaine Stewart. I appreciate—"

"There is no need to thank me. My name is Ruth de León. I'm supposed to be the director, which means I do everything.

The institute cannot afford more staff. It can barely afford me."

I answered with a polite, noncommittal murmur. Ruth glanced at her watch. "You can look at the mural, but I cannot allow you to linger. I am too busy to entertain drop-ins."

The small room we stood in looked like a miniature school gymnasium. Backboards hung at both ends of the room. Sun streamed through the skylights, lighting up the mural on the far wall better than any spotlight could have. I stood on the free throw line and studied the painting.

The workers' faces glowed in the sunlight as they celebrated the end of the workday. They sat on the cleared edges of a sugarcane field, their scythes lying on the ground. One man tuned his guitar, another passed around a bottle to his compatriots. Ominous storm clouds hovered over the festivities.

The painting was more fluid, more relaxed, than those in Corrye's house, but the bold style was unmistakably Mendieta. I moved closer for a better look, then backed away without taking my eyes from the painting.

Ruth folded her arms across her chest and watched me. A slight smile appeared on her face.

"Augustin spent the summer of 1969 painting that mural. He said it reminded him of happier times at home."

"Home? You mean Cuba, right?"

"Augustin hoped happier times would return to Cuba. His painting was a gift to all who come to the institute looking for compassion and the sharing of memories—and hopes."

"He was a wonderfully talented artist. Tell me about the institute. How did Augustin come to be part of your work?"

In a singsong voice, Ruth quietly recited, "The José Martí Cultural Institute was founded in 1900 by a group of Cuban exiles. We have provided our countrymen with a place to meet ever since. We run classes and holiday events for the children. We try to give financial support to all those who need it, especially our exiled artists. Perhaps our biggest service is simply giving people a place to meet and talk."

"I am afraid my education has a major gap. I have very little knowledge of the history of your country. Who was José Martí?"

"A great patriot. José is often called the George Washington of Cuba. He led the fight for freedom from Spain. In Cuba, José Martí's name means freedom and liberty. In 1892, José Martí founded the Partido Revolucionario Cubano—the Cuban Revolutionary Party. They labored in New York to plan their invasion of Cuba.

"José sacrificed his life for his country; he was killed a month after the battle started. This institute was built to honor his sacrifice to make our country free. We keep his memory—and his dream of a free Cuba—alive."

As we spoke, Ruth walked me back to the door. I tried to break away, but Ruth's gentle hand kept me on course.

"You should be proud of your work. How do you keep the institute going?"

"We hope. We pray. Everyone contributes. When that isn't enough, we charge. The groups who meet here pay a small fee." She shrugged. "It works. Somehow."

"What's Los Pinos Nuevos?"

Ruth stared at me as if she didn't understand my question. I pointed to the bulletin board hanging in the lobby. A notice with a black-and-white reproduction of the Mendieta mural had caught my eye.

I haltingly read, " 'Los Pinos Nuevos.' Forgive my awkward pronunciation. I recognize the painting. Are they somehow connected to Augustin Mendieta?" I translated the Spanish out loud. "The New Pines. Are they an environmental group?"

The woman laughed. "In 1892, José Martí came to Florida to preach revolution. He told a gathering of his countrymen they should rise up like new pines and unite. Los Pinos Nuevos was born."

"And this group—what is its purpose?"

"When our bodies die, our dreams continue. Los Pinos Nuevos is keeping the dream alive."

Chapter 22

Ruth shook herself out of the trance she'd fallen into and looked at her watch. "I'm sorry to have detained you for so long with stories about our past. You have made a great audience, but I must let you go. As a result, I have lingered too long and neglected my duties. I am sure there are many other places awaiting your exploration."

Ruth took my elbow and politely threw me out. But not before I memorized the name and address of Los Pinos Nuevos' contact. I left and went straight to the address on the flier.

I walked down the narrow alleyway between the houses and felt my misgivings grow with each step. Had my fragmented memories of high school Spanish lessons made an accurate translation of the note scrawled in red ink at the bottom of the flier?

Dar una buena pelea, llama Bobby. Put up a good fight, call Bobby.

Flamingo Alley, the street where Bobby lived, had none of the charms the name brought to mind. Instead of passing through rows of colorful birds, I carefully stepped between broken beer bottles, a variety of garbage, and used condoms. Tiny palm trees sprouted from the cracks between the walk's bricks.

The house, 22 Flamingo Alley, was almost completely hidden

behind a wall of trees and lush vegetation. A wobbly old man shuffled down the stairs and watched my approach with suspicious eyes. I was glad he wasn't carrying a shotgun.

The man put his hands on his hips and said, "You've gone to a lot of trouble to hear that we don't want whatever you're selling. Well, we might want it, but we can't pay for it. Didn't your boss tell you this is a flophouse? Anybody gets money, they trade it in for a bottle as quick as they can."

"Sorry, I don't have a single thing for sale today. I'm looking for Bobby."

"Bobby?" He squinted at me. "Now, what on earth could you possibly want with Bobby? Bobby don't talk to strangers."

"Why don't we let Bobby decide that?"

"Okay." He shrugged his shoulders with an eloquence that showed he thought I was wasting my time and shouted through the torn screen door, "Bobby! Bobby, get your butt down here! Somebody wants to see you."

A voice rumbled in return; I wasn't close enough to understand the words. The man listened and impatiently shouted, "Bobby! I want Bobby. You know, that kid that sleeps in the hall. Bobby, I know you're awake. Get your ass down here. I won't stop yelling till you do!"

The guy was persistent. He kept yelling until he heard feet clumping down the stairs. Then he turned to me and tipped an imaginary cap. "Heeer's Bobby!"

I almost gave him a few bucks, but changed my mind. I didn't want to contribute to a fellow alcoholic's binge fund. I simply said thanks and made believe I didn't see the wavering outstretched palm. I smiled. He cursed and wobbled away.

I didn't expect the bedraggled waif who stumbled through the doorway. Her close-cropped dark hair, dark eyes, and gaunt face gave her the look of a preteenager. She yawned and rubbed her knuckles against her eyes. Her voice was hoarse from a long night of smoking. "Who are you? You know, I was sleeping. I don't like people who wake me up."

"Neither do I. I've come to talk to you about Los Pinos Nuevos. I saw your flier at the institute."

"You're not a *compañero de armas*. You look like you've just come from the *comisaría*."

My rudimentary Spanish abandoned me. I understood the comrade in arms, but *comisaría* . . .

Bobby noticed my confusion. "Fucking cops. *Comisaría,* police station. Couldn't they find one who speaks Spanish?"

"Lo siento, solo hablo un poco de español." I hoped I was apologizing for not speaking more than a few words of Spanish.

Bobby's face remained impassive. I quickly said, "I'm not a cop."

"Yeah, they all say that. Prove it."

Sometimes you carefully plan the next step in an investigation. Sometimes you just open your mouth and listen in amazement to what comes out. Without thinking, I ad-libbed, "My brother's Dick Aldridge. I have one of the AK-47s you want to buy from him. I want to arrange a test shoot."

"You're bullshitting me. I don't know anything about guns. Besides, Dick's in jail. I saw it in the papers."

"You're behind on the news, Bobby. He's out but he's got to keep out of sight. The cops are looking for him."

Her eyes grew to large dark circles the size of half dollars. She whispered, "How did you find me? Dick said he didn't tell nobody about me."

"Well, he did. I'm making the deals now, not Dick."

"Dick warned me that people might come nosing around like a hungry dog looking for a bone. How do I know you're not one of the mongrels?"

I dragged my wallet from the bottom of my purse and flipped it open. Years ago, Eileen had given me a thick envelope as a Christmas present. The envelope was filled with wallet-size family photos. I teased Eileen about her sentimentality, but carefully placed the best of them in my wallet.

I showed Bobby a picture of a man and a woman standing in front of the Statue of Liberty. Even though the picture had been taken half a dozen years earlier on my brother's last visit to New York City, Bobby recognized Dick. There was no mistaking the lady with the bright red hair for anyone but me.

Bobby studied the picture, then squinted at my face. She thrust the wallet back to me and shrugged her shoulders. "So you're Dick's sister. You know, he owes me twenty bucks."

Since my wallet was out, I pulled out a twenty and gave it to her. "Now you're even." I gave her another twenty and said, "Now I'm paying. Unlike my brother, I don't believe in IOU. I believe in COD. Do you have your money together?"

"If you're looking for money, how come you're passing it out so fast?"

"Good faith, Bobby. I'm just proving that I'm not interested in playing games."

I told her where I was staying and strode away, hoping I looked like a cocky gun dealer. As I walked down the alley to my car, two thoughts ran through my mind: *What have I done? How is this going to solve my problems?*

I needed to think. Some people meditate to think; others take long walks. I like to drive. My rental car was a poor replacement for my Porsche, but it had air conditioning.

I turned the air conditioner on high and drove in the direction of the Atlantic Ocean. Instead of wide-open roads, I found traffic. By the time I reached Smathers Beach, I had run out of patience. I swung the car out of the line of traffic and pulled into the sandy area across from the beach.

The car was an automatic, with the gearshift in the center console. I looked down to put the car into park and froze with my hand on the knob.

A large, brightly colored snake was slithering from beneath the passenger's seat and moving up the console. Its head was inches away. Its eyes locked on my hand. I stopped moving. I stopped breathing.

Narrow yellow bands separated the snake's wide red and black bands. Being a city kid, I don't have any experience with snakes. I looked at the bright colors and wondered if they had any correlation to the strength of the venom.

I had hoped to avoid being punched, poisoned, shot, or stabbed on this trip. Getting bitten by a snake never entered my mind. Until now.

Chapter 23

I stopped moving, stopped breathing. My arm shook from fear. I slowly lifted my hand from the gearshift. The snake quivered but didn't move. I moved my hand away. Slowly, slowly, slowly, until my hand was resting in my lap.

The snake hovered in the air, undecided about attacking or retreating. The console was the only thing between my bare legs and the snake's fangs.

I watched the snake and wished I'd watched the nature shows on PBS. How much time would elapse between a snakebite and a horrible, painful death?

Without taking my eyes from the snake, I slowly moved my hand and turned the engine off. Then I pushed the door open. The snake bent its head over the console, alarmed by my slight movements.

I closed my eyes so I wouldn't see the snake bite me and dove out the open door. My shoulder hit the sand, and I rolled and landed face first on a small pile of rocks. I scrambled to kick the door closed. While my pounding heart slowed to a normal pace, I sat against the car and carefully checked my arms and legs for the marks of a puncture.

"Hey, are you okay, lady?" I stopped my self-examination and looked up.

Two boys who weren't quite old enough to be teenagers

stood in front of me. Both were tan and sun-bleached blond; both were wearing baggy shorts and faded T-shirts. The admiring looks on their faces puzzled me.

The taller boy grinned and said, "You exploded out of that car like there was a bomb or something. I've never seen anybody do that before."

The other boy chimed in, "Cool. A slow-motion explosion, just like in the movies."

I brushed sand from my legs and pushed myself to my feet. I smiled, glad to be safely outside the car. "No movie. Just a little problem with a snake."

"A snake? Cool. How'd it get out of its cage?"

"I have no idea. I didn't even know it was in the car."

I peered through the window. The snake stretched across the seat, its fangs extended menacingly.

The boys crowded next to me. They cupped their hands around their eyes to block the sun's glare and looked inside. The taller boy whistled. "Holy shit, that's a coral snake."

"Are coral snakes poisonous?"

"They sure are." The taller boy, who was also the blonder boy, stepped back and gave me a very suspicious look. "Isn't that your snake, lady?"

"No, it's not. I have no idea how it got there. Can you guys go call the cops? I don't want to leave the car. You know, in case somebody decides to break into it."

The boy didn't need any time to think about it. He yanked on the back of his friend's T-shirt. "Ernie, come on. Let's go. Hurry up!" He pulled on his friend's shirt again and dragged him away from the car. "I want to get back before the cops get here."

My bad luck deepened. I recognized the silver Lexus that bounced into the sandy area and pulled up behind my car. The sunroof was open so the occupant could work on his tan.

Ray Meltzer slowly got out of his car and walked over to me, dragging his feet in the sand. I watched my reflection in his mirrored sunglasses—I looked like a wide-eyed wild woman. I couldn't see Ray's eyes, but the frown on his face showed his disgust.

"I was on my way home for an early dinner when I heard

the call, so I said I'd take it. I figured it was some kids playing a prank. If I'd known it was you, I would have kept on going."

"Sorry. Would you like a few bucks so you can buy a sandwich to make up for the missed dinner?"

Meltzer touched my cheek; the gentleness of his touch surprised me. "That's quite a scrape. Make sure you put something on it. Want to tell me what's going on? The call said a snake was on the loose."

"Not on the loose—in the driver's seat."

Meltzer looked as if he wanted to touch my forehead to see if I was running a fever. I pointed over his shoulder. "Look in there. I seem to have picked up a hitchhiker."

The detective bent to look in the window, then straightened up to look at me. "You don't do anything easy, do you? I don't suppose you know how that thing got in there, do you?"

I didn't bother to shake my head. The disgusted look reappeared on Ray's face. My shaky nerves quickly turned to anger. "I don't suppose you want to call somebody who can get that thing out of there, do you?"

He didn't take the bait. Meltzer slowly walked back to his car. He held the radio microphone up to his mouth and talked.

I turned to the ocean. There's a Jimmy Buffett song about watching for waterspouts—I felt as if I were caught in one.

My blond friends returned and ran across the sand to me. The tall one, who said his name was Rob, decided to teach me more about snakes.

"Coral snakes aren't very jumpy, you know. It probably wouldn't have bitten you. But if it had, you woulda been dead. Wham." Rob smacked his fist against the palm of his hand. "Just like that. It only takes a minute with coral snakes."

I shuddered.

Meltzer came back and rudely interrupted. "Somebody will be along in fifteen or twenty minutes. Think you can wait that long?"

I nodded. Anything I said would have made me sound as ill-tempered as Meltzer. I kept my mouth closed and stared at my feet. How long had the snake been in the car? Had it been put there while I was at the institute or at Bobby's?

The two boys lost interest in us and drifted back to the car.

Ray and I didn't speak until the ASPCA showed up. As the men unloaded a long pole with a clamp at one end and other equipment from their van, a battered pickup truck stopped in the middle of the street.

A woman jumped out and ran to my car. She had a 35mm camera hanging from her neck and a notebook tucked under her arm. I turned and walked away; I didn't want to talk to a reporter.

I crossed the street to the beach and found an isolated palm tree where I could sit and watch the swimmers. I don't know how much time went by before Meltzer plopped down next to me.

"Are you sure you're okay? It's not unusual for shock to set in after something weird like this happens. I've seen it happen lots of times before. Nothing to be ashamed of."

"I know all about shock. I'll be fine. I'm getting impatient with my role of damsel in distress. Is it safe for me to leave?"

"Yep. Everybody including the snake and the reporter is gone. I don't think she managed to get your picture, but she knew who you are. Watch for tomorrow's paper—I'm sure you'll be in it."

Meltzer balanced his clipboard on his lap and tapped a pen against the clip. "Well, if you're sure you're okay, that's it. I don't see a need to file a report or open an investigation. Do you?"

"No, nothing will ever come of it." Taking advantage of the concern on his face, I asked, "Ray, can you persuade the paper to kill the story? I don't want to see my name all over the front page. My family's gotten enough bad publicity."

"I'll see what I can do, but don't get your hopes up. You probably won't wind up on the front page anyway. It's not like you killed somebody—I'm sorry. I didn't mean . . ."

I waved Ray's apology away. Still blushing, he touched his forehead with a gesture he'd learned from John Wayne movies and said, "Call me tomorrow. I want to be sure you're okay. I'll see what I can do about the paper. Maybe I can pull some strings."

Meltzer got into his car and drove away. I sat under the tree until the shakes stopped. I wanted one thing and one thing only: a drink.

Key West is a terrible place for an alcoholic—unless you're ready to dive off the wagon into a bottle. I drove back to the hotel, acutely aware of every bar I passed. Even though the air conditioning was pushed to its maximum, I was dripping wet from the effort.

When I got out of the car, I'd successfully passed every bar. All I had to do was get to my room, where I could collapse in private and hide until morning.

Old habits automatically resurfaced. I stopped in the lobby to pick up my messages. The woman behind the counter smiled at me and said, "There aren't any messages. Your husband took them up to your room."

The woman looked dismayed as she watched a surprised smile cover my face. She squealed, "Oh my God, I've given away the secret. I promised I wouldn't say anything."

"Did you say my husband's here? When did he get in?"

"He came in about an hour ago. He said it was a surprise. I'm sorry, I didn't mean to spill the beans."

I was too happy to hear that Dennis had decided to fly down to mind. After thanking the clerk, I hurried across the lobby and darted into the elevator just as the doors were closing. The elevator seemed slower than usual. When it finally stopped at my floor, I ran down the corridor and rushed into the room calling, "Dennis, where are you? I'm so glad . . ."

I looked at the man sitting on the sofa. It wasn't Dennis. My voice dwindled to a whisper. I slammed the door behind me and turned the lock. "What are you doing here?"

Cal stood and held out his hand. His khaki slacks, loafers, and light cotton shirt made him look like a businessman who'd escaped the pressures of the boardroom, if only for a weekend.

"Forgive my intrusion. Forgive my deception. I had to speak with you. Face to face, not over the telephone."

"How did you find me?"

"You used a credit card for your airplane tickets, your rental car, and this lovely room. Finding you was easy. It only took a phone call or two."

"And I bet you didn't even have to buy information from the credit bureau like I do. I bet you have a whole department set up to handle those tiresome chores." I tossed my purse on the bed and folded my arms across my chest. "What do you want, Cal?"

"Our conversation had an unfortunate ending. I apologize for losing my temper. I want to talk to you about your brother—"

"I told you . . ." I glanced suspiciously around the room. "I've caught the paranoid conspiracy flu. Is it safe to talk in here?"

"Completely. I checked." Cal smiled. "I do have the latest equipment at my disposal."

"Good for you. Let me tell you something. I don't know where my brother is hiding. Whatever possessed you to pose as my husband?" As an afterthought, I added, "You're not sleeping here."

Cal held up his hand. A gold room key dangled from the tip of his index finger.

"My dear, your virtue will not be compromised. I didn't fly down here to seduce you. I reserved the suite next door for my son, your stepson, in case he decides to join us. The woman at the front desk believed my story. She was delighted to make space for our happy family reunion. Come sit down. We have a lot to discuss."

I could continue leaning against the door with my arms folded across my chest or I could follow Cal's suggestion and be comfortable. Neither choice seemed right. I wanted to get away from the tense air in the room.

"Why don't we go outside? If we leave now we can get a ringside seat for a fabled Key West sunset."

"My dear, I would prefer staying here."

"I would prefer going outside."

"You leave me no choice. I don't have time to debate with you." Cal smoothed his pants and straightened his shirt. He unzipped the small overnight bag that was beneath the table, took out a Marlins baseball cap, and settled it on his head. "That should do. Lead the way."

The Seaside House takes advantage of its prime sunset viewing location. A pier stretches out a hundred yards into the water. Every inch is covered by blue tables with blue umbrellas and blue chairs. Tall blue bar stools line the back railing so latecomers have an unobstructed view.

We pushed through the maze of chairs to the table at the far end of the pier and carefully sat facing the water.

Cal lit a cigarette and tossed the pack on the table between us. "About our last chat: it's not often I'm caught off-guard, but this morning you managed to do it."

"So you decided to return the favor? Okay, you win, Cal. I'm surprised. Why are you here?"

"Blaine, the heat and humidity do not agree with you. They make you ill-tempered. We should have stayed in the air-conditioned comfort of your room."

"Men impersonating my husband don't bring out the best in me." I turned away to watch a catamaran slide by on its way to a sunset "booze cruise."

A waitress appeared at our side. Cal ordered two seltzers; she returned in minutes. Cal declined her offer to run a tab and slipped a ten-dollar bill onto her tray. "Thanks, and keep the change. We'll wave if we need refills."

The large tip brought good humor to the woman's face; she smiled and walked away. I sipped the seltzer until she was out of hearing range. "You've gone through a lot of trouble to come talk to me about Dick. Why?"

He hesitated. I leaned forward and pushed his sunglasses down to expose his eyes. "Be honest. I'll listen if you'll tell the truth."

"I've come to relate your brother's history to you. I know more about Dick than you do. More than anyone in your family knows. Hear me out. You'll understand things better when I'm done."

Too many shocks were having an effect. I sat back and folded my hands in my lap before Cal noticed the shakes.

"Law enforcement instincts flow deep in your family's blood. We first became aware of your brother when he was in college. He's been with us ever since he graduated."

Without thinking, I took a cigarette from Cal's pack and

barely managed to light it. The nicotine rush steadied my nerves, but I still felt as if I'd sat through an earthquake. "Cal, are you telling me that my brother works for you? For the CIA?"

"That's precisely what I'm telling you. There is a section called Domestic Collection. It's my section. Dick works for me. Your brother is quite talented, quite dedicated. A good actor."

"A great actor, if what you're telling me is true." I took another deep drag on the cigarette and slowly exhaled. "I can't believe what you're saying." I sounded calm, but inside I was spinning out of control.

"Believe me. Coming here and telling you this is risky. Risky for you, risky for me. But it's worth the risk. I'm hoping we can work together."

Ugly thoughts circled in my head. "Cal, if Dick works for you, why did he call me for help? Why didn't he call you?"

"Unfortunately, your brother no longer trusted me."

"If Dick didn't trust you, why should I?"

"Because you have in the past—quite successfully."

"That's not good enough. People change, Cal." I held my temper down and quietly asked, "Why didn't Dick trust you?"

"Blaine, I am sorry. I was trying to make this easier. It wasn't a question of trust. Your brother did come to me. I had to turn him away."

My temper—and my voice—rose. "Dick called asking for your help and you refused? Is that how you treat your help?"

"Dick knew the rules. I couldn't intervene without jeopardizing the entire operation." Cal held up his hand, attempting to hold back my anger. "I didn't abandon your brother. I arranged counsel for him. I also arranged to pay all the fees."

"Does that include death row appeals?"

"Blaine, listen—"

"No, you listen, Cal. You dumped Dick and now you want me to clean up your mess. I'm not going to do your dirty work, Cal."

Cal leaned over the table and spoke in a quiet, angry voice. "Now you listen to me. You have a problem. I have a problem. If we can work together, we will solve this dilemma. At the same time, we can save your brother."

"Details, Cal. I want details."

"What do you know about conditions in Cuba?"

"Is this civics lesson really necessary?" Cal nodded. Instead of arguing, I said, "I know Castro's regime is crumbling. There have been a lot of stories in the papers down here about flotillas, riots in Havana, and threats of mass exodus from Cuba. Other than that, I don't know much."

"Most of the refugees first touch American soil in Key West."

"What happens after they land?"

"The INS interviews them. The FBI interviews them too. We listen in to see if we can learn anything useful.

"From there, they usually go to the Transit Home for Cuban Refugees on Stock Island. They use the José Martí Center when the home is overflowing. Most eventually move to Miami or other cities to join friends and relatives. Anyone with a really serious criminal record gets sent back to Cuba."

"How often does that happen?"

Cal shook his head. "Not very often. So far this year about thirty-five hundred refugees have survived the ninety-mile voyage across the Straits of Florida. The number's growing geometrically, because Castro's encouraging them to leave. More than five hundred were plucked from the water today. Only a few hundred have been turned away this year."

Cal answered my unspoken question. "There is no immigration check. The refugee signs a paper saying he, or she, hasn't committed a felony. That's it—no check. But that's not our concern here tonight."

"I know what my concern is. What's yours?"

"Revolution."

Chapter 24

I dryly said, "So that's what my brother's been doing all these years—plotting to overthrow Fidel Castro. And we thought he was wasting away in dead-end jobs."

Cal frowned. "This is no joke. Have you ever heard of a group called Los Pinos Nuevos?"

I nearly dropped my cigarette but managed to shrug nonchalantly. "I assume they're doing the plotting. Is the CIA backing them?"

"As much as we'd like to see Castro replaced, we don't back fanatics who will use any means, including terrorism, to free their homeland. This group believes that a bloody, armed revolution is the only way to bring Castro down. No, we couldn't assist a group that's planning assassination."

I laughed. "Since when are you playing by the rules? Weren't you guys planning all kinds of ridiculous assassination schemes back in the sixties? What happened to the exploding cigars you were trying to plant in Fidel's humidor?"

"Blaine, my dear, I'll say it again because it's obvious that you did not understand me the first time: I am not joking."

"Sorry." I puffed my cigarette and sat back and tried to relax. Cal would set his own pace; my pushing wouldn't hurry him.

"This new version of Los Pinos Nuevos is a paramilitary group advocating open warfare in Cuba. They've been conducting war games in the Everglades and preparing for Bay of Pigs II. They're also collecting money to buy arms to send to Cuba. That's where your brother comes in."

I managed to keep a calm look on my face. "He's been arranging arms sales, right?"

Cal smiled approvingly. "I do admire your skills. That's why I am here. I knew it wouldn't take you long to uncover information we'd prefer to keep secret. Believe me, Blaine, I prefer to have you working with us, not against us."

"Flattery won't work. Cal, I'm not working with you or against you. I'm working for my brother. He needs someone on his side."

"You don't understand the security implications—"

I pounded my cigarette out in the ashtray and jumped to my feet. "That's it. I don't want to hear any more of your spy-versus-spy bullshit. Why don't you go back to Washington? I can muddle through on my own. I don't need your help, and Dick certainly isn't expecting you to help. I've already made a connection with this group—and I'm going to follow the lead wherever it takes me."

Cal put a steadying hand on my arm. "Blaine, be careful. We think these people killed Corrye because she wanted to stop sending them money. Even worse, she appeared ready to betray their plans. They have a long reach, one that extends beyond Key West, beyond Miami, all the way up north. These people feel they have the moral right to use any means necessary to overthrow Castro. Nothing will stop them. It doesn't matter if a few innocent lives are lost."

I pushed Cal's hand away and stood with my hands on my hips. "Are you threatening my family?" My voice was icy cold, but not nearly as cold as the anger running through my veins.

"Blaine, your very involvement in this case is threatening your family. Believe me, I'll do everything in my power to help you protect them."

When I spoke, my voice hadn't lost any of its coldness. "Now you're appointing yourself as a guardian angel. Am I to believe the CIA is going to watch out for my family?"

"We're already doing it. For example, there's a situation with your husband. Without your knowledge, he has started his own investigation."

"How do you know it's without my knowledge? Maybe Dennis is sharing all his information with me. Maybe he's following my directions."

Cal's smile answered my question. My wiretapping fears were more than paranoia—they were real.

"My dear, you must tell your husband to stop. He's endangering more than his career. My protection can extend just so far."

I stared into Cal's eyes. He nodded slightly to convince me of his sincerity. If Cal's story was true, everyone, not just Dick, was in danger. I brushed Cal's hand aside and fled the pier. Cal hurried after me.

I pushed my way through the crowd on the sidewalk. The sun had set, but the heat and humidity lingered. We walked along Duval Street, dodging the groups of families on their way to an early dinner and ignoring the T-shirt vendors who invited us into their air-conditioned shops.

Cal gently steered me down a street I'd never been on before. The street slowly changed from commercial to residential to overgrown fields. The street ended at the entrance to the city power plant.

Cal touched my arm and pointed to a building on our right. "Let's have dinner. We have more to discuss."

"I'm not hungry." The walk had cleared some of the anger from my head, but I still wasn't ready to listen to more of Cal's veiled threats.

"I am. Humor me. We need to talk on neutral territory. You can sit and smoke while I eat."

I agreed. Now that I'd calmed down, I wanted to hear the rest of Cal's story.

The restaurant was crowded and noisy. It looked like a million restaurants across the country—simple wooden tables and chairs, a low candle burning on each table, hanging plants. We turned down a table in the courtyard that didn't have any air conditioning in favor of a corner table in the smoking section.

Cal looked at the empty tables surrounding us and at the people waiting for tables in the nonsmoking area of the restaurant. "Smoking seems to have a few benefits left. It's much easier to get a table. This is nice."

I frowned. "Too bland. I'd rather be at Mike's."

Cal looked puzzled. "Mike's?"

"Sorry, I'm feeling a little homesick. Mike's Bar and Grill is a great place. It's on Tenth Avenue, a little far from my house, but worth the trip. They always make me feel at home—the food's good too." A waiter who was as nondescript as the restaurant strolled over to the table and interrupted my reminiscing. He smiled at Cal and said, "Nice to see you again, sir. Let me tell you about our specials tonight. We have . . ."

The waiter's voice droned on. He recited a list of fish and special sauces. *Nice to see you again, sir.*

Cal asked the waiter to give us a few minutes to decide. After the waiter walked away to refill the water glasses at another table I casually asked, "Have you been here before? I thought this was your first trip down here."

Cal looked into my eyes with the steady gaze of one who has studied the body language guides that say that's the way to show you're telling the truth. "This is my first visit to Key West. The waiter obviously mistook me for someone else."

I didn't believe him.

We ordered tuna that had been swimming in the ocean only a few hours earlier. I took a few bites and pushed the dish away. I didn't feel like eating. Neither did Cal; he left his plate untouched and amused himself by drinking martinis.

The silence became too much for me. I lit a cigarette. Cal stared at the olive in his glass.

"I don't know what to believe. Your story is too fantastic. I've spent too many years thinking of Dick as a floater."

"Believe me, Blaine, your brother hasn't been floating. He's been . . ."

Cal glanced around the room. His paranoia was infectious. I found myself looking around, trying to spot anyone with an abnormal interest in our conversation.

"Your brother has been playing a role. Regrettably, he could not share his adventures with his family. The question now becomes, what will you do?"

I wanted to run away and hide until my head stopped spinning. I wanted to take Dennis and Eileen with me until I was sure we'd be okay.

"I'm feeling a great deal of sympathy for those Cubans in their rafts. I feel like I'm drifting on currents that I don't understand. Currents I didn't even know existed."

Cal spoke harshly. "You don't have time to drift. Blaine, you said you're negotiating a deal with Los Pinos Nuevos. What have you done?"

I told him of my meeting with Bobby. "I don't know what I was thinking. The words just flew out of my mouth."

"You have placed yourself in very grave danger by attempting to pose as a dealer. Either you decide to play this game to the final inning, or you get out of here tonight. Don't wait to take a plane in the morning. Leave now."

"And if I leave, what about Dick?"

"Your brother has fended for himself all these years without assistance from you. Let Dick take care of himself."

"And if I stay—what's your advice?"

"Keep on with your investigation. When you're contacted about making a delivery, call me immediately. I'll handle everything from there. All you have to do is make the arrangements and pass them on to me. Do you have a gun?"

I thought of the hidden AK-47; it wouldn't be easy to carry it without being detected. "No."

"I'm leaving in the morning. You'll have one before I leave. You'll need money too."

"I don't need your money. I have my own."

"You may not have enough. We can't have you searching for an automatic teller machine that accepts your bank card, can we?"

Cal's casual air surprised me. Even though I didn't feel carefree, I tried to match his tone. I didn't succeed. Concern was growing too fast, too deep.

"How long do you think it will take to make the deal?"

"It depends on how desperate and how scared they are. If

they're desperate, they'll act fast. If they're scared, they'll take time to check you out. Control your impulse to rush. Slow it down, see what you can learn about their plans."

"Cal, I'm not interested in their plans. I only want to find my brother and clear him."

"Do as I suggest. We're convinced this group is responsible for Corrye's death and your brother's disappearance. Trust me. You'll find your brother."

Cal's advice didn't satisfy me—I hoped to promise the guns for information on my brother. I asked, "What did my brother uncover?"

"My dear, I am sorry to report that your brother did not share his secret with me. If he had, I might have helped him avoid these unfortunate incidents."

He drained his fourth martini and signaled to the waiter. "I have already told you more than you need to know."

The waiter brought a check. Cal tossed a hundred-dollar bill on the table and pushed his chair back. "I'm sorry. Did you want something else? Coffee, maybe dessert?"

I shook my head. What little appetite I had had was gone. We walked back to the hotel in silence. My head spun from nicotine and Cal's revelations.

The circle of people I trusted had shrunk—and Cal was inching closer to being outside that circle. Claiming the need for a pack of cigarettes, I left Cal in front of the hotel and walked down the street.

Chapter 25

I wanted to talk to Dennis but didn't dare call him at home. I walked along Front Street until I found a deserted telephone booth. I dialed a number and waited to hear a friendly voice.

"RiverView Bar and Grill. Don't ask, we're open till two."

The deep voice made me smile. "Ryan, this is Blaine. How's business?"

"Well, hello, stranger. Business would be better if I saw your face once in a while. Your stool's been awfully empty lately. What's the matter, won't that brand-new husband of yours let you out of the house? Just say the word, dear; we'll bust down the doors and liberate you."

The RiverView Bar and Grill—the View, as it's known in the neighborhood—has been a part of my life for years. When I was drinking, it was my home. When I stopped, I missed my friends at the View almost as much as I missed alcohol. Ryan and Bobby, the owners, make sure my mug of seltzer is always full and my favorite stool, the one near the cigarette machine, is empty whenever I want it.

I laughed. "Thanks, Ryan, I'll keep that in mind. I don't need liberating just yet, but I do need a favor."

"Say the word."

"Dennis should be home by now. Could you send somebody over there to get him? I have to talk to him but I can't call him at home. Get Dennis to the bar. I'll call back in ten or fifteen minutes."

"Business, huh?"

"Serious business, Ryan. Can you help me out?"

"No problem. I'll take care of it myself. Call back collect if you want. I don't care, I'll overcharge Dennis for his beer. Talk to you in a little bit."

He hung up. Instead of standing around waiting for the ten minutes to pass, I bought a chocolate ice cream cone and walked around the block a dozen times. After eight and a half minutes, I couldn't wait any longer. I started dialing.

"RiverView Bar and Grill. Don't ask—"

"Ryan, it's Blaine. Did you have any luck?"

"Sure did, honey. Your husband's on the way to the back office. You'll be able to have a nice, quiet love chat."

"Thanks, Ryan, I really appreciate it. I'll buy you a beer when I get home."

"Anytime. I'm going to put you on hold now so your husband can pick up. Be gentle. He looks a little anxious."

As soon as Ryan's voice faded, Dennis spoke. "Blaine, what's wrong? Ryan came pounding on the door, insisting that I come with him. I thought he was crazy. He practically dragged me out of the house. He wouldn't tell me why until we got into the bar."

I smiled at the vision of short, stubby Ryan dragging Dennis down the street. "Sorry. I guess Ryan got carried away. We have to talk."

"You couldn't call me at home?"

"No."

Dennis didn't ask why. He's been in the business long enough to know the reason. "What's up? Do you need help with something?"

"You've been investigating Dick. Did you find anything useful?"

"Not yet. I just started . . . Wait a second. How do you know what I'm doing?"

"Dennis, drop it. Please."

"Why?"

"Because I'm afraid of things I can't explain."

"It's that serious?"

"Yes, Dennis, it is. Life-or-death serious." I laughed. "Don't I sound melodramatic? I don't have time to tell you the whole story. You'll just have to trust me—and keep an eye on Eileen and Sandy. I'm worried about them too."

I expected to hear long-distance silence, but Dennis answered immediately. "Okay. As far as I'm concerned, the case is officially closed. When are you coming home? It's getting lonely up here."

"I wish I could tell you I'm on my way home, but I can't. I'm tangled in a mess and I'm not one step closer to finding Dick."

I pictured Dennis sitting behind Ryan's cluttered desk and sighed. "It's getting lonely down here too. I'm hoping the darkness-before-dawn cliché is true, because I'm lost in the darkness. I can't even see a trace of light at the end of this tunnel."

Dennis laughed. The cold ball of fear filling my chest melted a bit. "Sounds more like you're lost in cliché-land. Whatever you do, be careful. Blaine, you're hiding something. What else do you want to tell me?"

I hesitated. "There is one more thing. I haven't told anybody else—not even Eileen. It's bad."

"What is it?"

Dennis sounded alarmed; I immediately felt guilty and quickly said, "I started smoking again. I couldn't help myself. I started smoking again."

"Now that is serious. I have an idea. Smoke as much as you want. We'll worry about quitting again when you get home. Call me here tomorrow night around nine. I'm sure Ryan will let us use the View's phone. Blaine, I love you. Promise me you'll be careful."

I promised. I always try to keep my promises.

I couldn't sleep that night. I tossed and turned, worrying about Dick and trying to decide if Cal had been truthful. Mostly, I worried if I'd been completely truthful when I answered Dennis's question. Would I drop a case given the same circumstances? Would Dennis?

The next morning, banging on the door separating my room from Cal's woke me up. I had a nicotine hangover: a pounding head and a dry mouth that only a quart of seltzer would fix. I cursed and rolled over to look at the clock on the nightstand. Six-thirty.

The pounding got louder. I heard Cal's muffled voice. "Blaine, are you awake? Come on, open the door. It's me, Cal."

I shouted, "Goddammit, I know it's you, Cal. Stop that banging. You'll wake up everyone on this floor."

I never wear a nightgown, pajamas, or even an oversized T-shirt. And I never travel with a bathrobe. I rolled out of bed. Yesterday's shorts and T-shirt were on the floor where I'd dropped them the night before. They'd do. I slipped the clothes on as Cal impatiently tapped on the door. I unlocked the door; it swung open before I turned the knob.

Cal, looking dapper in a seersucker suit, crisp white shirt, and tie, stood before me. He held a white envelope in his left hand and a black pistol in his right.

"What, no coffee?"

"I'm sorry. I didn't think of coffee. You got in late last night, Blaine."

"I didn't realize you were waiting up for me, Dad. I had a lot of thinking to do. I think better when I'm walking." I nodded at the objects in Cal's hands. "Are those for me?"

"Yes, my dear. I am sorry to have awakened you, but I have an early flight. I bring you money." He handed me the thick white envelope. "Thirty thousand dollars. If you need more, contact me. You're on the honor system—no need to keep receipts.

"And this." Cal gave me the pistol and took a box of ammunition clips from his jacket pocket. "This is to be sure you don't give any of that money away, unless you want to. It's a Para-Ordnance forty-five automatic. An excellent combat handgun, made in Canada. The clip holds thirteen rounds. High quality, wonderful accuracy. It's legal. I pushed through a permit last night. You can carry it as a concealed weapon. You'll find the permit in the bag.

"I'm sure you'll be happy with this pistol, although I sincerely hope you never have the occasion to fire it."

I nodded and asked a question that had bothered me all night long. "Was Dick's room wiped clean under your orders?"

Cal nodded and quickly gave me a few more instructions about making contact with him and about being careful. I rubbed my eyes and tried to listen, but my mind kept wandering off in unsettling directions.

By listening to Cal's warnings, I cut myself off from Dennis, Eileen, Brad—everyone. I would be drifting in the ocean, tethered to solid ground by a thin line of trust extending from Cal to me—and that line was severely frayed. Cal would be my lifeline, my lifeguard, my swimming instructor. And not a very trustworthy one. If I failed he'd try to remove all traces of his involvement, just as carefully as he'd tried to clean Dick away.

I watched Cal walk down the hall and felt that ball of fear freeze up again. The elevator doors opened. As he stepped inside, I called his name. He stopped, half in, half out of the elevator, and looked at me. What was I going to say? Don't go, I'm afraid? I waved. Cal returned my wave and disappeared. I closed the door, wishing I had stopped him from leaving me alone. Even if you're not sure of your companions, it's better to not be alone. The middle of the ocean is a very lonely place.

Chapter 26

I sat on the bed with the envelope of money and the pistol in my lap. Cal had given me everything I needed—everything except a plan.

The next two days were wasted. I made a nuisance of myself with Ray Meltzer, Laska Brown, and anyone else who crossed my path. In return, I received a sunburn, advice to leave town, and warnings.

Early in the morning on the third day, I called Eileen. I gave her another no-progress report and waited for her reply. Instead of questions, I heard silence.

"Eileen?"

"I'm trying to think of a way to help you. I've called everyone I know, but no one knows more than he's read in the papers or seen on TV. When are you coming home?"

Even though Eileen sounded sympathetic, her question strained my patience. I hate to admit defeat.

I plucked a deadline from the air. "Eileen, I'm tired of running down dead ends and I feel like I'm making things worse, not better. Give me two more days. If I haven't turned up anything by then, I'll get out of here."

"You sound impatient. That scares me. Blaine, please don't do anything dangerous—or stupid."

What could I do, except promise to avoid stupid, dangerous

situations? As the words floated from my mouth, I felt misgivings stir. Sometimes, no matter how hard I try, I can't keep my promises.

I hung up. The bright light filling the room mocked my gloomy mood. The only good way to get rid of a depression is to sweat it out. I dressed in my running clothes and went out for a run.

It didn't take long to raise a sweat in the humidity. As I wiped perspiration from my eyes and struggled to keep running through the thick air, I decided to spend my last two days trying to enjoy the sun and getting used to failure.

I've had cases fall apart before. I've had to tell clients that continuing an investigation would be a waste of their money and my time. I've never had to admit defeat on such a personal crusade.

What about Dick? I thought of Cal's confident declaration that Dick could take care of himself. If only I shared Cal's confidence.

When I returned to my room, I was dripping wet and exhausted from the effort, not exhilarated. I dragged myself to the shower and stood under the cold water until the shock forced me to get moving—if only to go out and eat breakfast.

The best way to take my mind off my problems was to immerse myself in bigger troubles. The hotel gift shop had day-old copies of the *New York Times*. I eagerly grabbed one without grumbling about the price or the stale news. I planned a leisurely breakfast, interrupted by nothing but events in remote parts of the world. Day-old civil wars, corrupt politicians, and natural disasters would do.

I strolled around town with the newspaper tucked under my arm, searching for that leisurely breakfast. An outdoor café on Duval Street, tucked between an art gallery and a souvenir store, won. I walked down the narrow passageway and stepped into a small courtyard filled with tables. I chose one in the farthest, most isolated corner of the courtyard.

The waiter was cheerful and efficient. He put a menu and carafe of coffee in front of me. I ordered fruit and wished a thick

New York City bagel were available. After settling for a basket of home-baked muffins, I poured my first cup of coffee, lit a cigarette, and cracked open the newspaper.

The front page contained its usual selection of bad news: civil wars in countries on three continents, Washington budgetary battles, drug-resistant strains of old diseases, and students killing other students for leather jackets.

Most people might have been depressed after scanning the front page, but the stories had the opposite effect on me. I found myself smiling. Things could be worse.

The national editions of the *Times* have most of the articles I really enjoy removed. The quirky stories of life and deal-making in the city are gone, leaving only the national news and special sections. I quickly flipped through the Living Section—cooking doesn't interest me—and turned back to the national news. A headline on the article in the top right corner of the page caught my eye:

DC's Midnight Burglar Strikes Again
Ranking CIA Official Slain During Holdup

By ELAINE BONNER
Special to The New York Times

WASHINGTON, June 23—The body of Calton Wolff, a high-level CIA administrator, was discovered in his George-town home on Tuesday afternoon. According to a CIA spokesperson, Wolff apparently surprised the serial "Midnight Burglar" and was slain after a violent struggle.

The so-called Midnight Burglar is blamed for more than two dozen robberies in the Georgetown area. Named for his penchant for breaking into homes in the middle of the night, the burglar apparently takes great delight in robbing homes while the occupants are inside sleeping.

Sources denied any connection between Wolff's murder and his assignment at the Central Intelligence Agency. "Cal-ton Wolff was a valued senior member of our administrative

staff. We are shocked and baffled by his untimely death," a
spokesman said.

My eyes filled with tears. I used my napkin to wipe them
away, then continued reading.

Wolff's body was discovered late yesterday afternoon by
his personal secretary, James Ulysses. Ulysses, alarmed at
Wolff's failure to appear at previously scheduled meetings,
gained access to the house and discovered the body.
Wolff, a thirty-year career employee at the CIA, was mar-
ried once. He and his wife, Joan Simpson, were divorced in
1975. Ms. Simpson died in 1992. He leaves no children.

The tears blurred my vision. I crumpled the paper and tossed
it on the table. I threw a handful of money on top of it and
stumbled out to the street.

I'd cried too many times since I started this case; I didn't
want to cry again. The operator listened to me recite the telephone number and my credit card number—I was having too
much trouble getting my shaking fingers to punch the right
numbers.

I caught Dennis in his office. "Blaine!" He sounded happy,
but worried. "I didn't expect to hear from you today." He
paused, and I listened to his unspoken comment: *Why are you*
calling me here?

"Dennis, I had to call." I wiped my hand across my eyes and
came to my senses. Who knew how many people were listening
to our conversation? "I miss you. I wanted to hear your voice."

"I'm glad you called. I'm getting lonely. When am I going to
see you again?"

I closed my eyes and tried to send Dennis an unspoken message. *I need you.*

"Blaine? Are you still there?"

I opened my eyes. "Unfortunately for both of us, I am." I
sighed. "It's back to work for me. I'll call you tonight."

Dennis caught the subtle question in my voice. "Better not.

I won't be home until late. Got some stuff to do. I'll be out until at least nine."

That was our not too subtle code that Dennis would be waiting at the View for my call. I had twelve hours to fill, but I wouldn't fill them unarmed. I went back to my hotel room, retrieved the pistol Cal had given me, and hurried back to the street.

Chapter 27

Key West is a paradise for many, but there's one problem with paradise: you let your guard down. In New York, you're aware of a hidden streak of violence that can erupt at any moment, for any reason. You're always ready. Always aware that the person walking past you on the street, sitting next to you on the subway, or buying the *Daily News* from a corner newsstand could instantly become a lethal threat. In Key West, my suspicious nerves relaxed, lulled to sleep by the warm breeze, the sunshine, and the pretty flowers.

The sight of a black van slowly cruising down Whitehead Street snapped me out of my tropical inattention. I'd seen that van too often. The woman buying lemonade at the stand I'd passed a few moments earlier now seemed vaguely familiar. And the man patiently waiting for her to complete her purchase—he looked familiar too. How many times had I seen them since leaving the hotel?

Key West *is* a small town—but not that small. The hairs on the back of my neck quivered and rose. I was being followed by a team—a very professional team.

I remembered, much too late, the warning Dick had passed on through Eileen. *Cal is bullshitting you and you shouldn't believe anything that creep tells you.* Had I made the biggest mistake of my life in believing Cal's stories about Dick? Or was I making a mistake in believing the newspaper article announcing Cal's death?

I kept walking. Let them follow me to Brown's office. Let them follow me all over town until they were tired, sleepy, and bored. Then when I needed to disappear, it would be easy to disappear.

Brown's office was on Whitehead Street on the courthouse block at the end of a row of houses converted to lawyers' quarters. I crossed the street and walked inside.

The reception area had been a living room at one time. A sofa sat against the wall near the door. The rest of the room was filled with filing cabinets and office furniture.

A secretary sat behind a desk typing on a word processor. She looked up when I walked in, hoping I'd bring excitement to a dull morning.

When I asked to see Laska, the woman pushed her glasses up on the bridge of her nose and frowned. "Mr. Brown doesn't like to see people who don't have appointments. Oh hell, he isn't doing anything but ordering me around. Go on back. If he gets mad, I'll tell him you sneaked past when I was in the bathroom. Go down the hall. He's the next-to-the-last door on the left."

I followed the secretary's directions. All of the rooms, except the bathroom and kitchen, had been converted to offices. All the doors, except Brown's, were closed. His abrasive voice was loud enough for me to hear without straining.

"Don't worry. I have the situation under control. Yeah, I know she's back."

I stopped and waited to hear something—anything. What I heard left me disappointed.

"Everything's going according to plan. The paperwork is here. We're almost ready to go. We just need to arrange the closing." He paused to listen, then shouted, "Fuck that! You'll get paid when the money comes in."

Brown slammed the phone down. I waited for thirty seconds, then stuck my head into Brown's office. "Bill collectors nagging you?"

A scowl ran across the attorney's face. "Everybody wants

money these days." He forced a smile. "Well, hidey-ho, the big shot private investigator is back in town. Too bad you didn't stay away. I hope you manage to keep yourself out of trouble this time."

"If not out of trouble, at least out of jail. Sorry I didn't stop to visit you sooner; I've been busy. What do you hear from Dick?"

"Not a thing. What about you?"

"I told you, counselor, I don't know where my brother is. I'm sure you do."

Brown pushed his wheelchair from behind the desk and rolled up to my feet. "I'm a busy man. What do you want?"

"I want to talk to you about your school days." I nodded at the wall behind Laska's desk. "That's an impressive display of diplomas. Is your Yale diploma hanging there?"

"What's your point, Stewart?"

"Did you meet my brother at Yale? He graduated a year behind you."

"Yale's a mighty big school, and a year makes a big difference. I didn't hang with the youngsters."

"But you did hang with the Snakes and Vipers. Didn't you?"

I'd been warned that club members will immediately leave if the secret name is uttered by an outsider. Laska proved the theory. Without saying another word, he pushed himself out of the room.

I'm convinced you don't have to be smart or lucky to get by in this world, you just have to refuse to give up. As I plodded along the hot pavement, I reminded myself that perseverance is the only key to success.

A cruise ship had docked for the afternoon, and the crowd reached the center of town just as I did. The streets and alleyways were filled with people wearing bright buttons that marked them as tourists from the boat. I fought the crowds with pleasure, knowing they would make the job of the people following me more difficult. I wandered around the areas most favored by the tourists taking pleasure in leading my tails around in a frustrating circle.

When I reached the aquarium, I decided to take a break. I bought a soda and a half-dozen conch fritters from a stand and found a shady bench at the aquarium's entrance. From my spot on the bench, I could see the aquarium's entrance and the Wrecker's Museum.

Perseverance paid off. Tab Dixon came wobbling down the street. He wobbled and staggered and bounced off the tourists until he made it to my side. He fell and managed to turn and plop down on the bench. Tab laughed, spit a wad of chewing tobacco on the ground, and winked at me. The curious, guarded eyes of the strolling vacationers watched.

"Howdy, mate. Do I know you?"

Tab's breath had enough beer on it to make me drunk. His clothes were soiled and torn. I leaned away and said, "No, you don't know me."

Tab squinted at my face. "Don't lie to me. Old Tab's not a drunken fool, you know." He lowered his voice and leaned closer. "I've been looking all over town for you." The drunkenness left his voice. "A friend of mine asked me to deliver a message. He's been a good friend to Old Tab. I want to pay him back."

I moved as far away as the small bench allowed and lit a cigarette to cover the alcohol fumes. "What friend?"

"The one who's got the shaft. The one you came here to help. He said he's sorry he missed the wedding. He wanted to give you a Batman comic book as a present. Meet him at six o'clock at the abandoned marina on Middle Torch Key. It's on the map."

Tab bent over and started heaving as if he were going to throw up. "Be careful. Bad things happen on the Torch Keys. Bloody bodies. Unsolved murders. Good place to hide out." He spat again; the spittle landed inches from my feet.

Truly revolted, I got up and hurried away. Several tourists waiting in line at the aquarium shook their heads in disgust. One eager photographer held his camera up to take an action photo of the local drunk. I jostled the man's arm just as he snapped the shutter.

As I passed through the crowd, I muttered, "I came down

here to get away from this shit. If I wanted drunks puking on me, I would have stayed in Manhattan and ridden the subway all day."

Several people laughed. Others shook their heads in sympathy. Two, a man and woman dressed in new Key West T-shirts and stiff new shorts, simply stared at me.

I wandered aimlessly, following the human tide in and out of shops, making a small purchase here and there, and picking up brochures for sunset cruises, glass-bottomed-boat trips, scuba or snorkeling adventures. After two hours, I had souvenirs for my husband, my sister, my secretary, my staff, and half the population on Manhattan. I also had a detailed map of Key West. The newly clad tourist couple followed me wherever I went.

As I walked, I thought about Tab's message. No one else knew how I coveted Dick's comic book collection. How I never forgave him for throwing away his original DC Comics books when, at the age of thirteen, he decided he was too "grown-up" to have such kid stuff. The message had to be authentic—and I was desperate enough to believe anything.

I casually wandered back to the hotel, thinking about sneaking out of town. Only one road leads out of Key West. If I managed to escape from the watchers, they'd only have to drive to the bridge leading out of town and wait.

The couple that followed behind me stopped in the lobby. I took the elevator up to my room. The bright sunshine made the balcony look inviting, but the cool room was more appealing. I sprawled across the bed and opened the map.

I sat up. They could follow me if I drove out of town. What if I floated out of town?

I grabbed the telephone book and flipped through the yellow pages. Perseverance is vital, but I'll take a little luck now and then. Luck was with me. The eager young salesman, Ken, answered the phone. He eagerly agreed to my plan—especially after I promised to triple the fee.

The hotel thoughtfully provided a plastic bag for laundry. I wrapped Cal's pistol in a towel, wrapped extra ammunition clips in another towel, stuffed both rolls in the bag, and carefully knotted the top. I had two hours until Ken arrived. I stretched out on the bed and rehearsed my escape.

Chapter 28

The hallway was empty. I flung my pack over my shoulder and ran for the stairs. Before any prying eyes could spot me, I pushed the door open and headed down. I bypassed the lobby floor and kept going until I reached the basement.

After stealing a hotel jacket from a locker, I followed the dim lights that promised an emergency exit to the loading docks. Hoping that the jacket, baseball cap jammed over my red hair, and dark sunglasses would momentarily confuse anyone watching for me, I strolled outside.

The loading dock was on the street side of the hotel. I kept my head down and hurried around back to the pier. Ken was standing on the dock, anxiously looking at his watch. Behind him a small boat floated on the water. Its engine was idling, ready for a quick getaway.

I walked up to the young salesman and smiled. "Right on time, Kenny. I like promptness. As I said, I'm not sure how long I need the boat. But don't worry. My American Express card can handle whatever charges you pile on it."

His smile was shaky. "Are you sure you know how to handle a boat? My dad doesn't like to rent boats without checking out the driver."

"Don't worry, I'll be fine. Your boat will be fine, too."

I shook Ken's hand. He held on a moment longer than necessary. I could see him deciding to do the right thing and let his dad in on the deal. Before he could decide, I pulled my hand free and hopped into the boat.

Ken undid the ropes from the dock and tossed them into the boat. He pushed the boat away with his foot and stood on the pier, hands on his hips, watching me.

It had been years since I'd been in a small boat; even longer since I'd tried to pilot one. Fortunately, the Coast Guard wasn't watching. I oversteered, then overcorrected. The boat swung in a lazy circle. I pulled it back. The boat zigzagged away from the marina, barely missing a sailboat, two jet skiers, a catamaran, a yacht, and another sailboat. I felt Ken's eyes following me from the dock. I also felt his growing dismay at allowing an untrained novice get away with his boat. It was probably the last time he'd let a boat get away so easily.

From the solid dock, the water had looked deceptively flat and calm. In the middle of the channel, it was choppy. Wave after white-capped wave tossed the boat in the air; the hull bounced down hard enough to rattle my teeth. I clenched my jaw and concentrated on steering the boat.

I finally made it to open water without hitting anything. I slowly increased the speed until the boat skimmed across the water instead of bouncing on top of the waves. I pulled my baseball cap down to keep it from blowing away. A big grin stretched across my face—I was beginning to enjoy boating.

The keys, or *cayos*, I passed were tiny, dark lumps of land. They had narrow beaches and were covered with mangrove trees, their tangled roots dropping through the water to anchor them to the sand, and stubby pine trees. Eagles and other hunting birds circled over the keys searching for dinner. I shuddered and uttered a little prayer that I wouldn't be on their menu.

Despite the maps Ken had helpfully provided, I got lost. Forty-five minutes later, after several frustrating excursions down channels that led to the wrong key, I spotted a faded sign pointing the way to the Middle Torch Key marina.

I carefully wove my way through the narrow channel, ducking away from low branches that hung over the water and watching for rocks and submerged tree stumps. At the end of the strait, I could see a wide beach and a pier. The dock leaned to the left; it looked ready to fall at any moment. I steered toward the beach.

Remembering Ken's warnings about not letting the wake pound against the shore, I cut the motor a few yards from the key and let the boat drift until the hull scraped against the sand. I jumped out into the shallow water and tied the boat to the trunk of a tree that leaned out over the water. I waded ashore, stood with my hands on my hips, and surveyed the deserted lump of sand and trees.

The docks were crumbling into the water. A charred pile of wood marked the spot where the marina's office, burned by some long-forgotten arsonist, had once stood. A small tree sprouted in the middle of the rubble. The forest of pine trees was reclaiming the land. Seedlings grew on the edge of the forest. Tall grass covered the flat field that had been the marina's parking lot.

The heat and the silence pushed down on my lungs, making it difficult to breathe. Uncertain about my next move, I wiped sweat from my forehead and waited.

Birds exploded from their perches, frightened by movement under their nests. A man stepped out of the shadows of the trees. He wore baggy jeans cut off at the knee and a gray T-shirt that might have been white at one time, years ago. It was Dick.

He hesitated. I took off my baseball cap and waved. Dick ran across the clearing. He hugged me and said, "Blaine, I'm so glad you're here. I was starting to worry."

I pushed Dick back and examined him. "You don't look so good. You've lost more weight. Are you okay?"

Dick smiled; the worry lines in his forehead disappeared for a moment. "Don't worry—I'm as okay as I can be." I wanted to ask a thousand questions, but Dick didn't give me a chance. "Did you have any trouble getting here?"

"I got lost. And there weren't any gas stations to pull into for directions." I felt shy and awkward. "I've witnessed dozens of family reunions, but I've never had an active role in one. I'm not sure what I should say or do."

"Neither am I, but we don't have time for a big scene now,

Blaine." Dick patted my shoulder. "Let's save it for later, okay? How much gas does that boat have?"

"A full tank minus whatever it took to get here. Are you thinking of using that as your getaway car?"

"Well, we probably won't get all the way to Miami, but it will give us a head start. Come on, let's go."

I dug my heels into the sand. "Sorry, Dick, I'm not going anywhere until you fill in a few blanks."

Dick impatiently asked, "Can't we do this while we're moving? It's not safe around here."

"Tell me about your boat."

"I scuttled it so it couldn't be spotted from the air. I need to stay lost a little longer."

I folded my arms across my chest. "That's not what I meant."

"You really are stubborn, aren't you?"

A slight grin spread across my face. I nodded. "It seems to run in the family. I'll win, you know. I've had a few more years' experience."

Exasperated, Dick folded his arms across his chest. "What do you want to know?"

"How did you come up with the money to buy that boat? I've been doing a little research—"

"I've been saving."

"You've been saving." I shook my head. "You've never had a job for longer than a year, but you saved two hundred and forty-five thousand dollars to buy a forty-eight-foot boat. You should write a book and reveal your savings secrets."

"The boat's used."

"The boat is a 1986 Viking Convertible. Sold by the original owner. Only eight hundred and fifty hours on the engines. Holds six hundred and ninety gallons of fuel. Cruises at twenty-five, maybe twenty-six knots. The salesman said it has an amazing cruising range. At about five miles a gallon, how far can you go, Dick? Far enough to convince your clients that you can smuggle guns into and out of the country? Far enough to get to buyers in Cuba?"

"I don't know what you're talking about. I run a charter fishing business. I need a good boat to attract customers."

"The other captains on the pier said you don't know shit about fish. They said you go out empty and come back empty. What have you been doing down here?"

He didn't answer. I glared at him. Dick looked at the expression on my face and laughed. "I guess you won't believe me if I say fishing."

"No." Despite my intention to act stern, I smiled. I couldn't help myself—Dick looked like he'd been caught sneaking in late from a date. "Cal Wolff and I had a long talk about your career. I have my own theory about what's going on. I think the government's trying to set you up for something. Something big enough to get Corrye murdered."

"You talked to Cal? When?"

"Last week. He told me what you've been doing."

Dick responded by pushing me back under the cover of the trees. He parted the branches and watched a seaplane fly over the island. After the plane had moved out of sight, Dick took my arm and turned me toward the boat.

"They were flying a little too low. Blaine, the people in that plane could be looking for disabled boats or for drugs. They could also be looking for us. Let's get out of here before somebody spots us."

My legs were still rocking from my trip from Key West; I wasn't ready to go back on the water. "Who's going to find us here? We're in the middle of nowhere, and it looks like no one's been around here for years."

Dick patiently explained. "Blaine, you don't know anything about this area. The cops, the Coast Guard, and the Navy have a lot of experience tracking people in these keys. How long do you think it will take them to track us down? They probably already know you rented a boat."

He pulled my arm. "Come on; we can talk on the boat. Untie it while I get the engine going."

Dick's urgency convinced me. I stood near the front of the boat, the bow, and waited for Dick's orders. He took the controls and pushed on the throttle. A cloud of blue exhaust billowed from the rear. Satisfied the engine was revving properly, Dick motioned for me to push the boat out from the shore. I pushed until the warm water reached my knees, then jumped in.

Dick handled the boat with the confidence of someone who does it every day. Getting out to the bay took half the time it had taken me to get in. I sat in the stern, away from the branches, and brushed away hungry mosquitos.

When we finally pulled away from the shallow water and tangled mangrove roots, Dick pushed the throttle wide open. I grabbed my baseball cap as it flew off my head and stuffed it under a seat cushion.

I put my mouth to Dick's ear and shouted, "Where are we going?"

He yelled back, "Up to the Seven Mile Bridge. We'll wait there until it gets dark, then we'll cross over to the ocean. From there, it's up as far as this baby will take us before it runs out of gas."

That didn't sound like a good idea to me. Instead of arguing, I yelled, "When are we going to talk?"

"Later."

I shouted in his ear, "Cal's dead."

Dick flinched and turned the engine off. It sputtered once, then quit. The boat bobbed up and down on the water, but Dick didn't notice. "Cal's dead? Are you sure?"

"As sure as you can be about anything you read in the *New York Times*. I believed the story at first, but now I'm not sure it's true—it's too convenient. But Cal's gone to an awful lot of trouble to have somebody think he's dead."

Dick strung together a series of curses that made even me blush. When he finished, I asked, "Now will you tell me what's going on? Maybe we can figure a way out of this mess. Start with Corrye. Who killed her?"

"I don't know." Dick shook his head. "I really did love her. At first she was nothing more than a way into my target. I was trying to infiltrate a revolutionary group to find the source of their money."

"Los Pinos Nuevos." Dick raised his eyebrows. I smiled. "Detective blood runs deep in this family. Corrye was giving a lot of money to the group. You figured she would get you entree to the decision-makers."

"I came into town with a nice boat, a reputation for dealing anything that would make money, a love of poetry, and an eye for an older, lonely lady. Our list of contributors had Corrye's name on it, so I went after her."

Dick sighed and continued, "I hung out at Corrye's house doing repairs, running errands, and complaining that I couldn't get my business going. My real business, not my fishing business. I took her out in my boat. I told her stories about smuggling guns to the contras. That caught her interest. She introduced me to the group."

The boat drifted on the current. I sat, mesmerized by Dick's story.

"Unbelievable as it may sound, Corrye and I fell in love. Revolution wasn't so important to her anymore. The job wasn't so important to me anymore. We started making plans. We both decided to quit."

Dick cleared his throat. "Los Pinos Nuevos wasn't happy about our pending retirement. They wanted their guns. I think they killed Corrye because she told them she'd go to the authorities if they didn't leave us alone. I guess, in a way, I am responsible for Corrye's death. I misjudged the group's resolve. Cal told me I was making a mistake. I didn't believe him."

Dick turned away and stared at some distant spot on the horizon. I watched him run the back of his hand across his face and said, "Cal led me to believe that you had uncovered something vitally important. He tried to broker a deal."

Without turning around, Dick answered, "The money trail seemed to be leading back to another government agency. Cal was afraid I'd stumbled into another one of those Something-gate scandals. Being a good career man who was nearing the end of his career, Cal wanted to sidestep controversy.

"When they arrested me for killing Corrye, I called Cal. He said his hands were tied. I panicked; that's why I called you. I didn't know anyone else who might help. I didn't trust anyone I used to work with. Then Laska Brown walked in to represent me."

"Wait a second. Brown came to you? You didn't call him?"

"That's right. I've known him since college. He saw my name

in the papers. I was a schoolmate in trouble—that's why he came."

"Did Brown help you get out of Key West? Does he know where you are?"

"No to both. Skipping bail was my idea. I haven't talked to Brown; I don't want him to get disbarred because of me."

"Dick, there's something I don't understand. Why did you keep trying to send me away once I got here?"

"Calling you was a mistake. I didn't realize how big a mistake until I started getting threats. Threats that were aimed at you. That's why I tried to get you to go back to New York. I'd already lost Corrye. I didn't want to lose a sister too."

I couldn't think of anything else to say; Dick couldn't either. We sat in the bottom of the boat, staring at our bare legs and watching seagulls fly overhead. Rough waves rocked the boat, reminding me that we had to get moving.

I roused myself and looked at Dick. "Now what do we do? Going to Miami won't help us. I think I should go back to the hotel and check out, just as I told Eileen I would do. We can pick a place to meet. I'll get a car and pick you up. We can drive to New York and sort things out. Dennis and Eileen can help."

While I talked, Dick stood and scanned the horizon. He waited patiently until I had finished, then quietly said, "I can't drag more family members into this. I've been thinking about Cal. If being dead works for him, it could work for me too. That would get you off the hook too—at least for a little while. It should also give me time.

"No matter what happens, you can't tell anyone." He looked at me with desperate eyes. "Do you understand me, Blaine? No matter what, you can't tell anyone. You got that?"

I stared deep into Dick's eyes and softly said, "You know I can't promise that."

"I'm serious. I want you out of this. Out before you get hurt."

I folded my arms across my chest. Dick did the same—he sensed what my response would be. We glared at each other. I broke the silence. "It won't work."

"Yes, it will. And I'm not going to stand here all day arguing with you. We're in my territory now, so we're going to do it my way. This is what I'm thinking. The boat explodes. You tell the cops you were trying to bring me to justice but an unfortunate boating accident claimed my life. It's also unfortunate that my body won't be found. Laska will help you with the legal mess. You can trust him—I do."

"It won't work. You won't fool the people you really need to fool."

Dick came close to losing his temper. "Blaine, will you stop saying that? What happened to that positive-thinking stuff you used to preach when we were kids? It can work. You'll get some heat for a few days, but it will blow over. You just have to be convincing when you tell about losing my body."

The thought of describing Dick's body brought tears to my eyes. I blinked them away and said, "That shouldn't be too hard. Although I have to say—"

"I know what you're going to say, Blaine. It might be a stupid idea, but we're gonna give it a try. Here's the plan. I'm going to start a gas leak at the motor. A fire will start right away. It won't take long for the boat to blow, but there will be enough time for us to swim to that key over there." Dick pointed to a key off to the right.

"No one will have trouble believing it—gas leaks are a very common cause of fatal boating accidents. I'm going to start the engine so it's nice and hot."

While Dick played with the engine, I tried to think of a way to stop him. My gut told me Dick's plan couldn't work; my brain couldn't come up with anything better.

"Shit!" Dick's loud curse startled me. "I made the cut too close to the motor. The damn thing's already burning. Get into the water—now!"

We didn't move fast enough. An explosion shook the boat. The deck buckled and crackled as flames shot through the boards. A second blast tore the boat apart. The bucking boat catapulted me headfirst into the water.

I turned a quick somersault and clawed my way to the surface. Spitting a lungful of water, I wiped my face with the back of my hand and shouted, "Dick! Dick!"

No one answered my calls. Flames crackling and hissing as they hit the water were the only sounds I heard.

I furiously pushed aside pieces of Fiberglas, seat cushions, and other pieces of wreckage and swam in a circle, frantically screaming Dick's name until I was hoarse. The flames from the boat's sinking carcass illuminated my search. Tongues of burning kerosene floated on the waves. An oily wave smacked against my face, blinding me. I gagged and dove under the water to wash the fuel away. I grabbed pieces of wood and pushed them away, searching for my brother.

My lungs started burning and heaving. I burst through the water to the humid air.

I wiped the ocean from my eyes with the back of my hand. Tears ran down my cheeks. I blinked and forced them out until they washed my eyes clean.

A flaming circle on the water that looked like a dying campfire was all that remained of the boat. I dove and dove and dove until I barely had the strength to kick my way to the surface.

My energy disappeared along with the sunlight. The flames sizzled and died. The water and sky turned the same black color until I couldn't see where the water ended and the sky began.

Chapter 29

I kicked my legs as hard as I could and barely managed to keep my head above water. I shouted Dick's name until my voice turned to a raspy whisper and tried to fight off the feeling that no one would answer. Dick was gone.

My calf muscles started tingling and tightening. A cramp was coming on; total exhaustion wasn't far behind. I thought of finding a piece of floating wreckage to use as a raft. I slowly turned in a circle and saw a dark lump that had to be land. Reluctantly, I swam away from the last bits of wreckage. Fear and guilt made my arms heavy. I labored through the water, barely moving against the current.

Years of running and swimming took over. My arms and legs moved mechanically. I concentrated on breathing and keeping the water out of my mouth. Every time thoughts of Dick came to mind, I pushed them aside. I had to get to land before I passed out.

My legs scraped sand. Stupidly, I realized the water was shallow enough for me to walk. I put my feet down and walked, then crawled to shore.

The hot sun on my face woke me. I ran my tongue over my cracked lips and opened my eyes. They burned from the salt water and diesel fuel. My throat felt scratchy, as if I had smoked a full pack of cigarettes. Burns from pushing aside the flaming wreckage blistered my hands and arms. I sat up and looked around, expecting, hoping, praying to see Dick.

I saw chunks of Fiberglas on the beach and a few more pieces floating on the calm water. I saw the dismal trees and a lot of birds. I even saw a bald eagle soaring above the key. I didn't see Dick.

With shaky legs, I walked around the small island looking for a sign that Dick had made it to land. I spotted a life jacket bobbing in the water and waded out to grab it. From where I stood, I saw another island about a mile away. I stood with the water encircling my waist and stared across the open water.

Could Dick have swum to that distant key and safety? Or had our plan gone horribly wrong?

I heard an engine. In a few moments, a boat slowly glided into view. Its white hull, the railings, and every piece of equipment had been shined so bright the reflection from the sun hurt my eyes. A crisp American flag hung from a small pole set in the back of the boat. There were three men in the boat, one in the front, one in the back, and one in the middle. The one in the bow spotted me and waved. I stood waist-deep in the water and waited.

One of the men jumped out of the boat and splashed over to me. He took my hand and pulled me back to the beach. My legs started shaking; I quickly sat down in sand.

The men crouched in a semicircle around me. One put his finger on my wrist and carefully studied his watch. He said something that sounded like "shock." Another one wrapped a blanket around my shoulders. Even though the temperature must have been at least ninety degrees, I pulled the wool blanket up to my ears and shivered.

Someone held a canteen up in front of me. I grabbed it and took a deep swallow. The liquid burned my mouth. Before I could spit it out, it slid down my throat and settled in my stomach with a warm glow. Cognac. It felt like a visit from an old friend. I pushed the canteen away.

The man in charge said his name was George but didn't bother telling me his rank. He screwed the cap on the canteen and apologized. "Sorry it took so long to get to you. *Fat Albert* and his brother were down last night, so we were busy chasing down drug runners. One of our patrols spotted flames out here. Didn't you see the helicopter? We had one sweep the area."

I shook my head. "No helicopter. Who's Fat Albert and his brother?"

"Navy surveillance blimps. They had them down last night for repairs. When the blimps don't go up, the drug runners go out. What happened?"

"I'm not sure. It happened so fast. We smelled gas. The boat exploded."

"Gas leak. Happens every so often. You're lucky—sometimes we pick up nothing but charred bodies after a boat explodes. You said 'we.' Were there other people on the boat with you?"

I closed my eyes.

"Miss, are you okay? Was there someone else on the boat with you?"

"My brother. My brother was with me. I tried . . . I couldn't find him. He must have drowned."

The effort to tell the lie—and wondering if it was a lie or if it was the truth—made my voice hoarse. The young officer interpreted the harsh sound as an aftereffect of my close call. He stood up. "Okay, we'll call it in and take a quick look around. Let's get you in the boat and clean up those burns."

We cruised around the channel for nearly half an hour. I sat in the back and let one of the men wash and bandage my burns. Another man pulled pieces of my rented boat from the water and stacked them on the deck. As the pile grew higher, my fears grew stronger. Finally, the boat swung in a wide, lazy circle and we headed back to Key West.

George gently touched my shoulder. "Ma'am?" I broke through my daydream and realized the boat had docked. "I know this is probably the last thing in the world you want to do, but orders are to bring you to the police station. The gentlemen there want to talk to you about your accident. I told them you needed to see a doctor and get some sleep, but they insisted. Sorry, ma'am, I can't go against my orders. I'll take you myself."

I didn't argue with him. I followed him from the boat to a waiting car.

George escorted me to the door of the police station. I walked inside and saw a man waiting for me. Even though he had his back to me, I knew he was waiting for me—I recognized the wheelchair. I walked over to him, dripping sand behind me with each step.

Stepping around in front of the wheelchair, I remembered Dick's telling me he trusted Brown. I looked at Brown's shoulder-length hair, his scraggly goatee, and his rumpled shirt and tried to ignore my misgivings.

I sat on the chair beside him. "Well, counselor, fancy meeting you here. Are you waiting for me or are you stalking some other innocent victim?"

"If what Detective Meltzer is saying about you is true, you are hardly an innocent victim, Stewart. I heard you had a wild night. I decided to come see for myself."

"How did you hear about my night? You must have a lot of great connections, or you've been doing some good spying."

"Island telegraph. You can't keep anything secret down here. Well, you can, but not for longer than thirty seconds. In your case, the island telegraph's been working overtime."

My legs started shaking again. I folded them under the chair and quietly asked, "What exactly is it saying about me?"

"The talk says you're in town to deal. Guns, not drugs. If it was drugs no one would say a word. Drugs are a dime a dozen. But guns . . ." Brown whistled. "That's impressive, even by Key West's high standards. You're the talk of the town. Do you want to hear the rest? The part that describes your late-night adventures? I guess you're here because someone wants to talk to you about your boating companion."

"We have to talk."

Laska raised his bushy eyebrows. "Now you're not going to tell me you're a big, bad gunrunner, are you?"

"I'm too tired to spar with you. Dick said he trusted you. He said I should too." As soon as I said those words, my stomach rolled. Again I pushed my misgivings aside and repeated, "We have to talk."

For the first time since I'd met him, Laska Brown exhibited human qualities. He grabbed my hand and patted it. "We'll talk, but not here where Dick Tracy can hear us. Let's go outside. Even Meltzer can't stop you from talking to your attorney before you talk to him."

We went outside. I sat on the low concrete wall in front of the courthouse. Laska parked his wheelchair close beside me and said, "Okay, let's talk. You go first."

I told him the story that I'd been rehearsing since climbing aboard the Coast Guard boat. Laska listened. He didn't ask any questions, but the look on his face grew more and more skeptical as I talked.

"That's it." I lit a cigarette and waited for the attorney's reaction.

"Are you sure he's dead?"

My eyes filled with tears. "Yes. Dick was standing right next to the engine, trying to put out the fire, when it exploded. The explosion blew me into the water. I searched and searched. But . . ."

"You did what you could." He gently touched the bandage on my hand. "Has a doctor looked at you?"

"I don't think I need a doctor. One of the Coast Guard guys patched me up. To tell you the truth, I think he was a little overzealous."

"Well, I approve. They look very professional. How did your brother contact you?"

I admired Brown's style. I pictured him in a courtroom smoothly prying damaging information from a witness. But I wasn't an ill-prepared witness. I twirled my cigarette and watched the corkscrew of smoke drift away.

"Somebody slipped a note under my door. The note said Dick wanted to turn himself in and that I should meet him at the abandoned marina on Middle Torch Key. I wasn't sure the note was authentic, but I decided to check it out. The note's in my purse, which I guess is lying in about fifty feet of water right now."

"Convenient."

"Truth."

"If that's your story, stick to it. I don't want to know if you're lying. Why the boat? Why didn't you just drive to the key? It would have been a lot easier."

"Somebody told me that wandering around on the back roads in the Lower Keys is dangerous. I also thought it would be faster. I didn't want to get stuck behind a slow-moving RV. I've heard those trailers creep along."

Brown took a pen from his pocket and tapped it against the wheelchair's armrest. He opened his mouth to ask another question, but changed his mind. "Let's go talk to the lawmen. One word of advice: watch out for Ray Meltzer. The island telegraph says he's out to get you. He thinks you were trying to help your brother escape. He's a smart guy. He might even suspect that your accident was no accident."

"Are you done spreading gloom, or is there more good news?"

"The only bad news you're gonna get from me is the bill I'm going to send you. Remember to let me do the talking."

Brown wheeled his chair around in a circle and started up the walk. I hurried to catch up. As I pulled the door open for Brown, he winked and said, "One other thing. I called a friend who's a friend of the district attorney and reminded them of the false-arrest suit you declined to file. If you keep your mouth shut, I might just be able to keep you out of jail."

Ray Meltzer refused to look at me. He motioned for me to sit and pulled a chair away from the table for Laska. When we finished arranging ourselves at the table, he grumbled, "Why did you feel the need to bring your mouthpiece?"

Brown answered, "I thought it best to come along to this gathering. If you don't mind my saying so, your track record with Miss Stewart hasn't been very good."

"Okay, so you're a champion of civil rights." Meltzer flipped open his notebook. "This will be an informal statement. If necessary, we'll take a formal statement later. Okay, let's hear it."

Brown smiled encouragingly; Meltzer frowned at his pad. I took a deep breath and started talking. I finished, then sat back and waited for the detective's reaction.

The island telegraph proved to be accurate. Ray Meltzer used the exact words Brown had predicted. When he used those up, Ray took a deep breath and added a few more words.

When Meltzer finished, Laska sat back in his chair and laughed. "Aiding and abetting?" The attorney sounded incredulous. "How can you say such a thing? Ms. Stewart was attempting to bring her brother back to Key West. If she had been trying to get away with a fugitive, why did she step forward and admit what she had done? She could have easily said no one was with her on that boat. What proof do you have that my client was attempting to assist his escape?"

Meltzer thumbed his notebook as if he were searching for proof. "If I had my way—"

"If you had your way, you would have hung Dick Aldridge in Mallory Square at sunset. It's a good thing we don't follow your laws. What does the district attorney say?"

Defeat made Meltzer's voice husky. "He says no proof. Let her go." As I pushed my chair back, Meltzer added a warning. "He said let her go until I find proof that she's lying."

For the first time since we'd entered the room, Meltzer looked at me. "I want you to stay in town until we conclude our investigation." He glanced at Brown and triumphantly said, "The district attorney agrees with me."

Chapter 30

Brown's display of humanity continued after Meltzer dismissed us. He shook Meltzer's hand and motioned for me to follow him. I did as ordered.

As Brown pushed himself out the front door, he called over his shoulder to the policeman at the desk, "Hey, Gene, be a sport for once in your ugly life. Call a taxi for this despicable criminal. We'll be waiting right outside."

We returned to the spot of our earlier conference. I sat on the low wall and lit a cigarette.

Brown moved to be in the shade and smiled at me. "So, Stewart, let's talk about Dick. What did he tell you about the guns?"

"Guns? What are you talking about, Laska? Dick didn't have time to tell me much of anything."

"Oh yeah, the explosion. That bullshit may fool the cops. It doesn't fool me." Laska waggled a finger at me. "Young lady, lying to me won't help your cause."

"I'll take that chance." A pink taxi pulled up to the curb, saving me from Laska's response.

The usual messages from Eileen and Dennis were relayed to me by the hotel operator. I ignored them. It took all the strength I had to strip off my sandy clothes and take a hot shower. The burns didn't look serious, so I ignored them too and fell into bed.

I didn't sleep that night. I kept waiting for a sign from Dick, a sign that he was still alive. Shortly before dawn, I gave up the pretense of sleep. I dressed and hurried out to my rental car.

Not many people were up and on the road, so it didn't take long to get to Middle Torch Key. I drove past the turnoff for the marina and headed north, searching for the spot where our shipwreck had taken place. I had the wild idea that I could find Dick. Maybe I'd find him walking along the side of the road. Or sitting on the side of the road. Or waiting for me at a bar. Anyplace but washed up on shore.

I didn't find him on the road. Another wild idea took its place. If I couldn't find Dick from the road, maybe I'd have better luck from the water.

Fearing a nautical blacklist, I drove to a marina on the outskirts of town. The island telegraph didn't reach that far—I didn't have any trouble renting a boat.

My piloting abilities had improved. I headed away from the dock and made it to the channel without too much weaving. My confidence increased; I pushed the throttle down until the boat moved at a fast pace. I cruised past the entrance to the abandoned marina and continued north.

The Coast Guard had picked me off an unnamed key just west of No Name Key. I found it and turned the boat farther to the east, to another unnamed strip of land. A strip of land that might have been close enough for Dick to reach.

The water gradually turned brown as it grew more shallow. I cut off the engine and let the boat drift in water barely deep enough to keep it afloat. I tossed the anchor out and then hopped out and waded ashore.

The island was eerily quiet, like a cemetery on a deserted wintry afternoon. I called Dick's name; the sound was hushed by the pine needles of the low trees. A bird's harsh cry answered my call.

I found scattered debris that could have come from our wrecked boat. I had walked a quarter of the way around the key when I spotted footprints in the sand. They led into the trees. I followed them and was immediately engulfed by branches. The footprints disappeared in the carpet of fallen pine needles and scrub grass. I pushed through the trees. Branches scratched across my face, my arms, and my legs, leaving tiny raked lines on my skin.

Within minutes I lost sight of the water. Birds flew out of their nests and circled overhead, crying out to warn me away from their nests. The sun baked my head and neck. I kept walking east, keeping the sun behind my back.

I broke into a clearing about the size of a small car. This would have been a great place to find Dick or a trace of Dick, but I didn't. I found the remains of a campfire. I squatted beside the small circle of stones and poked at the ashes with a twig. Small tufts of grass poked through the charred wood. The burned remains were old. Too old to have been left by Dick.

Disgusted, I snapped the branch in half and tossed it on top of the charcoal. No one had been near that spot for months. I got to my feet and started bushwhacking again. After another ten minutes of walking and getting smacked in the face by branches, I broke through to a rutted dirt road.

Walking faster now, I followed the road to the beach and a rickety wooden bridge. About thirty feet in length, the bridge connected with another tiny key, which had another bridge at its far end. Beyond that key I saw a large mass of land. Beyond that I saw a long narrow bridge. Route 1. Sunlight bounced off the cars passing over it on their way to and from the Upper Keys and Miami.

If I had followed the road, it would have taken me about thirty or forty-five minutes to reach the main road. Instead, satisfied that Dick could have made it to safety if he had survived the explosion, I headed back to my boat. Not wanting to get slapped around by tree branches, I hiked along the beach. In the places where the mangrove trees extended to the very edge of the land, I waded along the shoreline in water warm enough to fill a hot tub.

The anchor had done its job; the boat bobbed up and down in the water waiting for my return. I pulled myself aboard and made my way back to Key West satisfied that Dick could still be alive. *If* kept sneaking to the front of my thoughts, and I kept pushing it back. I didn't want to think about *if*.

"The good news is that no one's found a body."

"You call that good news?" Eileen wasn't impressed. I had called a friend who rented a suite two floors above ours; she had dragged Eileen upstairs to her untapped—we hoped—phone. "What's the bad news?"

"If we're lucky there won't be any bad news. As soon as we hang up, I'm going to get another boat and head back there. I want to take another look around."

Eileen, who was thinking like an attorney, said, "We have to think about discussing this with the authorities. We're going to have to make some kind of deal to keep you out of trouble. I don't want to sound pessimistic, Blaine, but how long do we wait before we tell the rest of the family? They deserve to know."

I couldn't answer; I didn't even try. We were both silent for a moment. I tried to imagine telling the rest of my family that Dick was dead.

Eileen's imagination was torturing her too. When she started talking again her voice sounded muffled, as if she was choking back tears.

"Brad's been doing background checks on everybody you mentioned to him." Talking about business was safe. Eileen's voice grew more steady.

"Has Brad said anything about Laska Brown? Dick said he trusted Brown, but I don't trust anyone down here."

"Sorry, Blaine, Brad hasn't found anything suspicious. Laska Brown is a partner in a very successful practice. He owns a lot of real estate in South Miami Beach. Restored art deco hotels, a restaurant, and an apartment building. He's drowning in debt."

"Just like three-quarters of this country. What about his partners?"

"Solid as a rock. Ellen Greenspan is active as a board member for several nonprofit organizations."

"What kind of organizations?"

"Let me see if I can remember. Brad mentioned a group that

helps the homeless and a literacy project. Rodríguez and González are Cuban expatriates. They're well respected in the Cuban community; they spend a lot of money to earn that respect."

"What's that supposed to mean? Are they bribing people?"

Eileen laughed. "Not overtly. They donate a lot of money to Cuban community groups. Sorry, Blaine, there's nothing suspicious. When are you coming home?"

"I don't know. I'm not ready to declare this case over. I'm not ready to declare Dick dead."

It took Eileen a long time to answer. "Neither am I. Take your time, but be careful. If there's anything—"

"I'll call. You be careful, too."

We hung up. I had planned to call Dennis but stopped when I saw Bobby on the other side of the street in front of the institute. Her outfit, camouflage pants and an olive-green T-shirt, made her look ready for combat. She waved and ran across the street.

Her eyes were bloodshot but steady. "I've been looking for you."

"Well, you've found me. Sorry, but I don't have time for your revolutionary bullshit."

Before I could walk away, Bobby grabbed my arm. "Have you been working on our shipment? We're running out of time."

I pulled Bobby's hand from my shoulder. Before letting go of her hand, I squeezed it until she winced. "I'm not working on anything, because I don't remember receiving any purchase orders from you. And I don't take any other kind of orders from people like you."

"But—"

"But nothing. As far as I'm concerned, we don't have a deal until your people show some money. Why should I bust my ass if you can't pay for the goods?" I wanted to stall Bobby two more days, long enough to get out of town—with or without Dick.

"I thought you'd say that. We are ready to deal. Cash. Bring a suitcase large enough for three hundred thousand dollars."

"Three hundred thousand . . ."

Bobby snapped, "Ten percent. Like we agreed with your brother. Or are you changing that part of our deal too? If the money's not enough, you might want to show up anyway. We can help you find something you've been looking for."

"What's that supposed to mean?"

"That means you'd better come back here later. Two a.m. Alone. If you bring anybody, the deal's off and you'll never find what it is you lost."

Bobby didn't have to wait for my answer. We both knew I had no choice. I'd be there at two o'clock. Alone. Bobby turned and ran across the street; I watched her then went back to my hotel to take a nap.

The hall was dark. I stood in the lobby and waited until my eyes adjusted to the dim light. Bobby, the waif girl, appeared and looked over my shoulder.

"You didn't bring anybody, right?"

"Just like you said, I'm alone." And wishing I had a dozen Marines for backup.

She motioned for me to step inside, then locked the door behind me. Two men stood in the shadowy room. The Marlins baseball caps they wore hid their faces. One man, the one on the right, said something in Spanish. Bobby translated: "Do you have a gun?"

Lying would be stupid. I said, "Of course I do. Did you expect me to come here without one?"

"Give it to me. You'll get it back when you leave."

"No thanks. I'd rather hang onto it."

The men understood my answer. They moved fast, faster than I could react.

Strong hands grabbed my arms and twisted them behind my back. I struggled to free myself. Another set of hands quickly tied my wrists together. Once my hands were securely fastened, someone wrapped a soft cloth around my head, covering my eyes. The hands patted my body and pulled my pistol from my pocket.

Within a few seconds the battle had ended. I stood with my head bowed and waited. I heard heavy breathing as the men tried to catch their breath and felt a small rush of satisfaction. At least I'd made them break a sweat.

Bobby tried to reassure me. "Don't worry. This is just a precaution."

It's hard to sound confident when your hands are tied behind your back and you're blindfolded, but I tried. "Precaution against what? You invited me. Is this how you treat your guests?"

One of the men answered in a voice lightly colored by a Spanish accent. "Forgive us for our perceived rudeness. Unfortunately, we have many enemies. We are not placing you among them, but we must take reasonable precautions. You have nothing to fear. This is as much for your protection as ours. Others must meet with you before we do business. It is imperative that you do not know where we meet. Now please, trust us. We must go."

I adopted the man's formal tone and said, "Your words offer little comfort when your actions are so untrusting."

"Then I must apologize for my inadequate English. Now please, it is getting late."

Someone took my arm and led me through the darkness. I stumbled along, across the room, down a flight of stairs, and outside. I felt sharp stones through the soles of my running shoes. I heard the peculiar sound of a van's panel door sliding open. I was warned to duck my head and told to step up, and guiding hands helped me awkwardly climb into the van. I banged my shins against the seat, turned, and slid along the bench until I hit the wall. I sat and waited, feeling the panic build in my chest.

I heard another person climb in and felt the weight of a body settling beside me. The sour smell of sweat drifted past my nose. Bobby? I tried to lean away from the smell. The door slid closed and the lock clicked. Seconds later, the two front doors of the van opened and slammed shut. The engine started, and I barely had time to brace myself before the van started moving. The air conditioning came on full blast, blowing the smell away.

I concentrated on listening instead of panicking. The tires crunched on the stones for a few seconds, then bounced down the drive to the smooth pavement of the street.

We turned right, stopped briefly for what I guessed was a

stop sign, then drove straight for a few moments before turning right again. After a quick series of left and right turns, I abandoned the hope of keeping the directions in my head to retrace later—if I lived.

My hands tingled and throbbed as the ropes cut into my skin. I fidgeted and leaned forward, trying to decrease the pressure on my arms.

"That rope's not too tight, is it?" Bobby whispered in my ear. "If it is, I can loosen it a little—"

"*Callate!*" Shut up.

"I was only trying—"

"*Silencio!*" ended Bobby's protest.

The van turned and turned again until I completely lost all sense of direction and time. Finally, the van stopped making turns. We drove straight and fast. I remembered the bridge that led out of town to the north and Miami and knew we were no longer in Key West.

The van slowed, turned, and continued at a slower speed. Without warning, the driver veered off the road and stopped. The front doors opened and slammed shut. The sliding door opened. I tensed, knowing things could only get worse.

Two pairs of hands pulled me from the van. They walked me through a small patch of grass, over a patch of gravel, and up a flight of stairs. I didn't struggle. I didn't dare waste energy on futile struggles.

At the top of the stairs, we paused. I heard the sound of a door opening. The hands guided me through the opening. After a few paces, they stopped me and carefully turned me to the right.

The blindfold came off, the ropes didn't. The pressure of the rag left my eyes fuzzy and out of focus. I blinked; sharpness slowly returned. I didn't like the sight that greeted me.

Bobby and her two companions stood behind me. Another man, taller and thinner than the others, stood in the center of the room beneath a ceiling fan that was losing its battle to move the heavy, humid air. The shotgun that he cradled in his arms didn't scare me as much as what I saw directly in front of me.

A sofa had been turned away from the television set so it

faced the inside of the room. Dick sat in the middle of it. His scraggly beard, dark blond, covered his face. The portions of his face that weren't covered by the beard showed ugly purple bruises. His arms were pulled behind him.

I took a step closer to Dick. The man with the shotgun raised it and blocked my path. He turned and called over his shoulder, "Alberto, they have arrived."

I stopped at the shotgun barrier and tried to smile. "To paraphrase an inscription I saw on a tombstone in the cemetery in town, at least I know where you're sleeping tonight."

Dick didn't have time to answer. A man that I guessed to be Alberto came out of a room at the back of the house. He wore a sweat-stained olive-green T-shirt and camouflage pants that hung low on his hips. "This is a touching family reunion, but you are here to discuss business."

"I will not discuss business with my hands tied behind my back. What harm can I possibly do to you when you stand there, surrounded by three strong men, one with a shotgun? Either we talk as equals, or we don't talk."

He stepped closer until his face was inches from mine. Alberto's beard was heavy, his eyes bloodshot from too many cigarettes and not enough sleep. I stared back, not intimidated by the threatening glint in his black eyes.

Alberto turned to look at Dick. "What kind of a man are you? Do you always allow the women to take charge?"

"Blaine is a very stubborn person. As I am learning, you cannot order my sister to do anything. Nor do you 'allow' her to do anything. She does as she sees fit."

"Fine." Alberto stuck a wad of chewing tobacco in his mouth and started chewing. He nodded at the men who had abducted me. "Untie her. Leave him as he is."

The shorter of my two kidnappers pulled a switchblade from the back pocket of his jeans and flipped it open. I shuddered; the blade was longer than any I'd ever seen before. He stepped behind me and slit the rope. My hands swung free. I rubbed my wrists, trying to massage away the rope burns.

"You've gone to a great deal of trouble to bring me here. I'm flattered that you found it necessary to send three people to fetch me. Now, why have you gone through such trouble to arrange this meeting?"

"Blaine, will you—"

"Shut up, Dick. I'm dealing with this. It's my business now, not yours." I swung my gaze back to Alberto. "You seem to be in charge here. Do you have the money?"

"Do you have the weapons?"

My heart pounded. I coolly pulled my lips back in a thin smile and nodded. "It will take a few days to arrange delivery. Until then, I require a twenty percent deposit."

"He"—Alberto jerked a thumb in Dick's direction—"said ten."

"He's no longer in charge. We're doing business according to my rules now. I have expenses. I also need to be reassured that you're acting in good faith. Twenty percent. Small bills."

"We agreed on ten."

"Twenty."

We stared at each other like two dogs ready to fight. I held my breath and waited for Alberto's reaction. He spit a thin stream of brown tobacco juice on the floor. Drops splashed on the toes of my shoes. I didn't react.

"You'll get your deposit. As you can see, I already have mine. It's not that we doubt your ability to complete the transaction, but we are a cautious people. We've had many disappointments. This time we want to ensure that our expectations are met. Deliver the guns and your brother will be released. If you should attempt a scam, as you Americans say, your brother will pay the consequences. As you will also."

"And you will pay the consequences if you harm my brother. I promise you, I will find you and I will kill you."

Chapter 31

The meeting came to a chilling end. Alberto snapped his fingers. Bobby stooped and grabbed a long piece of rope from the floor.

I protested, "There's no need for that. Do you think I'll try something when you're holding my brother hostage?"

Alberto gestured for Bobby to drop the rope. She did and shook out the blindfold. I quietly kept my hands at my sides as she covered my eyes. She guided me out the door and along the porch to the staircase.

I grabbed the railings and tentatively walked down each step, trying to keep myself from falling head over heels. I miscalculated the distance between the last stair and the ground and lost my footing on the slick stair. I put my hands out to break my fall and caught myself on a smooth, rounded metal surface.

"Damn canoe. I told them to get rid of it." Bobby grabbed my arm and steadied me. "Hang on tight. We can't have you busting your head open and fucking up the deal."

I didn't thank Bobby for her concern. She held my arm and led me through the yard to the van. I heard the door slide open. Bobby pushed me inside, and I fell on the seat with a sigh of relief, exhausted from the tension.

The others got in. I smelled Bobby next to me. Doors slammed shut; the engine started. I rested my head against the back of the seat and tried to relax.

The van turned onto the highway. I concentrated on count-ing. One, two, three, four, five, six, seven . . . eight hundred thirty-two . . .

The van slowed. It turned left. Left again. Right. Assuming we'd crossed the bridge and were back in Key West, I settled back to wait. Finally, the van stopped. I heard doors open. Bobby pulled me across the seat and out of the van. Two strong hands caught me.

One of the men spoke to me. "When we are ready to deliver your money, you will receive a package. It will include instruc-tions on how to contact us when you are ready to deliver the shipment. Count to one hundred before you remove the blindfold."

Instructions like that may work in a movie, but they didn't work with me. As soon as the van drove off, I tore the blindfold from my eyes. The red plastic cover over the taillight on the right side of the van was broken. I watched the white light move down Caroline Street until it disappeared. I turned and ran to the hotel.

Twelve hundred sixty-four.

I bypassed the elevator and ran up the stairs to my room. Ignoring my nerves that were screaming for action—or collapse—I forced myself to sit at the desk and do some quick math.

Twelve hundred sixty-four. A little over twenty minutes—if my counting had been accurate.

I sat with my eyes closed and forced myself to think about every moment of the ride. I closed my eyes and tried to remem-ber every second of the journey from the van to the house.

No curb to step up on. Tall grass brushing against my legs. Stones under my feet.

The sound of a boat moving on the water. Waves lapping against a bulkhead.

A paved road leading to a house on a lagoon. An unkempt yard with high grass and stones. A twenty-minute ride from Key West. It wasn't enough. I squeezed my eyes shut so no light seeped in and forced myself back inside the van.

I massaged the splinter in the palm of my hand. Twenty steep stairs with a rough wooden railing leading to the main floor of the house. A large room. Ceiling fans. Sliding glass doors on the two outside walls. Thick maroon curtains.

The images were getting fuzzy and scattered; I wouldn't be able to drag many more details out. The smell of bird droppings and dog urine, but no animal sounds.

A left turn from the highway, then straight to the house. Reggae music, loud enough to be heard over the air conditioner, as we made the turn.

I sat with my eyes closed for a few more seconds and waited for another image. When nothing appeared, I opened my eyes and grabbed my car keys. Robert Louis Stevenson once wrote, "It is better to be a fool than to be dead." He was wrong—if you're not careful, you can be a fool and dead.

I didn't want to be a dead fool. I drove to the place that's billed as the Southernmost Point in the United States. I grabbed my knapsack, got out of the car, and walked across the street to Corrye's house. I quickly slipped through the gate to the back courtyard.

I groped around in the darkness and uncovered the AK-47. It took several more minutes of crawling around in the thick plants to find the ammunition clips. I stuffed everything into my pack, draped a towel over the top to hide the rifle stock, and hurried back to the car.

As soon as I drove over the bridge marking the end of Key West and the beginning of the Overseas Highway that leads to the mainland, I started watching the clock. Assuming that the van driver stuck to the speed limit so he wouldn't attract the attention of a patrol car, I did the same.

When you leave Key West, the mile markers on the side of the highway become your guide. Every direction begins with the mile marker. You don't turn left at the Exxon station, you turn left at Mile Marker 25. The restaurant isn't in Big Pine Key, it's at Mile Marker, MM, 33.

I drove across stretches of water, stretches of land, then water again. I passed an occasional gas station, hotel, restaurant, or bar. The road behind me was black and empty.

After eighteen miles, and several unsuccessful detours down

side roads, and no sign of a left-hand turn near a reggae bar, I began doubting my counting and calculating.

I made a quick, illegal U-turn and doubled back to Key West. After a few miles, I pulled off at a small gas station/grocery store/ restaurant. The store was closed, but it was a good place to take a break.

I sat on the car's trunk and looked around. The ocean lined the opposite side of the road. Palm trees and rows of dense bushes were all I could see on my side of the road. I took a deep breath and inhaled the scent of sweet flowers and palm trees.

Discouragement made me feel old and tired. I took a few deep breaths, then dragged myself back inside the car and headed north again.

At two-thirty in the morning, not many cars were on the road. I slowed and squinted through the windshield. Dark houses, beaches, the ocean, trees, and restaurants that had closed for the evening were all I saw.

Just past MM 17, I saw a narrow, unmarked road on the left side of the highway. I didn't see a bar or restaurant, only a small bungalow on the corner. Hoping they'd been having a party earlier that evening that featured loud music, I made the turn.

The road looked like the others I'd been down that evening. No lights, no sidewalks, no curb, houses on lagoons, boats in every backyard. Tears of frustration filled my eyes. I thought about giving up, then I thought about Dick. I angrily brushed the tears and the doubts away and let the car roll down the street.

None of the houses were on stilts. None except a house near the end of the street. The one with the overgrown grass in the front yard and the steep staircase leading to the main floor of the house.

I turned the car around and drove back toward the highway until I was out of sight of any hidden sentry. I parked on the side of the road, grabbed my pack, and walked back to the house.

When I was two houses away, I darted into the deep shadows beneath the palm trees and ran from shadow to shadow until I was a few yards from the house. I crawled into a bushy stand of low pine trees, pulled the AK-47 from the pack, loaded it, and stared at the house.

The lights were off. There were no cars parked out front or in the driveway. I rubbed the stock of the rifle for good luck and considered rushing in like a commando.

I crawled out of my hiding place. Bypassing the main staircase, I made a wide circle around the house, looking for another entrance.

On the far side of the house, I found another set of stairs. I crept up the staircase, cringing every time a board creaked. I held the AK-47 out in front of me, ready to shoot.

The stairs led to a narrow porch that ran around the house. I slung the rifle over my shoulder, dropped to my hands and knees, and crawled to the first window. It was open. Nothing, not even the sounds of snoring, floated out. I started to pry the screen open. It screeched and I stopped, afraid the screen would tumble into the room with a clatter loud enough to wake everyone in the house.

I repeated the routine at the next four windows. By then my knees were torn from crawling on the rough boards; I felt a splinter working into my shin. I crawled around a corner to the back of the house.

The sliding glass doors were open, inviting me inside—or setting me up for a trap. The invitation couldn't be ignored. I flipped the rifle to automatic and slowly eased inside.

The curtains fell closed behind me. The ceiling fans had been turned off; the humidity had built to an unbearable level. Sweat rolled down my face and dripped from the tip of my nose. The room smelled as if beer had been poured in the corners and sprinkled on the furniture.

After hearing nothing but my own soft breathing, I turned my flashlight on and swept the room. It was empty. I cursed and went from room to room. Each one was empty. Stray socks, packs of cigarettes, and clothes hanging in closets spoke of a hasty exit.

"Damn, damn, damn." My curses echoed off the walls, mocking my efforts to free Dick. Too late. Everything I'd done

in Key West had been done too late. I searched the house. The
mantra *too late* kept running through my head.

After leaving the house with nothing but a business card I
found in a kitchen drawer, I went back to the hotel. Not to sleep,
to hide the assault rifle. From experience, I knew sleep would
be impossible. The minute I stretched out on the bed, the walls
would close in until I couldn't breathe.

I decided to walk until the sun came up. I walked past bar
after bar, silently warning myself to keep walking, tasting the
cognac from the other morning. I almost made it to dawn but
Key West seduced me. A bar called the Osprey lured me inside.

From the moment I walked through the arched doorway that
was supposed to be modeled after a porthole and stepped down
to sit at the sunken bar, I knew what would happen. Following
the script, I sat at the bar and smiled at the bartender who
greeted me.

"Your timing is great. Fifteen more minutes and you
would've been locked out. We don't let folks in after four. We're
supposed to close at four, but"—he shrugged—"you know how
it is."

"I sure do. My favorite bar at home does the same thing."
Before my internal censor could stop me I said, "Margarita.
Rocks. Salt."

The bartender was faster than my conscience. When I tried
to imagine myself drinking again, I always thought I'd sit and
agonize—I didn't. I picked up the glass. I didn't stop to admire
the white rim of salt or the beads of condensation coating the
outside of the glass. I pushed the lime wedge away from my
mouth with the tip of my tongue, took a sip to demonstrate my
control, licked my salty lips, and took a longer, deeper drink.

My tongue tingled. My throat burned slightly. It tasted good.
It tasted better than good. Tequila makes me feel invincible, but
it couldn't stop the nagging voice in my head that scolded me
for being too late.

I stared at the ice cubes slowly melting at the bottom of the
glass. A voice interrupted my daydream. "Do it again?"

I looked up. The bartender had his hand poised to grab my

glass and refill it. I was tempted, but fear stopped me. I was afraid I'd keep drinking and forget about Dick. I shook my head, left some money on the bar, and stopped at the first telephone I came across.

Even though it was four o'clock in the morning, Dennis answered on the first ring. He managed to sound alert and wide awake. "Blaine, I've been waiting for you to call. Are you okay? I had dinner with Eileen last night. She told me everything."

"There's more. Dennis, I need you. I need you here."

Chapter 32

Dennis didn't ask for details. For a man awakened in the middle of the night by a telephone call from his agitated wife, he sounded remarkably calm.

"I have a bunch of vacation days saved up. No one will miss me." Dennis sounded bitter. "No one except a third-grade class at PS 31. I'll fly down in the morning."

Hearing Dennis's calm voice steadied my nerves. "Be careful—please. I love you."

"You're the one who needs to be careful." Dennis told me he loved me, then hung up.

I reached into my pocket for my cigarettes and realized I'd left them in the bar. For a crazy second, I considered going back. I knew I'd have another drink and another and another. The image of Dick sitting in that house was the only thing that stopped me.

I jogged back to the hotel. Without bothering to undress, I collapsed on the bed. After sleeping for a few hours, I took a long sweaty run around the island. I ran until all traces of the alcohol had seeped out through my pores. Only the memory remained. It would take more than running to make me forget.

Before pulling out of the hotel parking lot, I studied the map of the Lower Keys that was in the glove compartment. MM 17 was on Boca Chica Key, a residential neighborhood and a naval air base.

I drove back to Boca Chica Key and parked my car in front of the now deserted house. The windows of the house on the right were covered with plywood boards; the yard had the un-combed appearance of being recently abandoned.

The house on the left had a silver Cadillac parked in the driveway; a PBA sticker was stuck on the rear bumper. The front yard was covered with neatly raked gravel and meticulously trimmed trees. The noise of a sputtering outboard motor drifted out from behind the house.

I followed the sound and found myself in a yard cluttered with rotting boats, rusting motors, and other pieces of discarded marine equipment. Blue smoke billowed from the motor of the boat tied up at the dock that ran the length of the yard. The man bending over the engine with a wrench in his hand had thick silver hair and mustache. He wore baggy blue jeans that had been cut off at the knee and a dark T-shirt. Streaks of grease covered his arms and legs.

A woman watched from inside the house. I glanced at her face as she stared out the back door and wondered how long it would take her curiosity to push her out.

I stepped onto the deck and yelled, "Excuse me. Can I talk to you for a minute?"

The man looked up and turned the engine off. It coughed, roared, and died. He stuck the wrench in his back pocket and pulled a red bandanna from the other pocket. He wiped some of the grease from his hands and nodded at me.

"Morning. Having trouble with your car?" I shook my head. "Then I guess you're needing directions."

I smiled. "Wrong again. I'd like to ask you a few questions about your neighbors."

"Why should I be answering your questions? Are you with the police?"

"Not the police. I'm a private investigator from New York City. I'm trying to locate the people who were living in that house. I'm hoping you can help me."

"Private investigator, huh? I don't talk to strangers just because they say they've got a good reason to be asking questions. You have some kind of ID?"

I flashed my license and gave him a business card. He read it, then squinted to look at my face. "Looks okay. I'm retired from the Philadelphia police department. Guess that's where I learned to be so suspicious. Been down here ten years, but you never lose the habit. Why are you so interested in my next-door neighbors?"

"They skipped out in the middle of the night. The rental agency would like to find them to get some money for the damage they did to the house."

The man's eyes narrowed. "You came all the way down here from New York to find renters who ran out without cleaning up their mess?"

"The real estate agent who rented this place would love for me to find them, but I don't care about damages. I want to ask them some questions about a case I'm working on. I seem to be a step behind. Did you happen to see people moving out last night?"

"Moving out? Honey, they never moved anything in. One day, about two months ago, Mabel and I were sitting on the deck having breakfast and we saw new people over there. Now, I'm friendly, but Mabel's amazing. She can strike up a conversation with a telephone pole. Well, we went over to introduce ourselves. Never met such an unfriendly bunch. They just stared at us like they didn't understand English."

"Did they?"

"Did they what?"

"Understand English? Maybe they were from another country."

"Oh, they understood English all right. They mostly spoke Spanish, but we heard them talk English."

The heat didn't seem to bother him. It bothered me. I wiped sweat from my forehead and moved out of the sun. "How many people lived in the house?"

"Three guys. They had a woman friend who spent a lot of time here. A little bit of a thing. I took her for a little girl first time I saw her." He shook his head. "But I never saw a little girl drink like that one could."

The woman's curiosity forced her out of the house and over to us. "George, are you going to keep this poor woman out here until she keels over from heat stroke? Why don't we go inside for a glass of lemonade?"

"She's not visiting, she's asking questions."

I looked at Mabel. While her husband looked as if he'd crawled out from underneath a barrel of grease, Mabel looked as if she'd just stepped out of a beauty salon. Every blond hair on her head was firmly in place. The dried hairspray sparkled like ice in the sunlight.

"Did you see or hear anything suspicious last night?"

"Like I'd be able to hear anything over George's snoring. I saw the headlights of cars coming in and out, but I didn't get up to look. You know, these houses aren't too far apart, but the trees planted between block a lot of sound. We never hear much noise from next door. Is there something wrong?"

George answered. "It seems the Cuban contingent snuck out in the middle of the night. This lady's trying to find them."

"Oh my." Mabel's eyes opened wide. "I told you they were strange. Not at all friendly like everyone else around here."

Guessing they amused themselves by keeping close watch on the neighborhood, I asked, "Do you know what kind of cars they drove?"

"Lots of cars came in and out of here."

Mabel pulled on her husband's sleeve and said, "Tell her about the van."

"The van?" I looked at Mabel. "What kind of van?"

"I can't tell one car from another, but this van stood out. It's shiny black, and all the windows are tinted black too. It's got the name of some pet shop painted on the sides. Big yellow letters, you can't miss it."

I turned down Mabel's offer of a cold drink and asked a few more questions. As nosy as the couple appeared, they couldn't give me any more information. I thanked them and told them they could leave a message for me at the hotel if they remembered anything useful. I walked back to my car, knowing they'd never call.

Privacy was a jealously guarded commodity in this small community. None of the people in the other houses on the block could help. I was greeted by sympathetic shrugs and claims of having no knowledge of the people in the house near the end of the block.

Sunshine Realty. Sunshine Kelly, 3589 Duvall Street. I looked at the business card I'd found in the house and looked at the sign hanging from a curbside post. The yard was hidden behind a wooden fence. At five-eleven, I don't usually have trouble seeing over fences, but this one was tall enough to block my view. By standing on my tiptoes, I was able to peek through the diamonds cut into the top.

Buckets of palm trees and tropical flowers covered the front yard. The house leaned to the left, but the turquoise paint was fresh and bright. The gate swung open when I touched it.

I walked into the house expecting wicker furniture, ceiling fans, and palm trees. I found plush chairs and mahogany desks. The woman sitting behind one of the desks punched numbers into a calculator and mumbled the results into the telephone.

Although the office didn't have a tropical tone, her outfit did. The bright patterns on her shirt made the flowers on the desk look pale. The color of her desk matched her deep tan. Sunglasses dangled from a thick shocking-pink cord that was draped around her neck.

The woman watched my entrance and mouthed, "Be with you in a minute." She pointed at the coffeemaker sitting on the windowsill, then at one of the elegant chairs.

Following her instructions, I took a cup of coffee and sat. A cigarette smoldered in an ashtray on the desk. It's frightening how fast old, bad habits can take hold again. I'd bought another pack at the hotel, and now I lit one and sat back to wait.

After snapping "Screw you!" the woman slammed the phone down. She remembered that I was sitting in the chair and smiled sheepishly. "Sorry. I shouldn't curse in front of clients."

"That's okay, I understand. I have the same problem. Sometimes you just can't help yourself. Trouble?"

"Yeah. I rented a house to some scumbags who trashed the place and took off in the middle of the night. I'm sorry, I shouldn't be telling you my problems. I should be helping you with yours. What can I do for you?"

"I'm looking for Sunshine Kelly. I want to rent, maybe buy, a house."

My news made the woman happy; her smile reminded me of Jimmy Carter's. "Well, this could become my lucky day. I'm Sunshine Kelly. Are you looking for a vacation place or something long-term?"

"Long-term. A year, maybe longer."

The smile flashed again. "Great. It's fairly quiet this morning. Let me take you around town and show you a few places."

"That won't be necessary. I have my eye on a place. I think it's vacant. I hope it's available."

"Even better—that'll save us a lot of trouble. We'll go take a look at it if it's available. Where is this house?"

"Boca Chica Key."

Sunshine's smile faded. She took a nervous drag on her cigarette and said, "Look, can I be honest with you? You don't want to live out there. It sucks. You don't want to live next to a garbage dump. I can show you some great places right here in town."

"Let me be equally honest with you. Isn't the customer always right at Sunshine Realty? I want a desolate area. I like desolation. I'm trying to write a book. I want to be left alone. Frankly, there are too many distractions here in town."

"Okay, you win." Sunshine sighed.

She leaned back in her chair and folded her hands behind her head. "You want Boca Chica Key, you got Boca Chica Key. You've been out there, so you know what it's like. How much can you afford for rent?"

"I already spotted a house. I'd like to rent it. I might even want to buy it if I like the place and the owner's interested. I don't care how much it costs."

The magic words "I don't care how much it costs" ended Sunshine's petulant mood. "Great! This will save us a lot of time and trouble. Where's the house? Are you sure it's available?"

"I couldn't find a street sign or house number, but I can describe the house."

As I talked about the house, Sunshine lost her battle to keep the bright smile on her face. It faded slightly; I noticed only because I carefully watched her reaction.

"That house is rented. But other houses are available on Stock Island, several more attractive houses. Why don't we go look at them?"

"Are you sure that house is rented? It looked awfully empty this morning."

Blushing on demand is one of my greatest skills. I blushed and smiled with embarrassment. "I confess—I peeked in the windows this morning. It looked like your tenants disappeared in the middle of the night. They left a big mess behind. Of course, it will have to be cleaned before I move in. The place looks like it's been trashed."

Sunshine forgot about the deal she hoped to close. "Bastards. I never should have rented to those bastards."

In my most sympathetic voice, I said, "Tenants can be such a pain in the ass. I always ask for—and check—references. That keeps the trash out."

"References mean shit. I had references. Allen Lapin, a lawyer. A fucking pillar of the community. He said I'd be doing the community a favor. I wonder if the community is going to pay the damages."

"Probably not. Communities usually have a short memory. What did Mr. Lapin say?"

"Nothing. The bastard won't get on the phone. I keep leaving messages, but he's too fainthearted to talk to me."

The woman shook her head. "That's enough of my problems. Let's talk about yours. Now, about that house you're wanting to rent? I have a nice place right here in town. Don't worry, it's secluded. You can walk to the restaurants and bars, but it's on a street the tourists don't go down. I know it's not secluded like Boca Chica Key, but I think you'll like it."

As Sunshine gave me her sales pitch, I thought. Dennis would be arriving in just a few hours. I wanted privacy; a place where no one could tap our phones or bug our rooms.

I held my hand up. "Stop. I'll take it."

Sunshine stopped abruptly. "You'll take it? Don't you want to go take a look at the house?"

"Don't need to see it. You've told me enough. Can I move in today?"

"Sure—if you've got the money for a month's deposit and the first and last month's rent."

I did. I always carry a check in my wallet. I took it out and smoothed the worn paper. While Sunshine quickly filled in the blanks on a lease agreement, I sat back and tried to keep myself from breaking into a big, happy grin. I had a new home with guaranteed privacy—for at least one night. I also had a name I could connect to the house on Boca Chica Key. Allen Lapin. A lawyer. A pillar of the community.

Checking out of the hotel would be a mistake. I wanted to confuse the people following me—if only long enough to enjoy a reunion with Dennis. I threw my toothbrush into my pack and went to my suitcase to find some clean clothes. While searching for shorts, I found the plastic envelope of maps from Dick's boat. For no reason at all, I tossed them into my pack on top of my clothes.

Housekeeping had already been through the room. I spent a few minutes messing up the bed so it would look slept in and throwing towels in a corner of the bathroom floor. The message light on the phone was blinking. I called the hotel operator and listened to his message.

"You had a call. He said to tell you that E.T. called."

"E.T. Got it. Thanks." Brad's messages were getting more and more creative. I hung up and walked out of the room with a big smile on my face.

I didn't try to sneak out. Let them follow me. I knew I could lose them when the time came.

One of my first stops was at a secluded telephone booth. I lit a cigarette and thought about Brad's message. Brad spends too much time at the movies. "E.T." clearly meant I was to phone home. Not my home. Not Brad's home. I tried Brad's home away from home.

"Powerbuilders."

The voice was the familiar one that I'd known since kindergarten. I said, "Brad? Have you started a new career?"

"No, Babe, but you know I have to do something to keep my manly physique manly. Lifting weights is about the only thing that works for me. I've been hanging out here waiting for your call. They got tired of my harassing the receptionist, so they made me answer the phone."

"Speaking of work, Brad, what's so important?"

Brad sighed. "Is that cigarette smoke I hear pouring out of your lungs, Babe? Have you picked up nasty habits again?"

I thought of the margarita and licked my lips. I tasted the salt and tequila. "Don't ask about my vices and I won't ask about yours. I called because I thought you wanted to discuss work, not cigarettes."

"Let's talk about Swiss bank accounts instead."

"Whose?"

"Reginald Brown's. Laska uses Key West Federated to wire a lot of money. Brown's either extremely stupid or extremely confident. He hasn't gone to much trouble to hide his tracks."

"How much money, Brad?"

"Over the past three years, twelve million dollars."

"Drug money?"

"I don't know. The bank doesn't ask how he got the money. It just cheerfully accepts the deposit. Lots of money has been flooding from Brown's personal accounts to New York City to London and God knows where from there. If not Switzerland, there are at least a dozen countries that would be happy to hide money from the United States—for a small fee, of course."

"Is your information reliable?"

Brad's voice lost its playful tone. "I wouldn't have called you if it wasn't reliable. It sure would be interesting to know where that money's coming from."

I agreed.

After talking to Brad, I went to look at the house I'd rented from Sunshine Kelly. It was on Grinnell Street, a few blocks south of the graveyard.

Like most houses in the Old Town section of Key West, this one was hidden behind a tall fence and a front yard filled with overgrown trees and bushes. I walked past the house without stopping longer than any curious tourist would. I wouldn't go in until I had Dennis with me. By then it would be too late for bugging, wiretapping, and surveillance cameras.

Curiosity satisfied, I wandered around the corner to Truman and strolled the dozen or so blocks to Whitehead Street, to Lawyers' Row. Somehow the sign hadn't made an impression on me on my last visit to Whitehead Street. It did this time. Allen Lapin, Esq., had his office in the same small house that served as Laska Brown's office. Once again, I walked past without stopping.

I found Dennis sitting in the hotel lobby in the same seat once occupied by Al Tooney. Dennis's feet were resting on his garment bag. He didn't see me enter the lobby, because his nose was deep inside a newspaper. I walked up behind him and wrapped my arms around him. He folded the paper and tilted his head back to look at me.

"Blaine, I'm glad you called. I'd been thinking about flying down. Your call gave me the perfect excuse."

"Why did you need an excuse? I've been missing you."

Dennis took a deep breath. "Before you say anything else, I have to apologize. I've been doing something I always swore I'd never do."

My heart started pounding. Expecting the worst, I managed to say, "So, it's confession time. Exactly what have you been doing?"

"Taking my work problems out on you. I've been letting it drive a wedge between us. I'm sorry, Blaine. It's going to stop right now. . . ."

I answered by bending down and kissing him. Dennis arched his back and eagerly met my mouth.

"Let's go up to the room." Dennis's voice was husky.

My voice was equally hoarse. I stepped back and said, "Well, let's go."

Dennis grabbed his bag and followed me to the elevator. A small glimmer of luck struck; the elevator was empty. When the doors closed, Dennis dropped his garment bag on the floor and hugged me.

"I've missed you. I don't care how bad things are, I'm glad I'm here."

I pushed Dennis away. "I'm glad too, but we don't have much time to talk. We can't stay here; too many people know this is where I'm staying. I found a place where we can stay, but we're going to have to sneak out of here."

"Okay." Dennis kissed me. "I'll follow your lead."

The doors opened onto the fourth floor. The couple standing at the doors coughed politely to break up our embrace. Dennis grinned sheepishly; I blushed. The young couple watched us as Dennis grabbed his bag and we walked down the hallway to our room. When we reached my room and unlocked the door, they left.

Dennis pulled me inside and kicked the door closed. In seconds, we were pulling at each other's clothes with a desperation that couldn't wait for a more convenient moment. Sanity returned moments before we fell on the bed. I put my hands on Dennis's chest and pushed him away.

He groaned and reached out for me. I danced away from his hands and said, "Not until after we swim. Come on, let's get your bathing suit out of that bag. I know a really great beach."

"I don't want to—" Dennis watched a warning frown spread over my face. Without pausing for even a breath, he continued, "Actually, a swim sounds like a good idea. I'm kind of cramped from the trip. The warm water will loosen me up."

I silently applauded. Dennis grimaced and said, "I don't suppose I have time to take a shower."

I laughed and opened Dennis's garment bag. "Come on, dig out your trunks and change your clothes." As I spoke, I pulled out his toiletry kit and a few pieces of clothing and threw them into my pack on top of my clothes.

Dennis unzipped another compartment. He pulled out two pistols and several ammunition clips. "We don't want to forget the sunblock. I brought extra because I thought you might be running low by now."

I kissed his cheek. "You're so thoughtful. Give me a few more minutes and I'll be ready to go."

As I gathered a few odds and ends, Dennis sat on the bed and rested his head in his hands. He didn't look very happy. I ruffled his hair. "It will be worth every second—I promise."

We walked across town from the Gulf to the Atlantic Ocean

and back, just to see who was following. After we were both satisfied that no one was taking too much interest in our movements, I led Dennis to our house.

I swung the wooden gate closed behind us and led Dennis up the short gravel driveway to the house. As I walked, I unbuttoned the top buttons of my blouse. Dennis did the same with his shirt.

My fingers lost their agility. I fumbled at the front door with the key until Dennis impatiently took it from me. He pushed the door open. We darted inside and slammed the door closed behind us.

"There's no food or anything. Sorry, I didn't have time to shop."

Dennis wrapped his arms around me and hugged me. I slid my hands under his shirt and touched his bare back. His skin was warm, almost hot, beneath my fingers.

"Your housekeeping skills don't interest me." Dennis rubbed the back of my neck. "Your muscles feel like someone's been practicing knot tying. Do you want to tell me what's been going on down here?"

I lifted my head and kissed his chin. "We can talk later. I don't know if there are any sheets."

Dennis laughed. The hands that had been massaging my neck slipped down my back. "Since when have sheets been a necessity? Let's—"

I put my fingers over his mouth. "Let's stop talking."

Dennis's lips moved against my fingers. I shivered and stepped back. His fingers touched my rib cage and lightly traced the bones. The thin material of my blouse suddenly became an obstacle that had to be torn away. Our hands tangled as we fought to undo the buttons. Finally, I let my hands drop to my sides. The last button fell away. Dennis's warm hands touched my skin. I let out a long breath and turned to him.

Dennis stood still, his chest heaving, while I unfastened buttons and zippers. Clothes, his and mine, fell to the floor.

Chapter 33

Dennis rolled over and grabbed for my legs. He missed. I walked out to the living room and returned with the pack that had been thrown into a corner. Dennis watched. "Hey, where are you going?"

"I need to take a run. I've been using the heat as an excuse to slack off."

"You've also been smoking too many cigarettes."

I pulled my shorts on and sat on the edge of the bed to put on my socks and running shoes. I thought of telling Dennis about the drink, but stopped. I didn't want our reunion to turn into a tearful confession. "That too. I need to sweat my system clean."

"Want me to go with you? I think I can keep up—if you take it easy."

I stretched out on the bed so I could reach Dennis's face. I kissed him on the cheek and said, "Why don't you stay here where it's cool and read the papers? Look at the ads and pick out a place to take me for dinner tonight. Let's stay out all night dancing. We can finish the evening by watching the sun rise and then stay in bed all day tomorrow. We've earned a day off."

"Pipe dreams—like you'd take a day off right now. I have a better idea. Stay here with me." I shook my head and moved to get up. Dennis tried to hold me down on the bed. "We can call for a pizza later—if we get hungry. You can run in the morning."

I should have listened to Dennis, but I didn't. I kissed him again, then went out for my run. I left Dennis lying on the bed, hands folded across his chest.

I ran along the streets, thinking about the temptations of Key West. I'd already given in to the tobacco temptation. Now all I had to deal with was the temptation of the bars. Or so I thought. When I came to Whitehead Street, a new temptation hit.

Whitehead Street, the street where Laska Brown had his office. The low wrought-iron fence invited me to jump it—so I did. The leaves of the large palm tree drooped and touched the ground—and covered me as I sprinted to the back of the building.

The alleyway behind the house was filled with garbage cans and bowls of cat food and water. There was also a window—it was locked—and a door. Laska Brown should have paid more attention to security; the door wasn't locked. So I went in—and stepped on a cat's tail.

Noisy air conditioners in the windows covered the sound of the squealing cat. I opened the door; the cat scurried away from the clumsy human. Once my eyes adjusted to the dark, I left the tiny utility room and tiptoed down the hallway to Brown's office.

His office was in the back of the building. Even though its windows opened on the back alleyway, I didn't turn on the overhead lights. Instead, I turned on the small banker's lamp Laska had on his desk.

Standard snooping procedure dictates that you start with the desk. I followed standard procedure. I pulled a chair over from near the door, sat behind Brown's desk, and started opening drawers. The problem with standard snooping procedure is that most people who have something to hide know the rule. I didn't find any bank statements or other useful things in Brown's desk.

I moved the lamp to the edge of the desk and turned to the credenza behind the desk. I paged through the files, occasionally stopping to read one.

The air conditioners betrayed me. By the time I heard the creak of the floorboards, it was too late. The room exploded with light.

Laska Brown's mocking voice said, "Looking for something?"

I dropped the file I was reading but didn't move from the chair. The pistol in Brown's hand stopped me.

"I bet you're surprised that a cripple in a wheelchair could be so quiet. Quiet enough to sneak up on snooping people. Did you find what you were looking for?"

He swept a stack of papers to the floor. "Maybe it's under there. Did you look in the top drawer? I hide lots of good stuff there." Brown looked at me with frozen eyes. His voice was equally icy. "What were you looking for?"

I didn't answer. My silence rekindled Laska's fury. "That's right, save your breath. It doesn't matter. I can guess what you're looking for. You won't find anything here. I'm too smart for you."

"You're crazy. Not smart. How many people are you going to kill?"

"I'll kill anyone who gets in my way. There's too much money to let petty bureaucrats or would-be heroes like you stop me."

Anger rose in my throat. I swallowed it and said, "You're strong, you're smart, but you're still in a wheelchair. How did you kill Corrye? What about Al Tooney—did you kill him too? The heart attack seemed a little too convenient."

Laska laughed. "Is this where I'm supposed to confess to all my crimes before killing you? Fuck you, I don't follow scripts. Especially trite, second-rate scripts. You'll have to be more creative."

"You're cracking, counselor. You just admitted—"

"I admitted nothing!" Brown waved the pistol. "Let's get out of here. You first."

"Is this the part where I'm supposed to meekly obey your orders? No thanks, Laska. I'm not moving. We can finish our business here."

Brown pointed the pistol at my chest. "Move or I'll shoot you right here, right now."

I put my hands on my hips. "Go ahead. Shoot me. You're going to have a hell of a time cleaning blood splatters from the floor and walls. Do you think you'll be done mopping the floors and scrubbing the walls before your first appointment shows up tomorrow morning?"

Brown's eyes narrowed to tiny slits. Tiny, deadly slits. "You don't understand. I'm not playing games. Give me the telephone. I'll show you how serious I am."

"Get it yourself."

"Fucking bitch." Laska grabbed the telephone by the cord and pulled it across the table until he could reach it. He stabbed at the numbers; I moved slightly, hoping to take advantage of Brown's momentary distraction with the telephone. He pushed down on the trigger. I stopped moving.

"It's me. I have a problem here. . . . Nothing I can't handle. You got him there? Put him on for a second."

Laska waited. He caught my eye and winked. "Just be patient. You'll appreciate this."

My stomach tightened. Brown grunted into the phone and handed it to me. I held the receiver to my ear and tentatively said hello.

"Blaine? Is that you? What—"

"Dick?"

Brown grabbed the phone from my hand. "Get off the phone, you dumb bastard." He winked at me again. I froze, too furious, too sick, to react.

"If we're not there in half an hour, kill him. He's no fucking good to me anymore."

Laska slammed the receiver down and tossed the phone to the floor. He smiled at me. "What do you say? Do you want to hang around and debate? Or would you prefer to hit the road? It's your decision. Of course, if it were my brother, I'd be anxious to get moving." He glanced at his watch. "You have twenty-nine minutes."

It wasn't hard to recognize defeat. I raised my hands in the air. "You win. Where are we going?"

"Out the front door. Remember, time's a-wasting. Start a fuss and you won't see your brother until after he's become a corpse." Brown looked at his watch again. "You have twenty-eight minutes. Better hurry."

We walked out the front door. My hazy plan to break away

from Brown fell apart when Alberto stepped from the shadows and silently grabbed my arm.

Laska chuckled. "I always carry insurance. Now, why don't we stroll around the corner to my van?"

I resisted the urge to try to break free; I had to let them take me to Dick. Alberto dragged me down the sidewalk and around the corner. Brown followed.

Laska's van was silver, its windows covered with dark reflective material. The van looked like a thousand others made by General Motors, Chrysler, and all the rest. Except for one feature: the taillight on the right side was broken.

Brown slid the side door of the van open and grinned at me. "Get in. Hurry up. Clock's ticking. Go on, get in and wait. It'll only take me a minute."

I hesitated for only a second, then climbed inside the van. Alberto slammed the door and waited until Brown rolled his wheelchair up the lift and into the van before he ran around to the driver's side.

I looked out the window, praying I'd see Dennis. Thinking how easy it would be to open the door, jump out, and run away. Thinking how I'd never see Dick again if I did jump.

How much time would pass before Dennis started worrying? My fragile hope appeared and disappeared in a heartbeat. Dennis was used to my hour-long running sessions. By the time concern grew deep enough to make him stir from the air-conditioned house it would be too late.

Alberto started the engine. As the van pulled away, I turned in the seat to look at Brown. "Satisfy my curiosity. Who killed Corrye—and why?"

"I told you, I don't do confessions." Brown's loud theatrical sigh ended in a burst of anger. "Your brother tried to screw up my deal."

Alberto quietly said, *"Esmerase."*

Brown was too agitated to listen to the soft warning. "Don't tell me to be careful. That stupid fuck—after all I did to help him."

"When did you ever help anyone? You know, Dick said you were the only person down here that he trusted."

Brown forgot his boast about not confessing. He shouted, "Dick, Dick, Dick. You'd think he's a fucking saint. Well, he's not; he's a coward. He got me drunk. And then he was too gutless to stop me from getting in my car. My fellow Snake and Viper—someone I was supposed to trust with my life. Dick owes me. He feels guilty because I never blamed him. Because I never told anyone that he could have stopped me he thinks he can trust me with his life. Dumb bastard."

We slowly drove over the bridge leading out of Key West. Alberto uttered another warning, but Brown's resentment continued spilling out.

"I forgave him for betraying his sacred vow to protect a brother. I helped him. I gave him job references. I gave him money. When Dick decided to move down here, I helped him make the right connections. Shit, I even introduced him to Corrye."

Curiosity overpowered common sense. Even though I knew a question might stop Brown's ranting, I asked, "Why did you do that?"

Anger overpowered the attorney's common sense. "Dick wanted to make big money. So I set him up with Corrye."

I goaded Brown to keep his anger bubbling and his mouth moving. "Nice job, counselor. Was Dick going to sweet-talk Corrye out of her poetry royalties? How much did that come to—five, six hundred dollars?"

"It's more than that. My partners are Cuban. Wealthy Cubans with a lot of wealthy friends. They're passionate about freeing their mother country. They'll do anything—even fund a revolution. But revolutions need guns. The middleman—me—can make a lot of money."

Alberto interrupted. "Stop. You have said enough."

Brown couldn't be stopped. He snapped, "What does it matter? No guns. But no witnesses either. Tomorrow we start anew. Tonight we take out the garbage."

A queasy, electric silence filled the van. The desire to have the two men thinking about anything but taking out the garbage forced me to prod them. I said, "So you big boys decided to put together an army to go kick Castro's butt. Then you killed a poet because—let me guess—my brother couldn't deliver your toy guns."

"Fuck you, you know-it-all bitch. Dick claimed to have connections that could supply any type of gun we needed and in any quantity. She claimed to be a big supporter with a lot of cash. I believed both of them. Corrye stopped giving money and started asking too many questions."

I couldn't control myself. "So that's why you killed her?"

"Dick started whining about getting out of the business—and breaking our deal. Corrye would have made an excellent hostage. Dick would have done anything to save the great love of his life. She tried to fight me. She lost. I told her I'd shoot her, and I did. It worked out in the end—Ray Meltzer was all too willing to believe that Dick killed Corrye."

"Dick said he had sex with Corrye the night she died. I didn't believe him. Who raped her?"

"Maybe it was my friends. Maybe it was me. What's the matter, Stewart? Do you think a cripple can't get it up? Maybe you'd like to try. You might enjoy it."

I clamped my mouth shut and didn't say any of the things I was thinking.

We stopped for a red light. Alberto mumbled a steady stream of curses. I looked at the gun and measured the distance. I didn't move; there was no way I could reach the gun.

When the van started moving again, I asked another question. "Where did you kill Corrye? Meltzer said they didn't find any blood in the house."

"Nope," Laska boasted, "they won't find any there. But if they looked in the Martí Institute's basement, they might find some interesting spots. I told Corrye that she had to meet me there. She was wondering how Dick got that big fancy boat. I told her I'd uncovered some troublesome information about him. She assumed it was drugs."

"Will you please stop? You have told her enough."

"Shut up, Alberto. I'll decide when I've said enough."

"Yeah, shut up, Alberto. Brown's having too much fun painting you as his accomplice to listen to you."

"*Cómplice?* No, you are mistaken. He called me begging for

help. We did not plan to kill anyone. We helped dispose of the body. We helped dispose of the gun. That is all."

"And that's enough to get you the electric chair, you asshole," said Laska. "You helped me set up Dickie boy. He would have gone to the chair protesting his innocence."

I listened and watched out the back window for signs of a car following us. I saw a long string of blackness and the faint glow of Key West's lights on the horizon. Nothing else.

Brown chuckled. I pushed aside the fear that was sneaking into my veins and said, "Sounds like a great plan. But you screwed it up. Why did you ever let Dick call me?"

"Fucking cops. They felt sorry for the bastard and let him get near a phone. I thought you'd be a pleasant diversion—you know, keep him quiet—until I got him out on bail. After that, he would disappear."

"Then I screwed up your plans once again."

"You got that right. Dick thought he couldn't trust anyone but a dear family member. I quickly pointed out that you could suffer the same fate as Corrye. That's when he got scared and tried to send you home. It's too fucking bad you didn't listen to your brother. It's too fucking bad Alberto's trick with the snake didn't scare you away."

"What about Tooney? I assume you killed him, too. Why?"

"Another stupid fuck. It was easy to spice his cinnamon buns with just the right drugs." Brown's anger spewed out at anyone who interfered with his plans. "Thought he could blackmail me. Nobody pulls that shit on me. Corrye started worrying about all the money she'd given to her husband's revolutionary buddies. I don't know what Tooney found out, and I didn't care. He wanted a cut of my ten-million-dollar profit."

"So now you're going to add two more to your body count. Laska, don't you think you've killed enough people?" I swiveled around in my seat to look at the driver. "How about you, Alberto? Aren't you getting tired of hiding bodies for Attorney Laska Brown?"

Alberto cocked his head in thought. Laska laughed. "So what are you going to do, Stewart, offer us a deal? We're not interested. You have nothing to deal."

Laska was right—I didn't have anything to deal. The tenuous crack I'd started in Alberto's poise closed, reinforced by Brown's confidence.

Sitting back and waiting isn't my style, but it was all I could do. My fingers itched, demanding action. I folded my hands in my lap to keep them under control. Waiting was the only thing I could do.

As Alberto turned right off the highway, Laska said, "Stock Island's claim to fame is its dump, a golf course, a community college, a hospital, and a fine arts center. You'll get to the dump—eventually. But don't worry—you won't notice the stench."

I didn't have time to enjoy the scenery. The van abruptly swung off the road into a cramped trailer park. We drove through the rows of mobile homes, some battered and weathered, others shining as if they'd just come from the factory.

As we drove to the far reaches of the park, Laska played tour guide. "This is the local ghetto. The home of crack sellers, thieves, and people who've slid down as far as you can go. We'll have lots of privacy. Even the cops don't come back here at night."

We parked in front of a double-wide that looked ready to collapse at any moment. Its roof sagged in the middle; the television antenna dangled from a thin wire. The windows were closed; sheets of paper acted as curtains and blocked the view of anyone curious enough to try to peek inside.

Laska told Alberto to wait in the van. To me, he said, "Now you just sit here real cool, real quiet, while I get out. If you make a fuss, Alberto will have to hurt you."

I stared out the window at the dark empty street and tried to ignore the sinking feeling in my stomach. Fear made my heart pound. Laska moved fast. In minutes, he was outside the van. He pulled the door open and ordered me out.

Still hopeful that I'd find an opportunity to break away, I climbed down. Brown grabbed my arm with his iron grip and pulled me to his side. "Don't fuck up now or you won't live long enough for a tearful reunion with your brother."

Chapter 34

The humidity left me coated with sweat. Sweat rolled down my forehead and back. I felt my clothes grow damp. I listened to the restless squawk of the seagulls foraging at the dump and took a deep breath. The faint odor of rotting garbage drifted past my nose.

I stopped thinking. I stopped feeling. I held myself ready to do whatever was necessary to stay alive until I saw an opening.

Brown pinched my arm. "We're going up the walk to the trailer, nice and slow. You'll hold the right armrest and pull. I'll kill you right here on the sidewalk if you try anything."

We started up the walk, moving slowly and awkwardly. I followed Brown's instructions and pulled with my right hand. Brown wheeled with his left hand and used the other hand to aim the pistol at me.

I walked along as Brown ordered. My chance, maybe my only chance, would come when Brown tried to maneuver his wheelchair up the shaky wooden ramp in front of the trailer. My plan changed a few feet from the ramp.

Dennis stepped out of the shadows on the side of the trailer and blocked the sidewalk. "That's far enough, Brown. I'll take that gun, if you don't mind."

Laska pulled me to his side, trying to use me as a shield. He pressed the gun to my spine and cursed.

"Hotel clerks don't make much money. They always appreciate a few extra bucks and don't really mind gossiping about their guests. Could you be the handsome gentleman who showed up this morning inquiring about his wife's whereabouts?"

I didn't have to answer, Dennis did. "You bastard. You've gone far enough."

Brown chuckled. "I don't think so. Back off, asshole. I might not kill her, but I'll damn sure put her in a chair just like mine. Think about how much fun it will be to wheel your beautiful wife around the streets for the rest of her pain-filled life. Think about how much you'll enjoy making love to a cripple who can't feel a damn thing. Did you really mean that till-death-do-you-part shit, or will you bolt as soon as you can? Come another step closer and I'll send you both to hell."

I stiffened and tried to pull away. Brown pushed the gun harder against my back and wrapped his other arm around my waist.

"How about it, honey? How long do you think your dashing husband will hang around when you're moaning from pain—not pleasure—every night?"

He turned his attention to Dennis. "How about when you have to lift her out of bed every morning and push her down the street in an ugly chrome cart? How many times will you look at her useless legs and turn away really fast before she realizes you're thinking about your young secretary's pretty legs? How long will it take before you find yourself wishing that I had killed her? Wishing she'd die so you could get on with your life while you're still young enough to enjoy it?"

I couldn't listen to another disgusting word. Moving faster than I'd ever moved before, I spun around and grabbed the pistol. With all my strength, I pushed until the barrel brushed against his forearm.

Laska whimpered. The gun dropped to the concrete with a crack that sounded as loud as thunder. I ignored Laska's cursing and kept pushing his hand back.

Anger blinded me, turning me into something less than human. I wanted to kill him. I wanted to wrap my hands around his throat and squeeze until his eyes bulged and his face turned purple. Until his heart stopped beating and his brain stopped functioning. I didn't want revenge; I wanted to choke the evilness from his body.

Dennis tried to bring me back to humanity. He kicked the gun onto the grass and tried to loosen my grip. "Come on, Blaine, let go before you break something. It's over."

I wouldn't let go. A stream of foul words flew out of Brown's mouth. Dennis tapped my arm and sharply ordered me away. Without saying a word, I dropped Laska's hand and backed off. I stood under a palm tree with my fists clenched at my sides and watched.

A half-dozen people silently appeared from the darkness. Dennis gave directions and waited until Laska was wheeled away before turning to me.

He wrapped his arms around me and hugged me. My ribs hurt from the pressure. I should have felt relieved, but I didn't; I wouldn't until I saw Dick.

I took a deep shaky breath and tried to calm myself. Dennis anxiously asked, "Are you okay? That bastard didn't hurt you, did he?"

"No, he didn't hurt me." I rested my head against Dennis's chest and waited until I felt strong enough to hear the answer to the question I was afraid to ask. "What about Dick? Were you able to—"

"He's fine. Do you want to go see for yourself?"

"In a minute. I'm not sure my legs are ready to move. I feel like I've just finished running a marathon. How did you—"

"I can't take credit for this. Someone else organized this rescue party. Although I'm not quite sure you needed rescuing. You were ready to twist that guy's arm off his body."

"I wanted to twist his head off." I let my fears silently float off in the humid air. Dennis hugged me tighter and kissed the top of my head. We stood there, silently embracing.

The loud bang of the trailer's door flying open and hitting the outside wall roused us. I dragged my head from Dennis's shoulder and looked at the silhouette of the man standing in the trailer's doorway. He walked down the ramp; the light from inside the trailer shone on his face, and I finally recognized him. I gasped and broke away from Dennis.

"Cal! My God, you aren't dead. I thought—hoped—that story wasn't true."

Cal hugged me, then quickly stepped back as if afraid to hold me too long in the presence of my husband. Dennis stood by my side with an amused smile on his face.

"I'm sorry, my dear. It was a cruel, but necessary, deception. We let our unknown assassin believe his mission had succeeded. I hoped you wouldn't mourn. As our investigation continued, my suspicions about Brown grew. I am truly sorry I could not communicate them to you without jeopardizing your brother's well-being. I arrived here several days ago to supervise the operation personally."

"Cal, why did you try to offer me a deal when I was in Washington? Was that part of the plan?"

"Once again, my dear, I'm sorry. I used you, and I apologize. Your brother had dropped out of sight. I wanted to know how much information he had shared with you. Unfortunately for me, I had forgotten that toughness is one of your greatest strengths. My plan misfired. I am afraid my miscalculation spurred you to taking greater risks."

"Cal, stop apologizing. Tell me the rest of the story."

Cal took a pack of cigarettes from his pocket. He flipped the top of the box open and shook one out into the palm of my hand.

I let Cal light my cigarette and greedily sucked on it. "I was watching and hoping, but I didn't see anyone following. How did you—"

"Helicopter, boats, and a guide who knows the keys better than I know my own house. The tap on Brown's phone also helped. Trust me, we were following. I know you had more than a few bad moments, but we couldn't show ourselves until we were positive Brown was bringing you here to your brother. We didn't want to replace one hostage with another."

In a gently chiding voice, Cal said, "My dear, you gave us a number of rather frightening moments. However, I am glad you forced Mr. Brown's hand. I can only thank the Lord that we monitored those telephone lines. Once Brown made that call, we traced it back here. We had just enough time to strike before you arrived."

An uncontrollable shiver ran through me. Dennis took my hand and gently squeezed it. "Are you sure you're okay, Blaine? Do you want to sit down for a few minutes?"

"I'm okay, really. My nerves are beginning to wake up." I tossed the cigarette to the ground. "I really want to see Dick now. Is he inside?"

Both men nodded. Cal said, "He's a little battered, but structurally sound. I recommend we wait a few more minutes, give him time to catch his breath. Blaine, I know you have a thousand unanswered questions."

"I'll be thankful if you answer just one: Dennis, have you been keeping secrets from me? Are you working for Cal now?"

"If you don't mind, Dennis, I would like to answer that question." Cal awkwardly patted my shoulder. "I was aware that Dennis was in town. But rest assured, Blaine, your husband and I have never talked until approximately forty minutes ago—just a few minutes after you entered Counselor Brown's office. I immediately called your husband."

Dennis broke in. "And I hope I never receive another telephone call like that again, Blaine. Cal briefed me on the situation. I thought I'd go crazy."

"Since your husband is in the business, I called upon him for assistance. Of course, he agreed that interagency cooperation was indicated."

The trailer door opened. Cal nodded. I ran up the ramp. Dick stood in the doorway, his hands at his sides. The backlighting hid the expression—and the bruises—on his face.

I put my hands on Dick's shoulders and pushed him inside. The men flanking the door didn't move. I looked at them and said, "Do you mind? We'd like a few minutes alone."

They didn't reply, but they drifted out. The last man gently closed the door behind him.

Dick and I were alone. Since I'd last seen Dick, he'd lost even more weight. His tan was faded, leaving his skin with a jaundiced tint. The pale skin made the purple bruises look even more ugly and painful.

I gently touched his face. "Are you okay?"

"Okay enough." Dick threw his arms around me. "I guess it wasn't a very good idea after all. Do you want to say 'I told you so'?"

I stepped back and collapsed on the lumpy sofa bed. "My head's spinning. The explosion . . . what happened? I was so afraid . . . I thought you were dead."

Dick smiled ruefully. "My timing wasn't so good. I saw you hit the water; the blast threw me off in the opposite direction. I lost it for a few seconds. When I came to, I swam off to the far key. I heard you screaming my name, but I kept swimming. Blaine, I didn't want to put you through all that worry, but I thought you'd be more convincing if—"

"If I thought you were dead. I don't know if I should hug you or shake you."

"I used you." Dick's voice shook. "You don't know how much I regret that, how I'll always regret it. I compounded the mistake by telling you to trust Brown."

"School ties stretch just so far before they snap. What happened after you made it ashore?"

"I followed my own bad advice. I called Brown for help. He helped me, all right. I spent the time hoping you wouldn't go to Brown for help."

Silence filled the cramped trailer as we both envisioned a different ending to our adventure. I squeezed Dick's hand. "We have a lot of catching up to do. Why didn't you ever say anything about what you were doing?"

"I couldn't." Dick couldn't stop shaking his head. "It was exciting at first. But the thrill is really gone now."

"So what next, Dick?"

His words came out in a rush. "I've had it with this life, Blaine. I'm giving it up. Cal and I have been talking. I'm heading off to a suit and a desk job."

Dick's eyes filled with tears, but he didn't look away from me. The pain that I saw brought tears to my eyes. "I loved her, Blaine. They raped her. They killed her. All because of me."

"Dick, you can't blame yourself." The hackneyed words didn't comfort Dick. I doubt if they ever comforted anyone.

"Yes, I can. Corrye would have kept giving money to Los

Pinos Nuevos, but she'd still be alive. I'm sick of using people. Lying to the people I love."

There's a time when words offer comfort; there's a time when words are meaningless. I reached over and put my arm around Dick's shoulder. I didn't need to say anything else.

Chapter 35

A discreet knock on the door interrupted us. The door opened and Dennis stuck his head inside. "Cal's getting impatient. He sent me in to get you guys moving. There are a few people in town he needs to round up—Brown's buddy Allen Lapin, for one—and he wants to move now before they slip away."

Dick stopped me at the doorway. He hugged me and said, "It may be a few months before I see you again. But I promise you, one day I'm going to walk into your office and interrupt whatever you and Eileen happen to be doing."

"I'll be waiting."

Dennis pushed us through the door. "We'd better get moving before Cal sends in a SWAT team to get us."

Cal stood just outside the trailer nervously smoking a cigarette. He sent Dick off with the two men who'd been inside the trailer, then walked us to a car that was parked behind Laska's van.

After promising I'd hear from him in a few days, Cal held the door open while Dennis and I climbed inside. He gently closed the door and tapped the roof, signaling the driver to move.

I closed my eyes and rested my head against the seat cushion. Dennis put his arm around me and held me close. He didn't have to say anything; his touch said everything.

The driver left us off in front of our rented house. Dennis and I stood on the curb like zombies and watched the car drive away.

Dennis squeezed my shoulder. "Hungry?"

"No. Are you?"

"No. I lost my appetite when Cal called. Do you want to go in and try to get some sleep? It's been a long night."

"Not yet. I don't think I can sleep. I'm too hyped up to even sit."

Dennis looked at his watch. "Let's take a walk. Maybe we can put our nerves to sleep."

My legs twitched; I'd have to walk for hours before even thinking about sleep. "Are you sure? It's going to take a long, long walk to make me settle down."

"I am." Dennis took my hand and stepped off the curb. "Lead the way."

We walked and walked and walked and finally arrived at Smathers Beach. When we set foot on the narrow strip of sand, I stopped. Dennis tightened his grip on my hand. "Is there where it started?"

"No, this is where it ended for Corrye." I pointed to the infamous palm tree. "That's the shrine."

A lantern glowed at its base, throwing an eerie red glow over the icons left by fans. A man knelt in front of the tree, carefully arranging a bouquet of flowers. I whispered, "Dennis, that's Ray Meltzer. I have to go talk to him."

Dennis dropped my hand. I walked over to Ray and gently touched his shoulder. He stood and brushed sand from his bare knees. I quietly said, "It's all over, Ray."

"Yeah, I heard. I should apologize—"

"Don't. There's no need to apologize, Ray. Corrye was a lucky woman. I hope she knew how much you loved her."

Ray didn't answer. He turned to face the ocean. I knew that if the light had been brighter, I'd have seen tears in his eyes.

I listened to the wind blow through the palm trees and waited. Ray cleared his throat, then asked, "How much longer are you going to stay in town? Maybe I can show you around. You know, give you a better impression of Key West."

"Thanks, Ray, but we're leaving in the morning. What about you? What are you going to do?"

"Me?" He dug a hole in the sand with his toe and tried to sound untroubled. "I'll probably turn into a Key West eccentric and come out here every night to fix the flowers. When the fans stop leaving flowers and people start to forget Corrye, I'll bother everyone who comes near with stories about the great poet. Look me up next time you're in town. You know where to find me."

He shook my hand and walked away. I watched him disappear into the darkness. Dennis came up beside me and put his arms around me.

We watched until Ray was out of sight. Dennis rubbed my shoulder. "Are you okay?" I nodded. Dennis knelt in the sand and tapped my right foot. "Lift."

I grabbed his shoulders to steady myself and lifted my foot. He peeled off my sneaker and sock and dropped them in the sand. He put my foot down and tapped the other one. "And again." I did.

Dennis stripped off the shoe and sock and dumped them in the sand next to their mates. Then he sat and pulled off his own shoes and socks. He held out a hand.

I helped him to his feet and said, "I assume we're swimming."

"I was thinking wading, but swimming will work. Of course, we'd have to take off more than our shoes."

Holding hands tightly, as if we were afraid of being separated again, Dennis and I waded into the water until it lapped at our knees. Without speaking, we turned and walked north along the shoreline.

Dennis broke the silence. "We have to talk about what's going to happen when we go back to New York. I have to quit."

"Have to or want to?"

"Have to. I know I sound like a quitter, but I have to get out. I can't live with the way they tried to punish me for what you were doing. The way they pressured me to pressure you to quit."

"Don't quit for my sake. I can live with the pressure if you can."

I waited for Dennis to respond. He surprised me by quietly asking, "What would Jeff have done?"

Dennis's question stopped me cold. It had been weeks since I'd thought of Jeff, my first husband. Jeff, a DEA agent, had been killed—murdered—when an informant sold a deadly tip about an impending raid. His death had left me with a distrust of all cops and an excuse for a drinking binge that lasted for years.

Jeff's voice rang inside my head less frequently since I'd married Dennis, the man who had introduced me to Jeff. Dennis, the man I had recently married. I liked to think it was because Jeff approved of the marriage—not because my memories of that other life were dimming.

"Jeff always said, *Listen to your guts*. He meant, *Listen to your heart*. Dennis, your heart says you can't do it any longer. Quit. Do it tonight. Send a telegram so you don't ever have to set foot in Federal Plaza again."

Dennis didn't answer. I pulled him away from the shore until we stood waist-deep in the warm Atlantic. I pointed to the faint lights of a faraway cruise ship.

"When I first came down here, I was afraid of stepping into that blackness and falling off the edge of the world. I was afraid Dick had already gone over the side. And we made it back." I shrugged. "Quit before we get too close to that edge. We'll survive."

We stood in the water facing each other, arms wrapped around each other's shoulders. I softly recited Corrye's poem:

> *"Darkness wraps its warm arms around me,*
> * I am safe;*
> *Nothing can touch me*
> * until the harsh daylight shines again."*

Epilogue

Los Pinos Nuevos was noisily disbanded. For a few days, the plot to mount a Bay of Pigs II made the evening news, then it abruptly disappeared, replaced by a new royal scandal in England.

Six months later, Castro pulled his navy back from the coast of Cuba. Each day, thousands of people fled the country. They piled onto boats, rafts, inner tubes—anything that floated. Even if it would only float for a mile or two, they piled on. How many hundreds drowned during their freedom float will never be known.

Sometimes I taste the salt on my lips and shamefully remember that evening in the bar. I tell myself it's the taste of the Atlantic Ocean on our lips as we kissed that I'm remembering, but I know it's not. Then I remind myself that I made it back from the edge—just barely, but I made it back.

Sharon Zukowski enjoys hearing from her fans. You can write to her in care of the publisher, or reach her on the internet at 76372.2252 @ compuserve.com.

· A NOTE ON THE TYPE ·

The typeface used in this book is a version of Plantin, designed in 1913 by Frank Hinman Pierpoint (1860–1937). Although he was an American, Pierpoint spent most of his life working in England for the Monotype company, which he helped found. The font was named after Christophe Plantin (1514?–1589), a French bookbinder who turned to printing and by midcentury had established himself in Antwerp as the founder of a publishing dynasty—like Pierpoint, one who "made good" away from home. Plantin was not, however, a designer of type, nor was the modern font strictly speaking a revival (Pierpoint was unenthusiastic about Stanley Morison's revivals at Monotype in the 1920s). Plantin was based on what is now known to be Robert Granjon's Gros Cicero font, created for but never used by Plantin, which Pierpoint found in the Plantin-Moretus Museum. Later, its full-bodied but compact quality attracted Morison to Plantin as the model for Times Roman.